Deadly Chance

by

Talia Logan

Deadly Chance

Cover Art by *Rae Monet, Inc. Design*

The Wild Rose Press, Inc.
PO Box 708
Adams Basin, NY 14410-0708
Visit us at www.thewildrosepress.com

Publishing History
First Crimson Rose Edition, 2019
Print ISBN 978-1-5092-3024-2
Digital ISBN 978-1-5092-3025-9

Published in the United States of America

When she opened the door, he forgot his irritation. She wore a short suede skirt with a hip-hugging sweater. Soft leather boots wrapped around her calves. Everything matched in a deep shade of forest green, but with her dark auburn hair falling on her shoulders, the outfit did anything but camouflage her.

"I need to get my purse."

Chance sauntered inside and closed the door behind him. Ahead and to his left, he glimpsed a living room stacked with piles of mail and newspapers. Amused, he asked, "Do you ever read your mail?"

She reappeared carrying a small clutch. "I'm still sorting through everything that collected while we were gone. And I had a choice. I could either clean the apartment or get dressed."

His gaze fell to her chest. "You didn't have to dress on my account." He snaked his arms around her waist, dipping his head to speak in her ear. "In fact, undressed sounds like a much better idea."

She wriggled from his grasp, shaking her head. "I wish you'd make up your mind," she muttered.

"I made up my mind a long time ago. I just haven't decided what to do with you yet." He appraised the long lines of her body. "Or when."

Praise for Talia Logan

"Smart, dangerous and begging for a second read. I didn't want to let these characters go."

~Hunter J. Skye, award-winning author
of A Glimmer of Ghosts

Dedication

To the men and women of the United States military,
with respect and admiration for all you do.
Thank you.

Author's Note…

The seed for this story was sown many years ago when I went on my first tandem jump in Georgia. The experience was both terrifying and thrilling, and I wanted to incorporate it into a story. A friend of mine who was a retired Navy SEAL jumped with us, and later I spent a weekend in a house with several retired and active duty SEALs and their wives at a reunion in Pensacola, Florida. These men are a unique breed.

And for my southern friends who may have noticed the spelling of "crape" myrtle trees, yes, in Norfolk, Virginia, that's how we spell it. A little farther south, y'all say "crepe" myrtle. Don't flog me. However the word is spelled, our city has them planted everywhere, and summertime is a gorgeous burst of shades of pink and red.

As for the down and dirty writing of this story, I have to thank Jenna Jaxon and Hunter J. Skye for their continued tireless reading and suggestions, Dani Jace and E.J. Towler for their input. You ladies give me the courage to forge ahead. And of course, without my friend and editor from The Wild Rose Press, Amanda Barnett, this book would still be sitting on a shelf. Love and thanks to all of you. These people are HOW I have arrived here. YOU, my readers, are WHY I am here.

Chapter One

Democratic Republic of Georgia—the South Ossetia border
Friday, March 17—2:00 p.m.

From the shadows at the edge of the forest, Tempest Raines lifted her Nikon to snap pictures of the looping, heavy, barbed-wire fence dissecting the field. Earlier in the day, a team of workers had erected the barrier, but those men, while undoubtedly continuing their task, were now out of sight. Beyond the obstacle, a few widely-spaced houses dotted the landscape—forlorn and vacant. Except for an occasional glimpse of scattered Russian soldiers, the abandoned homes held no signs of life or inhabitants. But not by choice.

Next to her, a Georgian man gazed with sadness at his home. He had no place to go—everything he owned remained within those walls, behind the impenetrable barricade. Surrounding his house stood a carefully planted and nurtured vineyard—one he would likely never be able to wander through again.

He spoke to her in Georgian, and she turned to answer him. "Do you have anywhere to stay, Nikolai?"

His shoulders twitched, and he pasted a tiny smile on his face. "I have a brother in T'bilisi, but…" He left the sentence unfinished. "My neighbor, Timur—he tried to get through this—this fence. The bastards shot him. He wished only to gather some belongings, clothing for his family."

A tightness clutched her chest. She had seen the murder happen, had captured it on film this morning. She and her son Sloan had come to visit with Nikolai and his family, only to find the Russians breaking into the homes and forcing the residents out—shooting at the ground around them, kicking and dragging them across the dirt to the other side of the approaching boundary.

Sloan now stood several yards away, speaking to one of the displaced families, taking notes. It was no longer safe here. They needed to get out and return to the States. Why had she insisted they come back this afternoon? She started to move toward Sloan so they could leave, but Nikolai's words stopped her.

"We cannot go home." His voice barely a whisper. He straightened, his blue eyes pierced her, as if he knew her thoughts. "Your photographs will help—and Sloan's words. You must take them to your government."

How could she think only of herself and Sloan when these people...*her friends*...had no shelter, no refuge, no sanctuary? "Nikolai—"

He seized her arm. "The Russians have pushed the border to the oil pipeline, so they can control its use. They come in and build their fence and murder those who try to cross it. They will continue to do this until all of Georgia is once again under their rule. We cannot let them do this to us again, to force us to live under their despotic government.

"You must show the world what is happening here."

****

Friday, March 17—11:00 p.m.

Tempest paced through the small house, moved to the window, and pushed aside the thin curtain. The quiet of the black night sent a chill down her spine.

A full moon, high above the small Georgian village, flickered over the deserted street. Would this small hamlet be the next to fall to the Russians? She turned to examine her friend and guide, Alexei Baranov, intent on packing his few belongings into a small tote. He glanced at her and gave her a half-smile, but instead of lowering her fear, it filled her with unease.

The unsettled feeling coasted through her veins. Why was Alexei moving so slowly? She and Sloan had to get to Turkey. Tonight. But it wasn't the escalating unrest at the South Ossetia border that fueled her foreboding and the urgency for safety. Her work and travels often took her into dangerous situations, but the tension she fought against now—plucking at her nerves, making her head pound—she couldn't recall this level of dread, not even when she'd been in Libya during their civil war.

True, some of the soldiers had seen her taking pictures today—images that would surely help the Georgians in their fight to keep their independence. When those men reported to their superiors, they would want her film. They couldn't afford to let the free world have proof of their atrocities.

Yet even that certain knowledge didn't cause the prickling in the back of her neck. And because she couldn't pinpoint its source, this apprehensiveness concerned her even more. "Alexei, we need to hur—"

A staccato burst of gunshots popped. They sounded close. Too close. Had the insurgents found them? She dropped to the floor and crawled away from the window.

Alexei spun and bent to grab her arm. He yanked her up. "We must go!"

"No! I'm not leaving without Sloan!"

His grip on her elbow tightened, his tone terse. "It is too late for you to help him now. Those shots came from down the street—you know where. They have gone to your cottage." He started to pull her toward the door. "Where is your film? Did you leave it with Sloan?"

The question made her jerk to a stop. The crease in Alexei's brow made his eyes narrow, giving him a dark, forbidding expression. Thoughts flew through her mind in a jumble, so many at once she couldn't sort them into any concrete ideas. Except for one haunting impression. Sloan could be hurt, and her friend only asked about the film. A response tumbled from her mouth. "I…I don't have it with me."

The Russian straightened, loosening his hold. "Where is it?" His light blue eyes turned into slits.

She frowned. "I mailed it back home to the States."

He continued to stare at her.

His silence forced her to add, "This afternoon, when Sloan and I got back."

"Do you think this was wise? To send the film through the mail?"

The inquisition steeled her. "I thought it not wise to travel with it." She set her hands on her hips. "And apparently I was right." She spun toward the door and whispered to disguise the quivers in her voice. "I'm going to get my son."

Alexei's odd behavior could not distract her, even with her stomach in knots. No one, not even a friend, could be permitted to see she had any type of weakness.

"Stop," Alexei hissed. "Let me check the street first." He turned off the light and pushed by her, eased open the door a crack and peered outside. After several seconds, he said, "They are gone. Stay behind me. We must move quickly."

Tempest followed him into the curving, unevenly paved street. As they made their way past the aged, crumbling stone houses, she struggled not to break into a run. Every shadow seemed ominous, every sound threatening. She imagined movement around the house she and Sloan stayed in, but the street remained quiet and dark. Tightly drawn curtains in the surrounding homes let through little light. The villagers did not react to the frequent sound of gunshots and were not foolhardy enough to be curious. They would hunker down and await the morning to find out what had happened in their village.

As they neared the house, Tempest's throat began to constrict until she couldn't swallow. The front door stood open, hanging by a single hinge. She shoved past Alexei, darting to the first bedroom. *Empty.* Her son had disappeared.

Tears threatened, and she sagged against the doorframe, squeezing her eyes shut. "Sloan…" Her voice came out in a ragged whisper before she dragged herself forward to survey the other rooms. Tossed clothing and broken glass dotted the floors. And in the bedroom she used, her camera bag lay open—items scattered as if someone had rummaged through the case.

Looking for the film.

She yanked out her cell phone, her trembling fingers unable to unlock the passcode. "Open, damn it!" Finally, the screen popped up, and she punched the speed dial.

Her abrupt actions caught Alexei's attention. "What are you doing?" He sprang toward her and snatched the phone.

"No! I need to call Sloan!"

He held the phone behind him and thrust out his arm to stop her from lunging at him. "Do you wish to get him killed? If he has the phone on him, they will hear it ring."

"But he might be hiding. Maybe he escaped."

"Then he will call you when it is safe for him to do so."

His logical argument uprooted her rebuttals. She began to pace. "Who? Who are they?"

He drew himself into a rigid stance. "How would I know that?"

She stared at him. "I—I don't know. You spend—" The cold mask settling over his face nipped at her skin and stopped her in mid-sentence. A wave of disquiet gushed through her.

"I have no information regarding the Ossetian rebels."

"But…" The Ossetians? Why would they kidnap Sloan? They had no reason to want her film. "Why do you think the Ossetians are the ones who took him?"

He crossed his arms, his expression tight. "Who else could it be?"

The look on Alexi's face chilled her to the bone.

"I…don't know. It might be Russian soldiers. The ones from the raid this morning," Tempest argued.

"You obsess about the Russians. Do you not think I would know if they planned such an attack?"

His response didn't answer her question, exactly. In spite of his denials, could he have been aware of this? An icy rawness cut through her. She closed her eyes and forced the notion from her thoughts.

A familiar, unique ringtone launched from her phone. Before she could grab it, Alexei answered. She swiped at it and he spun, pushing her away. The short words he spoke in Russian gave her few clues about the conversation, until he said, "*Nyet*." He listened for a few seconds more, and then clicked off and handed her the phone.

She stabbed at the buttons, trying to open the recent call list. Her voice hit a crescendo. "Was that Sloan? Why didn't you let me talk to him?"

"It was not. You heard the conversation."

Her nerves frayed even more. "Your side only. Who was it? What did they say?"

"He is alive. They want your film. You must go home and bring it back."

She blinked. How simple he made this sound, as if she only had to jog down the block. A round trip would take days. "What if they kill him in the meantime?" Her voice cracked. "Damn it, Alexei! Who are they?"

"I do not know. Do you think they would tell me their names?"

The evasive answers triggered her anger, and she advanced on him, throwing up her arms. "You were speaking Russian to them. Were they Russian?"

His jaw tightened, and his voice became strained. "Does it matter? You know what they want. Your film is the only thing that concerns them. If you publish your photographs it will hurt their cause." Softening his tone, he urged Tempest. "My Storm. I will find him for you. You must trust me." He moved to her, running his hands down her arms. His gray-blond receding hair was scarcely longer than the closely trimmed beard hugging his chin. Deep creases lined his forehead and around his eyes.

The play on her name suggested they were closer acquaintances than they were. His tone and touch shot a stinging shiver along the back of her neck. The nickname he'd given her all those months ago suddenly seemed far too familiar. Alexei started to pull her closer, and she slithered from his grasp.

"I need to pack." Her voice came out in a croaking whisper.

A tiny spit of breath shot from his mouth, and he moved to another room.

Air rushed from Tempest's lungs as she stumbled to a cubbyhole and pulled out a tote bag to gather what remained of their gear. Her breath hitched in her throat. Despite her uneasiness about his actions, if Alexei could not find her son... The untenable notion hung in her mind, and her resolve strengthened. The film took a back seat in her mind as images of Sloan being hurt flooded her senses. Somehow, she would find him.

Sloan was all she had.

Chapter Two

Joint Expeditionary Base—Little Creek, Virginia Beach, Virginia
Wednesday, March 22—0830 hours

Tempest sat in the small utilitarian outer area of the Naval Special Warfare captain's office. She jiggled her foot as she mentally prepared her speech to the high-ranking head of the East Coast SEAL teams. She had known Captain Marc Dickey for years. If anyone could help her, it would be him. She had already contacted everyone she knew in Washington and received a firm *no*. Marc and his wife Sarah were close friends of hers, and their youngest son and Sloan had been buddies since they were five. Contacting Marc made sense.

At least it did in her mind.

Something had to be done to save her son. In a weak moment during the flight home, her mind had envisioned a picture of Sloan's father, but she'd immediately shoved it aside. The twenty-year-old image surely bore little resemblance to what the man might look like now. Plus, even if her exhaustive search years ago had shed some light on his whereabouts, that avenue had been blocked before the road ever got built. For all she knew, he might be married.

Or dead.

A deep sigh escaped her as the young lieutenant

who served as Marc's yeoman sorted through paperwork. A set of gold dolphins rested above his shirt pocket—a submariner when on sea duty, the young man had scored a coveted billet working as a secretary for the SEAL captain. Not unusual, since sub officers had top-secret clearances necessary to function in a job like this.

The door opened, and Marc emerged, breaking into a smile. "Tempest. It's great to see you. How've you been?" He embraced her and led her into his office.

She glanced around the walls that appeared to hold even more commendations and awards than on her last visit. Marc's chest sported so many ribbons it seemed remarkable he could maintain his upright posture. Once, she had queried him about what some of them were for, and he'd said only, "I can't tell you."

"Can I get you some coffee or anything?"

She refocused. Vodka probably wouldn't fly, but if ever she'd needed a drink, today hit the top of the list. With a smile, she declined. "I'm fine, thanks, Marc. How is Sarah?"

They spent a few minutes catching up on inconsequential events until she dropped her request. "Marc, I really stopped by because I have… I need your help." She launched into details, finishing with, "They abducted Sloan. I think they've taken him across the border into South Ossetia." With her mind and gaze the intensity of a laser, she peered at him, mentally willing him to give her the response she needed to hear.

The captain stared at her for a long moment, ran his hand over his mouth, then shook his head. "Who took him?"

A lump lodged in her throat. "I think it was the Russians—even if my contact there denied it. But Sloan and I saw the soldiers in the area that morning."

"I'm sorry, Tempest. Are you certain the White House won't do anything?"

"My contacts there said the president doesn't want to create an international incident. With the tension between us and their government..." She closed her eyes and shook her head.

He blew out a breath. "Tempest."

"Marc, I came to you because I have nowhere else to turn. I can't leave Sloan there to be killed. You're a SEAL—you have hundreds of men under your command. You—" She stopped. The sheer folly of what she asked began to filter from her addled brain into her stomach, taking away her voice. What was she going to do? Ask him to take her plea all the way up to the admiral? No way could he do what she needed. He—even the admiral—had to follow orders just as the lowliest seaman would. She picked up her bag. "I apologize, Marc. I don't know what—I'm not thinking clearly." She stood.

"Sit down."

She dropped into the chair. Even if she didn't fall under his authority, she couldn't ignore a command from a Naval officer. Particularly this one.

He stared at the wall behind her, tapping his pen on a yellow legal pad. He set the pen down, folded his arms across his chest, and stayed silent for another minute. Finally, he spoke. "I can't help you."

The knot in her stomach tightened as the walls of the office closed in around her. "I underst—"

Marc held up his hand to stop her. "I didn't say I

could do nothing." Lips pursed, his gaze plunged through her. "Look. You've already contacted the White House and been told no. I can't up and send a squad of SEALs overseas. Not without an *exceptionally* good reason and orders from someone much higher up the chain than I am." He shook his head and sighed. "One man under my command might, and I emphasize might, be willing to help you. Russia is his area of expertise. His retirement is coming up in a few months, and I've never known him to step down from a challenge. The man's the best there is. However"—he stopped and pointed a finger at her, jabbing at the air—"*you* will have to convince him to do this on your own. It will not come from me. I will have no knowledge of this whatsoever. If anything goes wrong, he and you could end up in jail." He paused. "Or dead."

The captain leaned forward and stared at her. His gaze drilled through her brain. "Do I make myself clear?"

An erratic pounding batted against her ribs, making her chest tight. A flood of joy surged through her. Yet his words made her uneasy. Her only response was to nod.

He tapped on the desk again. "All right. I'll get him up here. But the minute you leave this office, we never had this conversation. In fact, I've already forgotten it." His brow knitted into tight creases, eyes narrowed, lips drawn together. "And this is never"—he paused— "*never* to be mentioned to my wife. Or anyone."

"Okay." Her voice came out in a croak.

"Are your skydiving qualifications current?"

She tipped her head, frowning, then nodded and started to answer, but he continued.

"Good. I have an idea—just play along with me. Here's what I'm going to do." He spent the next few minutes discussing his plan with her, reached over to punch his phone intercom, then paused with his finger over the switch. "I believe you know the man. You asked me about Chance Adams once, soon after Sarah and I met you." His gaze stayed on her as he pushed the button without waiting for her response. "Lieutenant, call Commander Adams to my office."

Tempest could feel the blood drain from her face—making her lightheaded. She sucked in a breath and gripped the arms of the chair as acid burned the back of her throat.

He hung up the phone with another glance her way. "Tempest? Are you all right? You look pale. Are you sure you want to do this?"

****

Commander Chance Adams lifted his mug and took a swallow of the steaming liquid. The small dash of cream in his coffee did little to make the sludge more palatable, but Navy brew had its own character. He sifted through the papers on his desk and sighed. After Monday's full slate of meetings, his ten-hour day stuck at this desk yesterday had made no more than a small dent in the piles of work in front of him. The Navy's paperwork never ended. Like a self-reproducing amoeba, it seemed to procreate every time he turned his back.

"Multiply and conquer," he muttered, picking up another stapled set of sheets. Get through this small stack and he would take a break.

His desk phone jangled. "Sir, Captain Dickey wants to see you." The voice of his boss's yeoman filtered through the line.

"On my way." He threw down his pen as a low growl erupted from his throat. Hell. So much for his break. He set the papers down, headed for the stairwell, and jogged up the two flights. What could Marc possibly want from him now? He'd already sent up the teams' schedules for next week. If the captain wanted to change something, he'd be forced to rework the entire list.

The lieutenant glanced up when Chance reached the outer office. "You can go in, sir." Chance nodded his thanks, straightened his shoulders, knocked, and then entered the man's office. He paused after closing the door, waiting for a sign to gauge his boss's mood. He had worked with Marc Dickey for years, but the eagles on the captain's collar still demanded a certain amount of decorum. When his gaze fell on the back of a woman's head, he cocked his head slightly. Civilian females rarely made it into the inner halls of SEAL headquarters. She must be someone important. Some state politician, maybe?

"Chance. Have a seat."

He acknowledged his superior officer and settled in a seat next to the woman.

"This is Tempest Raines. You're familiar with her, I think."

The name rang a bell, but he couldn't pull up any recollections of her. He turned and acknowledged her with a polite greeting. "Nice to meet you."

She only shifted in her chair, tipping her head slightly away from him. With a tiny cough, she muttered, "It's a pleasure, Commander."

Her timid voice barely made it to his ears, and he

waited to see if she would look up, but her gaze remained riveted to her lap. He glanced at Marc—even the captain gave the woman an odd look. "Sir? I don't believe we've ever met."

She let out a faint sound. Something between a cough and a sharp intake of breath, with a little squeak attached. Her posture remained stiff, but she ran her hands across her dark blue skirt, as if smoothing out a wrinkle.

"Tempest is a photographer. You must have seen her work. She's probably shot off as many rolls of film as you have rounds of ammunition." He paused as a self-satisfied smile crept across his lips.

What the hell? Did the captain's own analogy actually make him smile? A lull in the conversation forced him to focus on this odd meeting. Was this one of Sarah Dickey's matchmaking schemes? It wouldn't be the first. "I'm sorry, sir, but I'm not really sure why you called me up here."

As Marc leaned back in his tall chair, his normal serious countenance returned. "Tempest wants to do a photo layout on our SEAL Teams. If I've understood her correctly"—he shot her a smile—"she'd like the emphasis to be on our jumping capabilities. With all the bad publicity the teams have had lately, I think it's a terrific idea."

Chance nearly choked and studied her profile again. Who was this woman? Marc acted completely smitten with her, and after years of working with the man, he'd never known his commanding officer to be influenced by a pretty face.

And even though she looked about as green as a seaman on his first cruise in the high seas, from what he'd been able to see, she had a hell of a good-looking face. Dark red hair brushed her shoulders, and with her hands folded delicately in her lap, she portrayed an air of innocence. He frowned and looked back at his captain. "I'll see that she's provided with an escort and shown around." He stopped, twisting his neck to direct his comment to her. "But you should be aware most of what we do is highly classified."

"I've explained all that to her, Chance. She understands she can't photograph the facility. Just the men. I'm counting on you to keep a close eye on her."

He tamped down a groan at the order. "I'll see what I can set up."

The woman cleared her throat. "Actually, Commander, I hoped to do this today. My time is limited." A little stronger now, her sultry voice swirled around him.

He scowled. Without letting his gaze leave her face, he addressed his boss. "Teams Four and Eight are off the base and the Team Two platoons are doing practice ops today, Marc. It's hardly conducive—"

"Perfect. Then she'll see firsthand what the men do. I suggest you get moving. They're probably already at the air strip."

The muscles in Chance's neck tightened. His schedule for the day hadn't included watching jumps. His mind pictured the amoebas on his desk mutating into gelatinous mountains of white paper blobs like a B-rated science fiction movie. Hell. Yesterday he'd put in a leave request for Monday, intending to take his bike and go on a long weekend road trip, but that little breather had now crashed into a concrete roadblock. He opened his mouth to argue with his commanding officer then clamped it shut. "Yes, *sir*," he managed through clenched teeth. He rose to leave the office.

"By the way," Marc said, "I think it would be nice if we showed her something a little out of the norm. She can get a bird's eye view and some unique shots if you take her on a tandem jump with one of the squads." A small crinkle at the edge of his eyes hinted at some enjoyment over this farce.

At the corner of his vision, the woman's head jerked around to stare at the captain, but Chance could barely pull together his own thoughts. Every ounce of his military training disappeared. "*What?*"

Chapter Three

Wednesday, March 22—0845 hours

The atmosphere in Captain Dickey's office chilled to a temperature colder than the Arctic. Still in her seat, the woman sucked in a breath. Chance's neck muscles strained as the cognizance of his insubordination crawled over him.

"Commander Adams. Did you not hear me? Must I repeat myself?" Marc's quiet response formed frost on every syllable as his clipped words sliced through the tension in the room.

Chance snapped to attention. "Sir. No, sir." He pulled back on his urge to debate this fiasco. Marc's reputation as a renegade was well-known, but as he rose in the ranks to a full-bird captain, his predispositions became more politically oriented and less reckless. Until today. This Marc Dickey brought back memories of the man Chance served under as a lowly ensign, when Marc pushed the limits as a wild-eyed maverick lieutenant.

He swung his head around to examine the woman again. In spite of the sheet of thin ice he was already skating on, maybe he could still disengage from this absurdity. "If you want to do this today, I'd hardly say you're dressed for it, Ms. Raines."

She smiled back at him sweetly.

For the first time, he got a good look at her face. Something about her…those eyes…had he met her before? No. He would've remembered eyes that shade of green—they held an eerie similarity to another woman's eyes—one he had sworn to forget. The unsummoned memory startled him, and he shook it off with a glance at Marc, but the captain had turned his attention to some paperwork. Did the man have a smirk on his face? Had the Navy come up with some new kind of behavioral response test? The woman's voice flowed back over him, seeping through his skin and into his brain, creating a slow trickle of thirst.

"I have a change of clothes in my car, Commander."

"Set it up, Chance." The slight smile gone, the captain's tone became brusque. "It's already oh-nine-hundred." With an air of dismissal, he stood and came around the desk to give the woman a hug. "It was good to see you, Tempest. Sarah and I will have you over for dinner soon." He paused then added with emphasis, "And Sloan, too."

Chance barely waited for her to say her farewells before he bolted from the insanity in his boss's office. Now he remembered. Tempest and Sloan Raines. She took pictures, and he wrote the articles. Pretty famous duo, from all accounts. But that hardly excused Marc Dickey's bizarre order. It went against every bit of protocol Chance had ever learned. Photographers never had permission to snap random pictures on this base, unless at some event taking place in a nonsecure area.

Something else had to be going on here—Marc hadn't just met her today—their friendship must span several years if the woman knew Marc's wife. Anger at his boss coursed through him, and he moved faster. He detested being played, and this entire scenario pelted him like a foul ball on Rec Day.

The woman scurried behind him, but he made no effort to allow her to catch up. Marc had stepped way over the boundaries with this order. At the stairwell, he yanked the door handle, shoving it open far enough for her to slip through…if she hurried. The thick metal banged against the concrete block wall as he jogged down the metal steps. Seconds later, the tap-tap of her high-heeled footsteps reverberated through the tunnel-like space with a staccato echo.

When he reached the landing, he spun around to confront her before opening the heavy steel door. "If you're going to spend your day chasing SEALs, you'd better keep up." His voice bounced in the small space. A few flights down, the sound of another door closing rang through the hall.

Her gaze spit fire at him. "I can keep up, Commander. But don't forget, Captain Dickey is most anxious to see this story published. I don't think he'd take too kindly to finding out you weren't completely cooperative."

Well, well, after her reserve in Marc's office, now the woman showed some spunk. Interesting. Then his resolve returned, and he glowered at her and punched a series of numbers into a keypad. He jerked on the door, let her step into the corridor before him, then took off around her down the passage. The massive door clanged shut behind them, resounding with a deep thud.

He halted in front of his office, the movement so abrupt, she bumped into him. "You writing anything to go with these pictures?"

His yeoman glanced up, eyes wide, undoubtedly curious about their...*guest*...not to mention Chance's out-of-character behavior.

"I, uhh, I'll probably write a short article. The photos should speak for themselves."

"Yeah?" With a quick glance and shrug at the senior chief, he pushed open his office door for Tempest then closed it behind her. "Why don't you just have the wordsmith you travel with write the article? Or did you figure you'd have better luck getting past Marc Dickey if you showed up by yourself?"

The woman looked as if she had been slapped. She swayed slightly. Her voice reverted to that same reserved tone she'd had when Marc first introduced her. "I thought you didn't know me."

Her quiet voice seeped through him. As pissed off as Marc had made him, he hadn't meant to be so churlish. No wonder his yeoman had been startled. Just because he wanted to challenge his boss over this ludicrous order didn't mean he had to take it out on Ms. Raines. The whole situation had caught him completely off-guard. After years of training to handle unexpected conditions, his irritation with himself for faltering ate at him even more than his aggravation with his boss. He refocused and saw her staring at him, waiting for an answer. A niggle of guilt over his harshness scudded through him, so he softened his tone and worked to ease the tension creasing his brow. "It took me a few minutes. I've seen your stuff in *National Geographic*. Didn't you win a Pulitzer or Nobel or something?"

She nodded and moved to sit in front of his desk.

He went around the side and sat in a high-backed leather chair, linked his fingers behind his head, and leaned back. The chair creaked. "What was it for?"

Her brow wrinkled, and she turned up a corner of her mouth, as if answering the question was distasteful. "A Pulitzer for some photos about the civil war in Libya."

He waited for her to say more, but she didn't elaborate. An air of competence swirled around her and yet, she seemed vulnerable. His growing fascination with this woman spiked. "You don't seem very pleased. I thought those things were a huge honor."

She hesitated for several seconds. When she spoke, a husky softness tempered her tone. "It…I saw…a lot of difficult things. It brings back some bad memories."

Her troubled expression gave him pause. She'd been through something—some kind of trauma. Probably watched too many people get killed. He'd seen similar reactions in men coming back from war zones. For some, the PTSD was so severe, they committed suicide. No doubt she'd seen some horrific acts. Empathy swelled through him. He crossed his arms over his chest, pressing her for a reaction. "Why? Your photos must have been exceptional. Do you feel like you didn't deserve the recognition?"

She didn't bite. The slight frown deepened on her face, her eyes narrowed. "I don't care for a lot of publicity. Do you?"

Quick retort. The woman had good verbal reflexes. And whatever caused her angst was buried. Deep. "No. But my job requires keeping secrets. Isn't yours about exposing them?"

"Yes, but that doesn't mean *my* secr—" She halted, twisting the gold band on her finger.

Well, that made her squirm. He'd hit on something

that ruffled her feathers. Maybe he could get her to open up. Chance shifted in his chair as the thought crawled over him. This unanticipated attraction to her rang some warning bells. At this point in his life he had no intention of getting involved with a woman. He moved on. "You never answered my question—you going solo on this story? Writing the article, too?"

For the second time, her entire countenance visibly drooped. "Shouldn't we be getting out to the airstrip?" Her soft voice drifted up as she stared at her lap.

A brief urge to ease whatever caused her pain slashed through him. Then the meeting with Marc resurfaced, and his annoyance over his disrupted schedule crept back. "Lady, I've got over a hundred men under my command. A half dozen platoons will be doing exercises all day. You'll get plenty of pictures, I promise."

Tempest looked at him for a few seconds before her gaze shifted to the wall behind him. She stared at it for a while, nervously tapping her fingers on the arm of her chair.

He started to turn his attention to the papers on his desk when he heard her let out a breath.

"Sloan and I were in Georgia—at the border of South Ossetia."

He jerked his head up and stared at her. His first thought was Atlanta, but his mind cleared. "Georgia? Why? What in the hell were you doing that close to Ossetia? Are you nuts?"

She returned his look with one of aggravation. "Georgia is a beautiful country."

"Yeah. Hovering at the edge of another war with Russia."

23

"They're just trying to keep their independence. They need help."

He opened his mouth, then shook his head. Regardless of his personal opinions on the topic, he didn't intend to have a debate over foreign affairs with this woman. Although she could no doubt hold her own in an argument. In fact, a match with her on any topic would likely keep him engaged. "So what did you do? Leave him there?"

She chewed on her lip. "He…sent me out. The mood had gotten too volatile."

Chance laughed. "You do have a gift for understatement. The border between South Ossetia and Georgia is teeming with Russian soldiers. Why didn't he leave with you?"

She averted her gaze again, studying the barren walls of his office as if they held priceless pieces of art. Her long fingers began to twist the ring again. "He couldn't."

The expression on her face cut through him like a sword. She couldn't seem to stop playing with the gold band. Her husband was missing. No wonder her moods jumped all over the damn place. He glanced at her hands, still fingering the narrow ring. The guy could've at least gotten her a diamond.

Yeah. Like the one you bought for Ginny?

An expletive shot through his mind but didn't escape his lips. The last thing he needed to dwell on right now was Virginia Randolph. Beyond this woman's green eyes, she bore absolutely no resemblance to that society bitch. In the short amount of time he'd been around her, he'd seen this woman's quiet class—far removed from the in-your-face

24

pretentiousness of Ginny and her family. An intelligence wove around Tempest Raines, an undisguised dedication, and an intriguing reserve. A small ache settled over him. Clearly, she loved her husband. For a second, he envied her—and the man she married—that depth of feeling. Self-reproach again creeping over him, he pushed the thought aside and softened his tone. "Did he get stuck out there?"

Her eyes glazed over, and she blinked rapidly, avoiding his scrutiny by looking down at her lap. She nodded.

Unable to stifle the rush of sympathy for her, he let out a breath and said, "I'm sorry. That's tough. I know—"

She looked up. The sudden burst of fire in her eyes burned through him. "I need you to help me get him out."

Chapter Four

A small compound in South Ossetia
Wednesday, March 22—5:00 p.m.

Sloan Raines strained against the ropes binding his ankles and wrists. He lay on his back, hands at the base of his spine, and started the leg lifts. *One.* Since he had been dumped here during the early morning hours on Sunday, his captors had kept the ropes around his wrists and ankles so tight he feared his limbs would become gangrenous before he got any relief. *Two.* Then last night, the man who brought his dinner had left them slightly looser after allowing him to relieve himself. *Three.*

Although he could hardly call the bowl of gruel they brought him dinner. But it provided sustenance nonetheless. *Four.*

His heartrate increased. A faint light shone through a small window, high above his reach. The shadows began to lengthen. *Five.* Concerned about losing track of the days, each morning he dragged himself across the dirt and scratched out a line with his heel—four so far. The futile exercise would not delay his fate—his captors would kill him eventually. The only reason they continued this charade of holding him captive was to lure his mother back.

He reached a count of fifty and began his sit-ups.

Pain shot through him with each movement, but pain was good. It kept him alive and aware. He couldn't afford to let himself grow weak. It would be at least a few days before she could return, and at some point, these rebels would make a mistake. He had to be ready. Maybe, with a little luck, he could escape before she came back for him. Knowing her as he did, he had no doubt she planned to rescue him.

But when she returned, the soldiers would kill them both.

A blazing light erupted in the ramshackle building. The sudden illumination made him squint. He squeezed his eyes shut, bracing for more abuse. Each time the guard came, the man kicked him. Arms, legs, chest...enough to bruise, but not break. They didn't want to kill him.

Yet.

A shadow loomed over him. "Sloan, my dear comrade. How are you today?"

Sloan cringed at the sound of the perfect English. The man he now despised, the one he and his mother had thought was their friend, had returned, and Sloan wouldn't validate his presence by giving him a response.

The silhouettes of two men moved into the space. "I have some wonderful news for you."

He closed his eyes again, attempting to shut out the words he dreaded.

"Our Storm, our Tempest, is working diligently to return. I spoke to her just a few hours ago. She is trying to find someone in your United States Navy to assist her. I am sorry your government does not think you are worth the effort."

Sloan let his head rest on his bent knees. As well as he knew his mother, and as much as he expected her to come back, he continued to pray she would not. Her return would not change his fate.

Alexei Baranov lowered himself to the ground, close to him. "You do not seem pleased. I should think you would be most happy that your captivity is so near its end. When our Storm arrives, I will bring her to see you. And then I will kill you both." He shook his head. "It is such a waste, but… We have become so close, she and I. Perhaps I will make love to her first. We almost have already, you know. She will be most grateful when I lead her to you. Yes. I will enjoy her body next to mine before I administer your final fate."

Sloan shot out his legs, connected with Alexei's knees, and knocked him down. In the shadows, a rifle cocked.

"*Nyet*," Alexei commanded. He jumped up and then struck Sloan across the face.

A trickle of warm blood oozed from Sloan's lip and trailed down his chin. Drawing his knees back up, he wiped his mouth across the filthy oversized pants they'd given him to wear.

His captor turned, snapping his fingers. A plate of food appeared in his hand. Alexei scooped up a spoonful and held it toward him. "Eat, my friend. I have no wish for you to die before our beloved Storm arrives." The bastard squatted but held the food just out of Sloan's reach.

Pushing aside his discomfort, he leaned forward, crushing his chest against his knees. The spoon touched his lips, and he sucked its contents into his mouth. He let his knees stretch out and bent forward again, taking another bite. The belittling process was meant to debase and humble him, make him feel inferior and grateful.

Instead, a heated angry defiance flowed through his veins.

Alexei shifted. The plate tilted and fell to the ground, dumping its contents on the dirt floor. "Ah. I am so sorry. I have spilled your meal." He set a cup of water nearby. "Perhaps the rats will clean up the mess for you."

The man stood and brushed off his expensive clothes with a meticulous air. "Do not strike me again, Sloan. I can make your stay with us so much more unpleasant—not to mention our Storm."

The two men left the cell, pulling the rickety door closed behind them. The sound of a bar sliding into place reached his ears.

Sloan gave his eyes time to readjust to the darkness. Then he rolled on his side and carefully ate the food off the floor. He had told his mother so many times before, "Eat. Keep your strength up. Don't let the atrocities we see conquer you. We can't help them if we fall prey to our emotions."

Slithering across the dirt to the cup of water, he slurped from it until the level became too low to continue. He pushed himself back upright then bent over and grasped the cup with his teeth, tipped it up and let the rest of the water flow into his mouth, trying not to spill any precious drops.

When he'd emptied it, he spat out the cup and leaned against the wall, eyes closed. A sense of defeat began to swell over him, and he honed in on the emotion, willing it into oblivion. He couldn't let these Russians trample him, crush his spirit—or his will to survive.

Alexei had kept him posted on all of his mother's travels—her safe arrival in Ankara, her return to the United States, and the government's reluctance to help her. The man said she intended to talk to someone in the Navy…it must be Marc Dickey. Yet, as persuasive as she could be, and regardless of their long friendship with the family, he doubted if the captain would risk his career to help her or him.

It hardly mattered. Even if she returned alone, she would have no trouble finding him. Alexei would lead her right to him.

Then his captor would kill her. After he raped her.

He swallowed hard. They had been so blind. Alexei had sucked them both in with enthusiastic, detailed plans for building a vacation haven on the Georgian coast. The promised development of the beautiful area into a resort would be sought by travelers from all over the world. Despite the Russian forces continuing their push into the Georgian Republic, Alexei convinced Sloan and his mother that his own intentions were solely personal—not political. He claimed a vested interest in the plans for redeveloping the coastline, although he'd never clearly explained that interest.

But they had overlooked the obvious. Alexei could accomplish that goal whether Georgia remained a country in its own right or became a part of Russia. It made no difference. No, Alexei Baranov's real interest, where he'd amassed most of his wealth, lay in the oil pipeline running between the Caspian and Black Seas.

When the Russians broke into their small cottage and grabbed Sloan, it didn't take long to learn why. His fluent grasp of their language, which he'd kept to himself during their trips here, benefitted his efforts. They intended to whisk both him and his mother to the border and kill them immediately, blaming it on the Ossetian separatists. Baranov wanted to eliminate them.

But she hadn't been with him. She'd gone to Alexei's cabin to talk to him. It nearly made him laugh. The friendship the bastard nurtured with her backfired and spoiled his own plan.

They allowed her to live and return home only because of the film. The Russians wanted those photos desperately, and Alexei determined if he let her go, he could convince her to return with the pictures in an attempt to save Sloan.

Apparently, the Soviet guessed correctly.

The last thing the Russians wanted was for Georgia to stay an independent nation and join NATO. As long as Georgia remained autonomous, they controlled portions of the oil pipeline.

Alexei Baranov wanted the Russians to have authority over that pipeline. He stood to gain much more from the oil than from building a hotel on the coast.

Sloan rolled over, trying to position himself comfortably enough to sleep. Somehow, he would find a weakness in their plan. He'd be damned if he would let that Russian, or anyone, lay a hand on the woman who had raised him.

He would kill anyone who tried to hurt his mother.

Chapter Five

Joint Expeditionary Base—Little Creek, Virginia Beach, Virginia
Wednesday, March 22—0900 hours

Tempest clenched her fists, but her gaze stayed steady on the SEAL.

Chance burst into laughter. "You can't be serious."

She stood and propped her hands on his desk, leaning across its worn surface. "I'm dead serious, Commander. I need help." Her outburst probably could have been timed—and worded—a little better, but she had no time to waste. She needed action.

A single eyebrow edged upward, but he said nothing.

She glared at him as his deep blue-eyed gaze shot through her. *Not now. Focus. Don't think about the past and get distracted.* This man had all the skills to get Sloan out of Ossetia, and she needed his expertise. Marc had gotten her this far. Now she had to convince Chance Adams, a decorated SEAL, to risk his entire career to help her. Winning the lottery would be more likely than him agreeing to this mission.

She dropped into the chair. Her fear he might recognize her had proven groundless, but she'd been a teenager when their paths crossed and bore little resemblance to the gangly eighteen-year-old from those days.

If she'd denied her feelings for Chance back then, she wouldn't be here in his office now.

She pinched the bridge of her nose and squeezed her eyes shut. So many mistakes. How could she ever explain the reasoning behind her actions? Would he understand? Did she even understand it herself? She had spent years in hiding and never expected to see him again. Twenty years ago, all her efforts to locate him had garnered her nothing but closed doors. As a result, no one knew who she used to be, not even her son. Her life brimmed with lies and half-truths. She opened her eyes to find him staring at her.

Silently, he scrutinized her with a disturbing intensity.

His inspection sent a chilling wave across her shoulders. She needed to break his visual lock on her. "I've got a lot of work to do—and I'm sure you do, too. Shouldn't we be getting out to the airstrip?"

He crossed his arms and leaned back. "Does Dickey know what the hell you're up to?"

The inference made her bristle. "No. Of course not."

Up went that eyebrow again. "So you admit you are up to something."

A snarl formed in her throat, but she held it back. Her best chance of saving Sloan's life still rested on this man, regardless of her *past* with him, whatever that encompassed. With Marc's command still echoing in her mind, she dissembled. "It's not unusual for me to stop in and see Marc when I'm near the base. When he suggested the photo shoot, the idea occurred to me...I thought maybe I could connect with someone who might…" She closed her eyes for a second then poured every ounce of femininity she could muster into her voice. "Commander…" She drew in a breath. "Chance, I need your help. Please."

His entire countenance changed. He set his hand over his mouth and for several seconds, observed her with an almost chivalrous expression. Then he blinked a couple of times and shook his head. "You're insane."

The declaration sliced through whatever composure she had left. "I'm far from insane, Commander Ad—oh, just forget it." She stood and picked up her bag. This futile idea wasted too much time. Precious minutes she could be using to figure out a way to get Sloan. "I'm sorry I took up so much of your morning. If you'll just escort me to the quarterdeck, I'll get out of your hair." *And your life. Once and for all. Not that you were ever really in it to begin with.* She moved to the office door.

Chance stood and crossed to her, grabbing his cover from the free-standing clothes tree. "Oh, no. I'm not about to get sent to Captain's Mast for disobeying an order. We're going to the airstrip."

She clenched her teeth. *Damn him.* "Fine. Let's go."

****

They rode the elevator downstairs and passed through the building's quarterdeck. Aggravation continued to slither through Chance's heated blood. He truly had no time for this today. As they approached the doors, the young watchstander posted at the entrance greeted him with a polite nod and "Sir."

Chance stopped with a glance at Tempest's visitor's badge. "You need to turn that in."

She unclipped it from her lapel and handed it to the sailor. Muttering his thanks, he marked it off his ledger. Chance plopped his cover on his head and held open the door, letting her step into the brisk air. "Where's your gear?"

She cocked her head and gave him a questioning look.

"Camera? Or is everything you need stuffed in that little designer bag you have?"

"Oh. It's in my car." She pointed to a blue Subaru Outback. "Over there."

He held his hand out for her keys, so she dug in her purse and handed them over without question. "Everything is in my camera bag, on the front seat."

He led her to his Blazer and held open the door while she slipped onto the vinyl seat without offering any thanks. He jogged to her car and retrieved the worn leather bag. As he started to work his way out, his gaze fell on a small compartment in the console. He saw a photograph and picked it up. A little boy laughed at something outside the camera's focus. Did she have a child? He didn't look much like her, but maybe he favored his father. Regardless, she hadn't mentioned any children. If she had a kid she'd dumped in some boarding school, it would eliminate any inkling of respect he might have for her work. He had no tolerance for parents who couldn't even care for their own child. If he had a kid—

Knock it off. You're forty-two years old. Those days are long gone. You missed your window, buddy.

Aggravated with himself, he backed out of the car, slammed the door, and started toward his Chevy. What little interest he'd tried to muster for this comical assignment had waned quickly. The unexpected feelings this woman stirred in him came from a place so buried it unsettled him. After his one serious relationship twenty years ago, he'd sworn off women and kept that single promise to himself. No one would hurt him to that extent again. He reached his car, tossed the camera bag in the back seat, and slipped behind the wheel.

She gave him a quick frown and glanced at her bag. "Could you be a little careful with that, please?" Without waiting for a reply, she stared out the window, either lost in thought or avoiding conversation.

Not that he gave a damn.

His jaw tightened. If he didn't care, why were her actions and reactions slinking through him like a teenager trying to sneak into the house after midnight?

He drove to the airstrip in silence. This woman had some deep secrets—something in her past haunted her. In spite of her obvious competence, a palpable anxiety lurked just beneath her veneer. Plus, the tiny spouts of anger that streamed from her, and her adept way of not answering questions, all pointed to stress. After years of studying people, the signs jumped out at him. And whatever she struggled with went deeper than this issue with her husband. If he could do something to help her, something that wouldn't cost him his job—or his life— he might consider it. He huffed out a breath.

Sure, Chance. And there's a cell at the brig with your name on it, just waiting for you.

He slipped the car into a space, and they climbed out. She opened the back door and retrieved her bag, hoisting it on her shoulder.

"Come on." With his hand on her back, he led her

through the lot and then across a tarmac to an open field. He checked his watch. "A couple of squads should be dropping shortly."

She angled away from him.

Huh. Interesting. His touch seemed to unnerve her, so he backed up a step. These inconsistent reactions puzzled him. Since the outburst in his office, her initial spirit had disappeared. Now she seemed even more vulnerable, more defenseless. He studied Tempest as she set the bag on the ground and pulled out a Nikon. Knowing the deeper motive behind this stunt did nothing to shake his fascination with the woman. Something about her was familiar, but unable to make any connection, he shrugged and continued to toy with an image of his arms wrapped around that slender body as he comforted her.

Yeah. No doubt her husband would appreciate you filling the gap for him while he's being held hostage in some Russian territory. Dumbass. Berating himself for his lapse in self-discipline, he blew out a breath and shook his head.

She opened the Nikon and inserted a fresh roll of film, then played with the settings and gazed at the skyline through the lens before looping the strap over her neck to wait.

"You still use film? Why?"

Her mouth opened, and a breath caught in her throat before she shrugged. "It's more honest. Photos, images, can be manipulated and enhanced, even faked. Negatives can't." She looked up at him. "For what I do, I don't want anyone accusing me of twisting the truth."

As she spoke, his assessment of her continued to climb.

They stood in the chill of the morning, watching the sky, until Chance pointed. "Here comes one squad now." Within seconds, eight men popped into sight, floating through the air.

Tempest raised her camera, catching them airborne, then landing, and finally gathering their equipment. The squad's leader, a lieutenant, barked orders, and they took off across the field.

"These first few squads are doing speed drills. They only have a few seconds to gather their things and move out. The next platoon will be practicing their landings—they'll have to hit one of those X marks."

When the first group from the next platoon came into sight, Tempest kept her camera on them in the air and followed them through the exercise.

A part of his mind kept track of his team, but his focus stayed on her. While in her element, the allure surrounding her grew. The next squad floated down, but Tempest focused on the men already on the ground, capturing the camaraderie between them. After several seconds, he asked, "What are you doing?"

"Anyone can take pictures of skydivers. I take pictures of people." She lowered her camera and scanned him. "It doesn't matter where you go, or who you are, or what the circumstances might be. Everyone is the same everywhere." She raised her camera and continued to speak. Her fingers tightened, and a terseness colored her tone. "If I can show that in my photographs, maybe someday enough people will start to realize it and stop the fighting."

Her sudden fervor intrigued him. All of his preconceived notions about her, all of his suspicions that she was vacuous, vanished with that one statement.

Then he retracted the thought. During the short amount of time he'd been with her, he had never really believed her empty-headed. He surveyed her. No, not even close.

Intelligent. Resourceful. Intense. As the list went on, the adjectives slowed, giving him time to consider the aspects persuading him to choose one description above another. *Impassioned. Provocative.* He paused. *Sexy.* He inspected her again, standing by him in her navy-blue suit, with legs that started—God knew where—and ended in those high heels. The woman looked regal and exposed at the same time. How the hell did she manage to do that? He drew a deep breath. *Definitely sexy.*

And married. Leave it alone. "Shit."

She turned to view him. "What's wrong?" Her gaze flitted over his face, and her lips puckered in a smile. "Not enough action for you, Commander?"

Chance pulled off his sunglasses, let his gaze sweep over her, opened his mouth, but then clamped it shut. He couldn't let her flirting suck him in and end up getting slapped in front of his men. Before he spouted off some impropriety and got himself in trouble, a gust of wind whipped across the field, and she shivered. His self-recriminations turned to concern. "Where's your coat?"

"In my car. I didn't realize how windy it would be out here."

The urge to protect this woman washed over him. Again. If he'd worn his overcoat, he'd take it off and settle it across her shoulders to give her some warmth. Then he'd wrap his arms around her to keep it snug.

If she weren't married, he'd protect her. He snorted. Like he planned to do for Ginny? No. Women these days didn't want protecting. They sucked you dry and left your ashes in the fire pit. He studied Tempest again and a new conviction struck him. No. Not all of them. Not this one. He hoped to God her husband appreciated what he had with her.

Damn, Chance. What the hell had gotten into him? Had he learned nothing from his past? He'd warded off the advances of women for twenty years—without regret. His job consumed him. As he'd progressed through the ranks, these young men and those like them became his family, and his instincts as a protector turned to them. They were strong, they were capable, and they were his men, his responsibility. Not this woman, no matter how attractive he found her.

He shook himself from his thoughts to watch her work. The rapid click and whirr of her camera strummed the quiet air. With swift and confident movements, her professionalism and passion mirrored his own dedication to his job, gaining his reluctant admiration. But he didn't intend to get sucked in by her, captivating or not.

Once the entire platoon hit the ground, she took a few more shots, then stopped, letting the camera hang idly around her neck. The men continued to gather their things, joking amongst themselves.

"Finished?"

"They've seen me now. They're posing, even though they're pretending to act casual. In fact, I'd say they're preening like peacocks."

He examined the group. The sight of an attractive woman standing by their commanding officer drew them like children on a treasure hunt. He scowled. "You're equating my men to a bunch of sixteen-year-old kids. They're not kids."

Her expression tight, she faced him. "Chance, they're people. The same everywhere. Exactly the point I've been trying to make."

"They're well-trained machines."

"I'm sure they are, under different circumstances. But right now, today, without the pressure, they're just young men with the same needs and desires as any young man." A fleeting expression of hopelessness passed over her face as she shifted her gaze back to his men. She blinked several times.

He frowned. She might be focused on her work, but her missing husband lingered close to the edge of her mind. If that photo in her car was their son, and she had to tell the kid his father had been killed…no mother should ever have to do that, but it happened. Far too often. A bitter fact he'd seen more than once. He forced the thought from his mind and refocused on her comment. Another gust of wind swirled around them, whipping through her dark red hair. He glanced at her shapely legs and couldn't stop his words. "The way you're dressed, what the hell do you expect?"

She looked down at herself, then with her brow knitted, back at him. "What's wrong with the way I'm dressed?"

A low hum vibrated in his throat. "Absolutely nothing." Although *nothing* period would be even better.

Lips pursed, she scowled. "Would you be happier if I tucked my hair under a ball cap and wore jeans and a T-shirt?"

He stopped to consider her question, surveying her from behind his dark glasses, creating that image in his mind. Hair up, providing him access to her long creamy neck. A tight T-shirt, low-cut, stretched across her chest, revealing a little more of the cleavage he could only glimpse now. Snug jeans wrapped around her hips and thighs like a second skin.

He took a step closer and started to bend over to speak into her ear, then pulled back. *Let it go. The woman is married, and you don't mess with married women. Ever. You and your brother made a pact.*

Yet, even though he reined himself in, his expression must have been clear, because she blushed.

An immense satisfaction rushed over him. Maybe he couldn't have her, but he could make love to her with words, and hopefully cause her as much discomfort as she caused him. Paybacks were hell.

And they go both ways, pal. Give her a break. She's got other things on her mind. "Do you want to take any more pictures?"

"I've taken six rolls. I think that's enough."

"Six and a half. You snapped ten off the roll that's in the camera now."

She planted her hands on her hips. "What were you doing, counting?"

His training took over, and he pushed aside his growing interest in her. "You bet your sweet ass I was counting."

Her mouth tightened, and her nostrils flared. "Why? Do you think I'm going to sell my photos to some terrorist group? Do you think I'm a traitor?"

He pulled off his glasses, narrowed his eyes, and crossed his arms. "I think you've spent a lot of time in a lot of places our government might consider subversive—you've already admitted you were in

Georgia and Libya. I have no way of knowing who's approached you and why. I don't take chances when my men's lives are at stake."

"You've been watching me for over an hour. If I pointed my camera at anything other than your men, you would have noticed." She glared at him, her expression frigid. "Unless you were looking at something else."

Her challenge made him bristle—because it held some truth. "My CO told me to keep an eye on you. I'm following orders." He took another step closer, staring into her green eyes. "I don't know you, and I don't trust anyone. For all I know, you might be Dickey's lover, some mole sent over here from God-knows-where."

A bright shade of red flushed her face. "How dare you!" Her hands tightened into fists. "I've known Marc and Sarah for years. I would *never*—" In a strained voice, she continued, "I'm not even going to respond to your insulting suggestion. I resent the implication."

Chance kept his gaze on Tempest. Feisty little thing. But his resolve stayed strong. He'd seen spies use less obvious tricks, and despite her explanation, the whole scenario might be some scheme she concocted to worm her way onto the base. "Resent it all you want." He held out his hand. "Now, give me your film."

Her voice rose a pitch. "No! You can't take my film."

"Ms. Raines, I can have your entire camera bag confiscated if I so choose. You're on a United States military installation. This is my domain." He waggled his fingers. "Hand them over. All the ones you've shot are in that little pocket on the side of the bag. You can leave that last roll in your camera until this afternoon."

Unmoving, she tried to stare him down then finally conceded. She unzipped the small pocket and extracted the six rolls. "Here. How am I supposed to develop them? They aren't going to do me any good like that."

"We'll take them to a photo lab and print them up."

Her voice peaked. "You can't do that. I don't want any amateurs messing with my film."

Across the way, a couple of his men glanced at them. He expelled a sigh. "Would you keep your voice down? My men aren't used to seeing a woman out here—they think I'm attacking you."

"You are." Her tight expression sliced through him.

Myriad cryptic responses popped into his mind. He pushed them aside. "I said *we*, as in you and I. We'll find a lab somewhere around here, and I'll stay with you until you're done. Till then, I keep the film." He paused and leaned closer. "Unless you want me to come to your…private darkroom. But I still keep the film."

A low growl rumbled in her throat. She spun on her heels and stomped toward the Blazer.

Chance called after her. "Should I assume you're done here?"

She didn't answer.

He grinned. The woman had pluck. Another plus. He slipped his glasses back on and sauntered across the tarmac behind her, watching her hips sway in the snug skirt.

When he reached the car, she stood facing the passenger door, arms crossed, waiting for him. He took his time rummaging in his pocket for his key and inserting it in the lock. "You've got quite a temper, don't you? I'm surprised it doesn't get you in trouble."

"Most people I deal with don't make a hobby out

of trying to provoke me."

He opened the door. "They don't know what they're missing."

Before she climbed in, she spun and glared at him. With a scowl, she plopped herself on the seat, throwing her camera bag on the floorboard by her feet.

"Careful. I'd hate to see your equipment damaged."

Chapter Six

Wednesday, March 22—1130 hours

Tempest huffed, yanked on the door, and slammed it shut—but couldn't shut out his chuckle. Everything the man did and said grated on her, as if he wanted nothing more than to tease and annoy her. Had he been like this twenty years ago?

No. Not like this. He'd been self-assured, not cocky—strong, but with a kindness under the surface. From what she recalled, he'd done everything possible to make that relationship with Ginny work. It hadn't been his fault the woman had treated him like dirt. He hadn't deserved her attitude, or the way she toyed with him. Maybe he did have a right to be jaded.

Thoughts of those days nearly brought tears to her eyes. Tears of frustration, loneliness, and longing for things she could never have. What wicked twist of fate had brought him into her life then? And again now?

Don't kid yourself, Tempest. You hoped for this. Isn't that why you looked for a job in Norfolk sixteen years ago? Isn't that why you furthered a friendship with Sarah Dickey when you met her and learned Marc was a SEAL?

Somewhere in a tiny corner of her mind, a minuscule fantasy had taken seed. Over the years, she had met and formed friendships with other SEALs and

Special Ops, but when she began cultivating her scheme to rescue Sloan, that seed of fantasy sprouted. Chance's name kept popping into her thoughts with disturbing frequency.

The motivating truth shot through her. The excuse that he was the best held no water. Nothing burrowed deeper, with more pain, than the hope that somehow, if they were together, he would see a woman and not a teenager.

She squeezed her eyes shut. Apparently, he didn't see a kid now. He toyed with her, then pulled back as if she were a leper. She sucked in a breath. Could he possibly have figured out her secret? Was his seeming unfamiliarity just a charade?

Did he know?

If he did, it would explain his attitude. He would have enough information to destroy her, and in turn, Sloan. The unacceptable thought made a tear slide down her cheek. She bent over to dig in her bag and pulled out a pair of sunglasses.

He glanced at her. "Bad time of day for the sun. You okay?"

Choked with emotion, she couldn't respond and just nodded.

The light at the corner turned red, and he slid to a smooth stop, his fingers drumming a perfect cadence on the steering wheel. "What's wrong?"

Tempest turned to face the window. *What kind of response would he accept? Everything in the world?* She floundered for the most believable excuse she could devise. "I don't like the idea of my film being confiscated."

He pulled off his sunglasses and wiped them with a

small cloth nestled in the console. "I'm not confiscating it per se. Consider it safe-keeping."

She glanced his way and grimaced. *Smart-ass.*

"I'm not going to do anything to damage your film." He turned his head and peered at her. In his eyes, a thoughtful kindness blended with concern.

Her resolve to keep a barrier between her and Chance crumbled, and she reached over to touch his leg. The hardness of his muscles sank into her flesh with a calming strength. Their gazes locked, and a flash of fire rose in her chest. For a brief second, she closed her eyes and drew in a hitched breath.

The light turned green, and he pushed her hand away, his mouth tight.

His sudden action made her focus on him—his stern expression. What had possessed her to do such a thing? Had she lost her mind? Chance thought her insane, and maybe the accusation held some truth. With a sigh, she turned toward the window. The silence in the car closed around them in a suffocating chokehold.

****

Chance threw the gear into second and accelerated. Her touch continued to burn against his skin as an unexpected disappointment hit him. He wanted to believe Tempest was different. Seeing the look on her face when she talked about Sloan, he truly thought she loved the man. This woman who had it all could give of herself and be a faithful wife. Men consistently took the rap for cheating, but he'd found many women followed the same path. Even in the teams, he'd encountered some wives who took measures to relieve their loneliness—and fear—when the men went on ops. One had come on to him once, and he put her to rights before she had time to move her hand from his cheek. He'd ended up giving his teammate a character reference during a particularly nasty divorce. The man hadn't warranted her duplicity.

And then a memory of his brother hurtled through his mind. No man deserved what had happened to Chance's older sibling, either. Between his own experience and Troy's, they'd determined no woman was worth the battle or the pain.

Best not to think of that right now.

An image of Tempest materialized inside his brain. He'd provoked her, teased her, played with her, and she took it in stride. Until she touched him. The heat of her gentle fingers on his thigh still seared his skin. He nearly clicked on the air conditioner.

Disillusionment stabbed at his chest. Even with this desire rippling through him, he hadn't expected her to reciprocate. He'd hoped she held to a higher standard than so many other women he'd known. Yet, even with his and Troy's abysmal experiences with women, not all of them were liars and cheats. Sarah Dickey for one had stayed loyal to her husband, as did the wives of several of his men. Which was why they continued to be married and off the market.

"Let me get my clothes out of my car. I'll change, and we can get this jump over with."

"After lunch." He drove past the turn for the hangars, wound through the streets, and headed for the NEX at the east end of the base.

"I'm not hungry."

"Fine. You can watch me eat."

She took off her sunglasses and tucked them inside her purse. "I thought you'd be anxious to get rid of me."

He pulled into a parking place, stopping the car with a jerk. "Babe, I'm not even close to being done with you."

The expression on her face caused a choking knot to form in his throat. Pain, regret, and grief engulfed her features. A fleeting sense of remorse gripped him, but quickly changed to anger. She didn't deserve his sympathy. Cheating wives sank lower than swamp algae. He'd slithered through miles of the green sludge and wouldn't hesitate to do so again—given a choice of getting mired in muck versus being in the company of a cheating wife.

He resisted the urge to slam his fist on the steering wheel. This continuing hunger to know this woman on a different level ate at him like termites decimating a rotten piece of wood. The first woman he'd met in twenty years who actually intrigued him. He could take her to bed, but would that really satisfy him? And even if it did, would the self-recriminations afterward be worth the sex? Chance absolutely never touched another man's wife.

So what is it that you think you want from her?

More than a roll in the hay, but not with a husband in the wings. Best drop this growing obsession before it plummeted him into a situation he'd regret. Anger with himself, Marc, and this woman escalating, he climbed out of the car and headed for the Exchange entrance without bothering to open her door. Guilt coated him for being an ass, but damn it, a woman who wasn't a lady didn't deserve to be treated as one. A part of his brain registered her scrambling to catch up with him, and he didn't care.

****

Chance's sudden hostility was baffling. Mild antagonism and annoyance, she could understand. After all, she'd managed to finagle her way into his schedule. But this vibe of sheer loathing rolling off him seemed abnormal. What had she done to incur such resentment? Even if he remembered, would he despise her that much for the things she had done as a teen?

She caught up to him inside the building and grabbed his arm, forcing him to turn around. "Why are you being so hateful to me? You don't even know me."

His mouth tight, eyes narrowed, he stared at her for several seconds then shook his head.

The cold gaze stabbed her like splinters of ice, and she cringed. He turned his back and entered the sub sandwich food line. In a daze, she wandered to the opposite side of the room, picking up a pre-assembled croissant with chicken salad. With a cola and the sandwich, she paid the bill and found an empty table in a corner.

The scent of the freshly baked pastry made her stomach turn. She stared out the windows, watching the activity in the parking lot. Chance's expression continued to dance in her mind. He didn't claim to know her, but had he somehow sensed her misdeeds? After all this time, did her actions from two decades ago color her that much? Or did he just have some special ability that let him sniff out any flaws?

In the last five days, the world had tumbled down around her. She'd lost her son, had the U.S. government pat her on the head like a little puppy before refusing to help, found Chance, and now, apparently, forfeited him. Again.

Well, not really *again*. That would imply she'd had him once before. Nothing could be further from the truth. Tempest feared that someday her transgression would be punished, but she hadn't known it would hurt so much. Squeezing her lids shut, she tried to ward off the stinging tears. A rustle at the table jerked her thoughts to the present, and she grabbed a paper napkin to dab at the threatening tears. Chance sat at the other side of the small table and studied her for a minute. As his gaze swept over her, his expression lost some of its hardness. Then he picked up his sandwich, digging into it as if nothing were wrong. "Eat your lunch. I don't want you passing out on me when we jump."

She cocked her head. "You're still taking me?"

"My captain issued an order."

Two sailors passed behind her, and she shifted her chair a little closer to the table. "It didn't sound like an order."

"Trust me. It was."

She picked a corner off the croissant and stuck it in her mouth. The light pastry normally would have made her moan in pleasure. Now it fell into her gut like lead.

"I've seen some of your photos and read Sloan's articles. Impressive stuff."

Regardless of everything going on, she smiled. Her son gave her multiple reasons to feel proud twenty-four hours a day. "Thanks. That would mean a lot to him. He works hard."

"The two of you have been in some interesting situations."

"A few."

"You should know how important it is to keep your strength up."

She looked up, scanning his face. Their altercation of a few minutes ago appeared resolved. Still, the need to trust did not give her cause to believe Chance either forgot or dismissed his harsh words of a few minutes ago.

"Sloan tells me the same thing all the time."

"Then he's a smart man." He bit off another hunk of sandwich.

She picked up the croissant and took a small bite. "I thought SEALs learned how to survive without the simple necessities of life like food and sleep."

He shook his head. "Misconception. We learn how to push our minds and bodies beyond what most people think is possible. It doesn't mean they starve you. Even during Hell Week they keep you fed." A crooked smile crossed his face. "If you don't mind a little dirt and sand in your bologna sandwich." He crunched on a potato chip. "They just don't let you sleep. They aren't trying to kill you. Only strengthen you. And weed out the ones who can't hack it."

"What about Hell Week? What's it like?"

His brow knitted in a deep V. He put down his sub and wiped a napkin across his mouth, then took a long swallow of soda. He fixed his gaze on Tempest as if gauging her reaction to his words. "It's five and a half days of the most grueling torture you can imagine. Twenty-four hours a day, one exercise after another, no breaks, no showers, no sleep. No time to think. If you start to think, you lose."

She tilted her head but kept her gaze on him. "Lose? You make it sound like a game."

He shrugged. "It is, in a sense. Winner takes all."

"But what's the point? Why do they do that to

you?"

"Because the ones who make it come out with a belief that there is nothing—" He stopped, emphasizing his last word. "—*nothing*, they can't do."

She shook her head. "It sounds like misplaced invincibility. A dangerous delusion."

"No. We just push a little harder, a little further, to reach our goals. The body's limits no longer hold any meaning. We understand those boundaries are an arbitrarily assigned standard. The body can do infinitely more than most people believe."

Lifting her soda, she paused before taking a sip. "I still don't see how you can survive the intense training. What sets you apart from the ones who don't make it through?"

He finished his sandwich, crumpled his napkin, and dropped it on the plate. "It's a simple brainwashing technique. You open your mind, listen to their drivel, and shut out everything else. When they tell you nothing can stop you, that you're unbeatable, you believe them. When they ridicule you, tell you you're lower than dirt, you tune it out. It's all mind games. *SEALs are ordinary men, doing extraordinary things.*"

She watched as he managed to take in everything around him, while still focusing on her. "A convenient quotation, but I don't believe it. There's nothing ordinary about any SEAL I've ever met. You wear your self-confidence like a medal."

"Because we earned it like a medal." He drained the rest of his soda. "You said people were the same everywhere. Now you're saying we're different."

She leaned over the small table and lowered her voice. "You aren't listening to me. Training may teach you to react faster, differently, follow orders. But emotionally, people are the same. We all hurt, we all feel joy, we all…love." She stared into the remains of her lunch. "You, me, your SEAL team." She raised her head and allowed a tiny smile to cross her lips. "We're not so different, you and I."

The comment hung over the table like a guillotine's sharp blade. At that moment, she would have sacrificed her soul to take it back. But it was too late. Chance glared at her, assessing her every thought, every movement. He stood.

"Yeah? We're not different?" His eyes cold, he leaned over slightly. "Then why aren't you out there rescuing Sloan yourself, instead of here, trying to get me involved?" He picked up his trash and headed for the waste can. He dumped his tray, then looked back over his shoulder, his glance a summons.

Her mind in turmoil, Tempest rose, threw out her uneaten lunch, and followed Chance in silence to his car.

Chapter Seven

Wednesday, March 22—1230 hours

Tempest shadowed Chance across the lot and into the hangar. Cabinets lined the sides of the aluminum building, but the huge center held nothing but empty space, with what appeared to be a small office tucked in the far corner. "What about the thirty-minute video?"

"Civilian stuff for insurance." One eye narrowed as he challenged her. "How do you know about that?"

"I've, uhh, had friends try to convince me to jump before."

A smirk creased his eyes. "What's wrong? Getting scared?"

"No."

He grinned. "You should be. There's a bathroom in the office over there. You can change while I try to find a spare jumpsuit."

She trotted to the back of the building. When she returned, he handed her a suit. It looked huge.

His tone all business, he said, "This is the smallest one I could find. Put it on."

She set down her bags and stepped into the jumpsuit. It didn't hug her as much as she was used to, but at least it fell within the small range. For a man. She zipped it up, knowing full well his gaze never left her.

He tugged at the front. "It's a little loose, but it'll

do." He held out a harness. "Step into this."

She slipped the black straps over her feet and pulled them up to her thighs. As he ran his hands along the wide bands, tightening them, she tried to shut out the surge of heat emanating from his touch.

The heavy, black skydiver's uniform made her feel like a cow. Not that the one bundled in her closet made her feel like a runway model, either. Why had Marc gotten her into this? Some logical premise had prompted his action—after years of friendship, she'd learned he did nothing without forethought and reasons. Suddenly peppered with misgivings, she started to pull away from the source of her unease.

Chance yanked on the straps.

"Ouch. It doesn't need to be that tight." She reached down to ease the tension.

From behind her, he ran his hand over the strap that encircled her midriff. His head bent close to her ear, sending chills down her arm. "I don't want to lose you..." He tugged again, pulling her against him. "...in midair."

Inside the suit, her heart pounded against her ribs. His hands drifted down to the straps running high on her thighs. He slipped his fingers underneath them, tracing treacherously close to her core.

She wrenched from his grasp and turned to face him. "That was uncalled for."

Chance stepped forward until the fronts of their jumpsuits met. "I was only checking to make sure they're snug enough."

Through clenched teeth, she spat, "They're fine."

"What about you? Are you fine?" He hovered over her, leaning down until his lips were inches from hers.

Sneaking his fingers under the straps on her shoulders, he pulled her even closer. "Maybe we should make sure. As good luck. For the jump."

Despite the cool air in the building, sweat drenched Tempest's clothes inside the jumpsuit. Chance's breath filtered over her face. She looked into his clear blue eyes, anticipating the press of his lips on hers—a sensation she'd imagined for over twenty years.

"Yo, Commander! You ready to roll?"

The voice cut through the empty hangar, echoing off the walls. Chance released her so rapidly, she stumbled backward.

"Yeah. Let's get her done." He jerked his head at Tempest. "Come on."

She grabbed her wrist camera and jogged over to the counter to stow her belongings, then dashed out behind Chance. The tethers around her pelvis threatened to cut off the circulation in her legs. A chastity belt two sizes too small couldn't have felt worse. "Chance, this harness is too tight."

He reached behind her, tugged and then ran his hands under the straps.

His caress over her rear end sent a shockwave of desire through every nerve in her body, but she didn't dare speak out. She wouldn't allow him to make her look like a fool in front of these men.

He yanked on the harness to keep her from moving away and played with the buckles. "Is that better?" He turned her to face him. His tone soft, he said, "Tempest, you can think whatever you want, but if I told you the stories I know about loose harnesses you wouldn't be bitching. Trust me."

As insane as it seemed, she did trust him. She

would trust him with her life.

And with her son's.

They crossed the tarmac to the waiting plane. Two young men held out their hands, helping her scramble on board. Pulling the door shut behind Chance, they and the rest of the squadron of eight men settled along the sides of the gutted plane, sitting in squat positions, relaxing as they went airborne.

Tempest strapped her camera on her wrist and tightened the buckles, tugging to check its stability, then leaned against the back of the pilot's seat and drew her knees to her chin, observing the group. Their collective cool and calm attitude not only impressed her, it filled her with ease.

"Why do you have a wrist camera? Do you get to use one often?"

Chance sat perpendicular to her, resting against the side of the plane. Their legs touched and could easily become entwined if they wished.

For her part, the wish dug deep into her being. "It's come in handy a few times."

He studied her, probably refraining from exerting his vocal cords to talk above the roar of the engines.

She glanced at her watch. "How high are we going?"

"About thirteen thousand feet. Takes about fifteen minutes to get up there."

His focus fell on his men for a minute, so she rested her face on her knees, blocking out most of her conscious thoughts. Except those of Sloan. He'd wanted to learn how to skydive, so for his sixteenth birthday, she signed him up for a tandem jump. He'd loved it so much, he wanted lessons and talked her into taking them with him. She'd agreed, but never enjoyed it to the extent he did. Since those days, she'd been on more than three hundred jumps, usually with him, convincing herself it might come in handy someday in her work. However, her wildest imagination wouldn't have brought forth this scenario. She drew in a deep breath. As much as she didn't care for the sport, oddly, this time she felt no anxiety. She would jump into Hell to save her son.

Assuming he wasn't dead.

Covered by the thunder of the engines, she tightened her arms around her knees and groaned, squeezing her eyes closed. She couldn't allow herself to even consider that possibility. The gut-wrenching option simply didn't exist. Rolling her head so her cheek rested on her knee, she found Chance staring at her with startling intensity.

"You okay?"

She lifted her head. "I'm fine."

"Second thoughts?"

She paused, looking him in the eye. "No."

"Good." He scooted close to her, talking in her ear but still raising his voice to be heard. "When they open the door, get on your knees, and I'll hook up the harness. Half the guys will go before we do. We'll slide up to the door. Remember what I told you. Just sit down and let your legs hang out of the opening. I'll give us the push to get out.

"Whatever you do, don't panic on me. I'm not going anywhere. And for God's sake, don't hold your breath. You'll pass out. Pay attention to yourself. If you're holding your breath, scream. It'll make you suck in air and get you breathing again. Any questions about that?"

She shook her head and hid her smile. Recollections of her first jump cascaded into her thoughts—and her terror over leaping into the open space.

"Okay. Just relax during the free-fall. Spread your arms out and enjoy the ride. It'll take about sixty seconds. I'll pull the cord at around 4,500 feet. When we hit the ground, we'll do it standing up. As we touch down, just jog along for a few steps. It should feel pretty natural." He glanced at his altimeter. "Twelve thousand feet. You ready?"

She gave him a thumbs-up, slipped the goggles over her eyes, adjusted the helmet, and stuffed her hair away from her face and into the suit. Rising to her knees, she shifted so Chance could kneel behind her. She felt him hook the steel clips to her harness.

Together, they lined up behind the first four men. The SEAL in front slid the door across the tracks, barely pausing before he jumped out. The men in front of her tumbled out in succession, and with each one's exit, Chance nudged her a little closer to the opening.

Concentrating on Chance's brief set of instructions, she scrambled to the gaping hole as the fourth man disappeared from her sight. She draped her legs over the edge and looked down. "Crap."

She had no time to register any other thoughts or speak any other words.

Chance pushed, and she fell into open space with no concrete points of reference to orient her scattered senses.

And as with every one of the three hundred times before, the muscles in Tempest's throat vibrated as she expelled a bloodcurdling scream she could feel, but not hear with the wind roaring past her ears.

Chapter Eight

*Thirteen thousand feet above Norfolk, Virginia
Wednesday, March 22—1330 hours.*

Tempest clamped her mouth shut and focused on her actions. *Pay attention!* Her brain screamed at her, making her wonder if another shriek had shot from her lips. Sensations battered her mind and body.

Air howled in her ears at a hundred and twenty miles an hour, as if she stood in the center of a category three hurricane. No sounds beyond the tornado-like blast reached her ears. The rush of wind pulled at the exposed skin on her face in a brutal attempt to rip it from her bones. The slightly too-large jumpsuit whipped around her body as if it might be torn into shreds.

Chance tugged at her arms. He spread them out, forcing her to fly like an eagle. They continued plunging at a hurtling speed, dropping a hundred and seventy-six feet for each eternal second, as if the dive would never end. It epitomized the longest sixty seconds of her life. Every single time. Why did she do this? Again?

To save your son.

She would do it a million more times if that's what it took. She dragged her arms back in to take some pictures.

****

A sudden jerk yanked Tempest. Above them, the blue and gold parachute spread across the sky, blocking the sun's glare.

An intense silence infused the air, bringing with it an awareness of life beyond the chaos of Earth. No breeze rustled the nylon fabric, no birds squawked, nothing broke through the enormous impact of the quiet. This was the other reason why. This was why she continued to do this. Every time.

"You with me? You didn't croak, did you?"

"I'm fine. I love this quiet."

"Yeah, it's something else, isn't it?"

Chance adjusted his body behind her. "Stand on my feet."

She shifted her weight, and he grabbed her harness and repositioned it. "Is that more comfortable?"

"Yes, thanks." The force of the wind had made the straps dig deeper into her pelvis. She looked down. "I can see your men. How did they get so far ahead of us?"

"They had their arms tucked in. They're anxious to get these evolutions behind them so they can down some suds and relax."

She felt his warm breath linger over her neck as she snapped off more shots.

"Nice perfume. The last guy I took on a tandem didn't smell this good."

Had it been physically possible, she would've pivoted around to strangle him. "Back off."

He chuckled, and the deep tone warmed her through the suit. "Did our jump put the fear of God into you?"

She declined to answer.

He shoved the cords into her hands. "Here. You can steer." Keeping his fingers wrapped over hers, he demonstrated. "Pull it this way."

She did, sending them gliding to the right, then the left. She curbed her desire to show off her skill and idly maneuvered the chute through the air. He let her play for several seconds, then reclaimed control.

"You'd better let me land. Where you're headed, you're going to dump us in that pond over there."

Relinquishing the ropes, she took a few more pictures and watched the ground come closer as he positioned them over the drop zone.

"See that X? I'm going to land us right in the center. Don't forget. When your feet hit the ground, start jogging."

After feeling as if she were in slow motion for the last two minutes, the spot Chance indicated loomed up quickly. Suddenly, solid ground struck her feet. She started the walking movement, but her legs went out in front of her, and she slid over the dirt on her rump.

Chance's legs wrapped around her hips, and Tempest nestled tight against him. The intimate closeness rocketed through her senses, and she stiffened. "I thought I was supposed to hit the ground running."

He started unhooking the clamps. "Sorry. A crosswind caught us. You weren't ready for the pull. It would have dragged us across the field." He hopped up, extending his hand to help her. "You okay? It was actually a pretty good landing."

"I'm fine." Refusing his offer of assistance, she stood and brushed off her backside.

Through narrowed eyes, he examined her. "You really think you don't need help from anyone, do you?"

"I can take care of myself."

He turned and made moves to gather his chute. "Yeah. I'll just bet you can."

As Tempest waited for him, two of his men strolled toward them.

"So, Ms. Raines, what'd you think?"

She smiled. "It isn't something I want to do every day."

The young man looked genuinely surprised. His companion grinned. "There's nothing like the first time."

With one eyebrow cocked, she grimaced. "A lot like your first fender-bender."

They laughed. "You jumped with the best. Couldn't have been in better hands."

An unexpected tingle ran through her. Chance's hands. These boys had no idea.

Chance straightened and walked toward the hangar. "Quit jerking off. Put up your gear and get your asses out to the obstacle course."

Amidst murmured "yes, sirs," the two men took off.

Tempest marched up to Chance and followed him inside. "That was rather harsh. They were just being polite."

"They're on duty. They don't have time to be polite." Turning his back, he dropped the chute on the floor and began to spread it out.

"If they'd been talking to anyone else besides me, you wouldn't make that comment."

His shoulders jerked, and he straightened to stare at

her. A fire blazed in his eyes. Without a word he sauntered over, roughly unhooked the harness, peeled it from her shoulders, and let it drop to the floor. He grabbed the front zipper on her jumpsuit and pulled it down slowly, keeping his gaze on its downward motion.

A chill ran through her. Although fully clothed under the suit, she felt stripped bare. His look undressed her as surely as if he had ripped her shirt off her body. She swatted his hand, knocking it away.

For a second, he seemed surprised. Then his expression changed, a frigid iciness edging into his blue eyes. He opened his mouth, then tightened his lips and spun around, bending over to fold his parachute.

A ragged breath caught in her chest. These vacillating moods of his confused her. "Where do you want me to put this?"

He tilted his head. "Leave it on that counter. I'll take care of it later."

She moved to the table, laid the bundled-up suit and helmet in a pile, and dropped the harness on top. Pulling her bags from the cabinet, she headed for the exit. "I'll wait outside."

****

Chance didn't acknowledge her words as she stalked out the door. The image he'd had of Tempest earlier, wearing casual clothes, fell somewhat short of the actual vision. Her hips shifted slightly in the snug denim, and the T-shirt hugged her slim form, accentuating every desirable curve on her body. She sucked him in like Charybdis, pulling in Odysseus and his entire ship.

He expelled a graphic curse. The woman meant

nothing but trouble, and his actions mimicked a damned teenager in heat. But that wasn't the whole story. *You're pissed because you want to get to know her, and she's off-limits.* Chance packed up the parachute and stowed it away, then shot a glance at her piled-up jumpsuit. He'd take care of it later this afternoon. Right now, more compelling thoughts filled his mind.

He could have been finished with Ms. Tempest Raines, but he still needed to go with her to the darkroom. Keeping tabs on her film would require them to spend several more hours together, while she developed the rolls and printed the shots.

That scenario alone caused him enough aggravation, but the fact he looked forward to the chore made his blood boil. If she'd only taken pictures on the field, he might have been able to skip keeping track of the images she'd captured, but with her aerial shots he couldn't risk having even an innocent likeness of a secure area slip through.

Yet, even that explanation didn't hold water. He didn't suspect her of any subterfuge. The entire ploy had crept into his mind as a way to stretch his time with her. And that pissed him off even more.

Expelling a long breath, he left the hangar and went outside. Tempest leaned against his car, with her head tilted back against the roof, eyes closed, as if she were taking a quick bask in the mid-afternoon sun. *What's your problem, Chance? Are you really interested in her, or is she just forbidden fruit? It's easier to turn away if you tell yourself that, right?*

Hell. He sighed. No. His interest didn't stem from sex. She pulled at him on a different level. And that admission sent a bolt of god-honest fear through

Chance. Getting involved with a woman didn't fit in his plans. Even if Tempest wasn't married, he had to walk away from her. Now.

Tempest's eyelids fluttered open, and unrelenting grief drenched her face. Her shoulders drooped. Her entire body sagged in defeat. Her expression, her body language, staggered him. Maybe he had been too harsh, too quick to judge. No one could fail to see her torment.

An unexpected stab of envy that she wasn't his pierced through him.

Self-reproach coated Chance with a bitter ache in his chest. He'd been brutally cruel to her...even if he didn't voice all his thoughts, he'd done little to hide them. He needed to suck up his ego and apologize to the woman. Approaching her, this time he kept several feet of distance between them. "Tempest, I—" He choked. The words wouldn't come. "I assume you're ready to go."

She nodded, so he unlocked the car's door and waited for her to climb in. Any attempt at conversation seemed pointless. He drove back to headquarters in silence, pulling into a space by the passenger side of her car.

Tempest crawled out, dragging her camera bag behind her, then trudged around the back of the SUV.

With the engine idling, Chance rolled down the window and watched her.

She set her bag on the passenger seat and pulled out her cameras, quickly rewound the film from both, popped open the backs and took the canisters out. Reaching in the bag, she withdrew a small card. She handed the rolls and business card to him through his open window. "Here's the rest of my film."

"You didn't have to give me that half roll—just the one from the wrist camera. I watched you closely enough."

She shrugged. "I don't want to get caught in some set-up, framed, and thrown in jail." Her attempt at humor fell flat. "The card has my phone number on it. I'm not on deadline, but I'd like to get this film developed as soon as it's convenient for you. The newspaper agreed to run the story when I turn them in."

"That's it? All this for the *Virginian Pilot*? No *National Geographic*? That doesn't sound like the Tempest Raines who has every magazine in the country scrambling for her photos."

She looked ready to lash out at him again, but only let out a tiny sigh. "I guess I could submit it to *Soldier of Fortune…*" A crooked smile passed over her lips, and her shoulders hiked a tic. "Or maybe *Gentleman's Quarterly*. I haven't really given it much thought."

To his ears, she sounded tired and beaten. That it might be partially his fault troubled him. Just because he wanted her and couldn't have her didn't excuse his actions. He shot out a breath.

She frowned, tilting her head toward the hood of his still running car. "Aren't you going to your office?"

"Nah. I've got to go back and put up the stuff we left out. It's after fifteen-hundred. Day's shot now anyway."

"I'm sorry I took up your entire day." Turning, she dropped her cameras back in her bag and started to close the door.

"Look, Tempest, I'm sorry I've been such an ass. I just… Dickey pissed me off. I didn't mean to take it out on you." It seemed the most believable explanation.

Maybe he could salvage the situation. If he could get her mind off Sloan for a little while, it might help clear her thinking. "I don't suppose you'd like to go out for a drink."

She twisted her head around to stare at him. The look of disbelief on her face answered his question explicitly enough. With a slight shake of her head, Tempest walked around the car and climbed in, started it up, and with a final glance at Chance she drove from the parking lot.

"Crap." He'd pushed her too much and hadn't backed off soon enough. Her glaring look didn't conceal the tears collecting in her eyes.

Chapter Nine

Sandbridge, Virginia Beach, Virginia
Friday, March 24—4:00 a.m.

The shrill ring of the phone jarred Tempest from the bed. She snatched the receiver and uttered a breathless greeting.

A static-filled pause reached her ear before the caller spoke. "My Storm?"

The heavy Slavic accent sent chills coursing through her. "Alexei? Yes, it's Tempest. Do you have any news?" She strained to hear him across the weak connection.

"We found Sloan…small camp…is near the foot…casus Mount…by the Kura Riv…"

"I can hardly hear you, Alexei. There's too much static. Have you seen him? Is he all right?"

"He is alive. I did not see him myself. But you must…your film…trade…"

"Alexei! I'm losing you! What did you say?"

The line went dead. "No!" She dropped the receiver back in the cradle and fell across the bed. Tears streamed from her eyes. She covered her face and rolled over as sobs of despair mixed with relief wracked her body.

He's alive.

Emotions overran her, and she let them. Trying to

stem the built-up tension from the last six days would be futile. She wept until the tears stopped, then stayed curled up in a ball until the dry hiccupping sobs relented.

After an eternity, she flipped on her back and faced the glowing red numbers of the digital clock. It flickered and read 4:50.

She groaned. The minutes stretched out interminably. Every day, every night, she prayed for the phone call that would tell her Sloan survived, so she could proceed with her plan. Now it had come, and inertia suspended her actions, her thoughts.

The preparations she needed to make hadn't been completed or even considered. After her initial arranging and charting and mapping things out, she had all but pushed her scheme from her mind. When she should've been finalizing details and looking for errors, she'd paced from room to room, folding dirty laundry instead of washing it, vacuuming the same square foot of carpet over and over, and scrubbing imaginary specks of grease from clean dishes. She could hardly function.

Her one absolute element, the only thing holding her plot together, was the thing furthest from her grasp. She needed Chance. His skill, his connections. Without them, without him, she had no hope of seeing Sloan alive again.

She hadn't spoken to the man since Wednesday, after leaving him in his car in the building's parking lot. Yesterday afternoon, he'd left a message on her answering machine—telling her to call him back if she wanted to develop her film this morning. She hadn't bothered to return his call to confirm.

More minutes ticked away. In a burst of energy, she jumped from the bed, ran into the bathroom, and turned on the shower. Manic, she bathed and dressed, dashed out the door and drove to the base.

The headquarter's parking lot had few vehicles in it during the dawning pre-work hour. She drummed her fingers on the steering wheel, waiting for the time when the building came alive.

Finally, she emerged from her car and approached the entrance. The watchstander stood alert, understandably cautious about a civilian entering the secure building at this early hour. After an extended conversation, he agreed to let her wait on the quarterdeck until Commander Adams arrived.

She tried to sit but couldn't stop her fidgeting. Showcases, models, and pictures dotted the entrance hall, so she amused herself by wandering around, examining every item of interest to her, and more that were not.

The sailor kept his vigil, not bothering to hide his obvious scrutiny of her actions.

As the beginning of the workday neared, men and women began filtering into the building, heading in different directions. She reclaimed her seat, surveying each person until Chance breezed through the door.

She jumped up to cross the room. The watchstander spoke to Chance, indicating Tempest's presence with a nod of his head. Chance turned as she stepped up to the podium.

Without so much as a *good morning*, he kept his gaze on her while asking the sailor for a visitor's badge. The young guard filled out the paperwork, and Chance scratched his signature, handing the pen to Tempest for her to sign. She took the badge and clipped it to her shirt, then followed him to his office.

Nervous energy swelled through her body. She wanted to grab him and shake him until he stopped long enough to listen to her. As they trekked down the halls, she crossed her arms as if the action could contain the energy straining to burst forth.

After unlocking his door, he stood aside to let her enter first. He hung his cover on the clothes tree, then moved to his desk and picked up a stained coffee mug that looked like it hadn't been washed in weeks. "Coffee?"

"Please. Just a little creamer and a packet of sugar." She plopped onto the chair across from his desk and rested her head in her hands. All this subterfuge had gotten her no closer to her goal. The burning itch of seeing Chance after all these years, being so near him and yet not close at all, crawled over her like leeches sucking out her blood. Somehow, she had to persuade him to help her.

So deep in thought, when he returned with the coffee, she didn't hear him until his chair squeaked with his weight. She stiffened and looked up. Steam rose in heated waves from the two cups on his desk. She reached out to grasp one but paused when her fingers wrapped around the lightweight polystyrene. Her hand shook, and she took a deep, steadying breath, then lifted the flimsy cup and leaned back in the chair.

Chance sipped his brew and observed her over the rim of his mug.

She crossed her legs, letting her foot jiggle. His silence unnerved her. Her gaze flitted around his office, focusing on anything besides him.

After a minute, he leaned forward, propping his elbows on the desk. "I wasn't expecting you today. You didn't call."

His voice made her flinch. She rested her arms on her lap and gripped the cup in both hands. "I was gone all day yesterday. It was late when I got home. I didn't want to…disturb you." In truth, she'd hardly left her apartment since Wednesday night, hoping Alexei might call. She'd allowed the answering machine to pick up Chance's call only because she'd just hung up on a persistent salesman minutes before.

"What are you so nervous about?"

She stopped her shaking foot. "Nothing. I'm just anxious to get started."

"You should have called before you came all the way out here—I could have saved you a trip. The base doesn't have any functional darkrooms anymore. At least not any I can access."

The look on her face must have been overt. Crestfallen didn't begin to describe her disappointment. A whispered, "Oh," slipped from her lips. She averted her gaze and lifted the small white cup to hide her dismay. The coffee made tiny waves as her hand trembled.

He watched her for a minute more, then sighed. "Where do you usually develop your film? I'll meet you there."

The unexpected situation made her muscles tense. She ran her hand over her mouth, then drew in a deep breath. "My condo. I set up a darkroom in a spare room."

The tiniest hint of a smile creased the corners of his eyes, and he leaned back. "Then I guess I'll have to go to your place."

His expression made her bristle. Having Chance in her apartment was not a good idea. She tapped her fingers on her cup. "I have a friend who owns a camera store in Norfolk. He has a couple of darkrooms. I used to develop my film there before I set up my own."

He watched her for a few seconds, then turned his attention to the papers on his desk. "Fine. Just give me a few minutes to take care of some things here."

While he went through a stack of forms, scanning them and scribbling his signature on each, she inspected his office. Nearly barren of personal effects, it looked neat and orderly. After spending years wondering about him, it struck her she had no clue about his private life. She studied him as he did his paperwork. Did he have a life outside the Navy at all? "Why don't you have any pictures or anything in here?"

The edge of his mouth hiked up, even as his gaze remained focused on the papers and he continued to sign sheet after sheet. "Waste of time. I'm in a new office every couple of years. Why bother?"

She lifted her shoulders a little. "I don't know. There's just nothing...of you in here."

The comment made him stop and glance up. "This is me. The Navy is my life. You're seeing all there is to see." He resumed his writing. "Besides, I'm retiring in July. Not much point in it now."

Marc had mentioned something about that, but at the time she hadn't realized he'd been talking about Chance, and since then Tempest had forgotten the reference. "Why? You could stay in for several more years. You should be making captain soon."

He set down the pen and folded his hands, lifting

his head to regard her. Several seconds passed before he spoke. "Because I decided it's time I got a different life." He pushed his chair back, opened one of his desk drawers, and scooped up her rolls of film. "Let's go. I can finish this stuff later."

Tempest sprang from the chair. Any kind of activity eclipsed sitting here, motionless and anxious.

They made their way to the quarterdeck, then Chance stopped. "Hell."

His tone made her jerk. *Now what?* "What's wrong?"

"I have some paperwork I need to get up to Marc's office—I forgot." His gaze breezed over her, and his eyes glimmered. "I was distracted. Wait here. I'll just be a minute." He hiked an amused eyebrow at her and headed for the stairs.

With his promise to be only a few minutes, she stood at the building's windows, gazing at the parking lot. After a moment, she dug her wallet from her purse and pulled out a picture of Sloan.

Her son. She would give up all she had for his safe return. The entire blame for his capture fell on her shoulders. After seeing the raid, he'd wanted to leave immediately, but she had insisted on returning to talk to Nikolai and some of the other families that afternoon. He rarely argued with her, but this time his disapproval had been vocal and fierce. He'd conceded, but on their way back to the small village, after she'd mailed her film, they had disagreed again. Sloan finally convinced her they should travel before daylight, which prompted her to leave the hut, seeking Alexei to let him know…and to soothe her ruffled feathers.

If she didn't get her son back alive, her life would

end.

He'd decided to start school in the fall and get his degree. They had discussed it for weeks. He needed to move on, do something different. With the twinkle that so frequently lit his eyes, he said, "I think you're old enough to take care of yourself now, Mom."

She had smiled at his teasing comment, even when her heart felt like it had been wrenched from her chest. How would she survive without him? She couldn't imagine life without him, couldn't even remember when he hadn't been with her. The rest of her life didn't matter.

Sloan was everything.

And he recognized her need. He never said as much, but it influenced his reason to leave. He didn't want his mother so dependent on him. With his usual mastery of words, he made up excuses and reasons and logical rebuttals to her objections. She'd never won a debate with him.

Until this last one. As it turned out, with that small victory, she lost much, much more.

She swiped her finger at the corner of her eye, wiping away the forming tear.

"Tempest? What brings you back?" Marc Dickey walked over and set his hand on her shoulder.

In an instant, she composed herself and gave him a charming smile. "Hi, Marc. Chance and I are heading to a darkroom to develop my film."

He dropped his hand and studied her for a moment. "Have you made any progress toward your goal?"

She closed her eyes and shook her head, then with her brow creased, looked up. "Why did you have him take me on a jump? I've been skydiving for years."

He looked past her for a second. "To give you more time. Get you a little closer. Jumping with someone creates a unique bond."

She almost snorted. It had created a bond, all right. But not a good one. "I'm afraid it didn't work."

A sigh slipped from him, and he shook his head, grasping her hand. "I fear your window is closing."

"Sloan's alive, Marc. I have a contact in Georgia who has…heard some things. He's being held in a compound just inside South Ossetia, near the Kura River." She paused to look around the quarterdeck. "I know what they want. Me. They're keeping him alive until I get back out there."

His eyebrows hiked a tiny amount. "All the more reason for you not to return."

She glared at him. "If he were your son, would you leave him there to be killed?"

"Of course not, but—"

"But what? Because you're a SEAL? A Naval officer? A…*man*?"

Air shot from his nose. His eyes narrowed. "Tempest."

She bent her head. "I'm sorry, Marc." She looked up and blinked back the forming tears. "I have to do something."

He gathered her close and gave her a hug. "Work on Chance some more. He has a heart." He paused. "He hasn't changed in that regard. You should know that."

She jerked and pulled back.

His gaze burrowed through her before he spoke. "You've known him for a while, haven't you?" Two sailors passed behind them, and he lowered his voice. "When you mentioned him several years ago, I recall you asked if I knew him and where he was stationed." His eyebrows hiked a slight amount.

"I—he—I met him briefly a long time ago. He was the first SEAL I ever met. But I haven't seen him since, and the circumstances were so…inconsequential…he doesn't remember me."

"I see." He studied her for a few seconds more, then squeezed her hand. "Tempest, what's going on?"

She frowned and tipped her head. "I'm trying to find Sloan."

His gaze steady, lips tight, he said, "Beyond that." He paused, his hard scrutiny chipping away at her. "Is Sloan Chance's son?"

The unexpected question rocketed through Tempest, splintering her thoughts, her entire body. Her knees buckled as she sucked in a breath and slumped against the wall.

Marc's expression softened, and he took her other hand in his to steady her. "Does Chance know?"

Unable to speak, she shook her head then looked up. Her voice weak, she rasped, "How did you figure it out?"

The question made him smile. "Sloan looks just like him. Sarah and I both commented on the similarities the last time we saw him. That and your questions about Chance. I don't forget those things when they involve one of my men." He released her hands and studied her for minute. "Tempest, this is none of my business, and forgive me for asking, but it falls a little outside my understanding how he could not remember you…under the circumstances."

She squeezed her eyes shut, then blinked. "I looked different then…I was barely eighteen and skinny. And I used to bleach my hair so I'd look more like my sister." She hitched in a breath, and her response came out in a croaked whisper, "And he was drunk."

He pursed his lips and expelled a long breath. His brow creased with a questioning awareness. "Was it at that party for Ginny Randolph?"

Her sudden intake of air caught in her throat and formed a painful bubble, creating a sharp ache in her chest. "You know about that?"

"He mentioned it. It affected him. More than he'll admit. I was a lieutenant, and he'd been assigned to my team. We got to be pretty good friends before he shipped to the west coast, and I pieced together most of the story from comments he made."

"Then you knew where he was when I asked you about him?"

"I knew where he was stationed, but I had no idea where he was. Sarah and I hadn't known you very long, and since you didn't explain your connection to him, I didn't elaborate. We don't talk in the teams."

She ran her hand over her mouth and nodded. "Please don't say anything to him. I—haven't decided how to broach the subject yet. I just want to get Sloan out of there."

"I can't advise you how to handle this. But I'll warn you, he has some very strong ideas about family. You need to figure this out soon. And keep trying. Right now, he's your best option." He gave her another hug and trekked across the quiet lobby.

She dragged her hand through her hair. Marc and Sarah had managed to figure out her secret...how could she possibly extricate herself from this morass? She had to tell Chance. But what if he didn't believe her? He didn't remember her, although she bore little resemblance to the gangly young girl he'd known. She focused again on the photograph in her hand. She'd been a child herself when Sloan had been born, but had pulled herself up, found work, raised him into a fine young man. Too good to die at the age of twenty.

No. With or without Chance Adams, or Marc Dickey, or even a platoon of SEALs, she would get her son out of there.

"Where are you?" Chance stood beside her.

She knitted her brow. "I'm right here."

He cupped her chin. "No, you weren't. You were a million miles away. Or at least several thousand. Thinking about Sloan again?"

She inspected him, looking for signs of sarcasm, but saw none. Still, she only shook her head. "No. I was just—talking to Marc."

"I know. I ran into him when I got off the elevator." For several seconds, he studied her in silence, then his expression cooled, and he asked, "Does Marc know Sloan is missing?"

His question made her twitch. "You asked me that Wednesday." She glanced around the room and stepped closer to him. Her voice a whisper, she kept her gaze steady on his eyes. "No. If Marc knew what I was asking you to do, he would never allow it. I need your help. Of course, I haven't told him."

His brows furrowed, mouth tight. He took her elbow and guided her toward the doors. "Let's go."

Clearly Chance didn't believe her, but the tiny pellets of Marc's words pinged at her. *He has a heart—he's your best option.*

Somehow, she had to convince Chance to help her.

****

Chance led Tempest from the building toward the parking lot. "Where is this place?"

"In Ghent, on Colonial Avenue."

"Aperture? I've been in there. I bought my brother a 35mm for Christmas a couple of years ago. The guy knows his stuff."

Her eyes lit up, and she smiled. "Dan's a film purist. His wife talked him into carrying digital cameras and supplies a few years ago. Otherwise he probably would've had to close the store."

"Good. Too many privately-owned shops in Ghent have already closed their doors."

She shot him a glance. "How do you know Ghent so well?"

"Because I lived there for a while. And I like the restaurants—I eat down there a few times a month." He walked up to his truck. "Why don't we just go together? There's no sense in driving two cars."

Her shoulders twitched, then she relented. "Okay. Let me get my things." She took off in a trot before he could stop her, so he climbed into the truck and started it up, following her through the lot. He pulled up to her car as she was locking it, and he stretched across the seat to push open the passenger door. Before she finished stowing her gear, her cell phone rang, and she moved a few steps away to answer. Her muffled voice floated through the air, but he couldn't clearly distinguish the words. Then she clicked the phone off and settled into the front seat, staring out the passenger window.

Something was bothering her. He put the truck in gear but kept his foot on the brake. "Did you get some news about Sloan?"

His question seemed to startle her, and she shifted her posture. "No—it was Dan. I had called to let him know we were coming over. I wanted to make sure the darkroom was available."

The answer was logical enough but failed to satisfy him. Still, he let it slide and left the base to head toward downtown Norfolk. He meandered along Shore Drive until she finally questioned him.

"Could you have taken a slower route?" Sarcasm laced her tone. "Why didn't you get on the interstate?"

"Maybe I'm enjoying our titillating conversation."

She grimaced, sighed, and turned toward the window.

He grinned and turned onto Colonial Avenue. By the time he found a parking place and they walked to the store, nearly an hour had passed.

The second Tempest stepped through the door, a burly man with a graying beard and ponytail swooped up and embraced her. "Tempest. You never come see me anymore."

Against his big chest, her voice came out muffled. "Not true. I was here a month ago."

He released her and faced Chance, extending his hand. "Dan Siebert." His eyes narrowed. "You've been here before. Bought a camera. For…your brother?"

Bemused, Chance grasped the man's hand. "Chance Adams. And yeah, I did. It was a couple of years ago. I'm surprised you remember."

One of his shoulders hiked up. "You didn't skimp. Is he happy with the gift?"

"Loves it. The next time he's in town, I'll bring him by."

Dan nodded, and his gaze dropped to the Trident above Chance's uniform pocket. His thick eyebrows twitched before he turned his attention back to Tempest. "Darkroom's open. Go do what you gotta do."

She headed for the back of the shop with Chance on her heels. While she located the supplies, she spoke over her shoulder. "Do you do that on purpose?"

"Do what?"

"Intimidate people that way. Or does it just come naturally?"

"What are you talking about?"

"I've known Dan Siebert for years, and I've never seen him react like he did when he saw your Trident. It impresses people, doesn't it?"

He folded his arms, leaning against the counter. "I suppose. I don't worry much about what people think." He paused. "Does it impress you?"

She jerked, setting down the container of chemicals she held. Turning to face him, she examined him for a long minute. The overhead light reflected off the pin on his chest, and she paused to study the details. The flying eagle's sharp talons clutched a trident, pistol, and anchor. The imposing symbol depicted everything a SEAL embodied. She tore her focus away, glanced at his eyes once more, then returned her attention to filling the trays with chemicals.

He moved closer until his arm brushed hers. "You didn't answer me."

"It might have, once. Not anymore."

He pressed against her a little more. "What impresses you now?"

A clamminess coated her skin. "After all the things

I've seen, not much."

"You're cynical." He reached out, brushing her hair away from her face.

She shivered.

"Cold? I've got a jacket in the car. Want me to get it?"

"No. I'm fine." Pulling away, she made her final preparations for her film. "I've got to turn the light off. It's going to be pitch dark. Maybe you should wait outside."

He smirked. "I've been in darkrooms before. I think I'll stick around. You might try to switch rolls of film on me."

She glared at him, then snapped off the light, continuing her work in the blackness. For an hour, she said nothing, concentrating on her task.

Even in the dark, Tempest sensed his gaze on her.

Chapter Ten

A small compound in South Ossetia
Friday, March 24—5:30 p.m.

Sloan pressed against the hard-packed dirt, rolled onto his knees, then pressed his back against the wall. Using the trembling muscles in his legs, he slid upward to a standing position.

A wave of dizziness swirled through his head, and he waited for it to pass. The quantity of food they provided him kept him alive, but weak.

Just as they wanted.

His mother's quest to reach him had, if he were to believe Alexei, hit a dead end. She'd had no luck obtaining assistance and planned to return on her own.

Or so his captor asserted.

The conversation Alexei had with his comrade before entering the cell didn't support his claims. He had called Tempest, but the connection had been so poor he didn't learn any new information. A surge of hope flowed through Sloan. Maybe his mother had found a safer way to return—one of which the Russian was unaware. Regardless, whether she did or not, Alexei would never tell him the truth—unless that truth benefitted his own cause.

He began to make tiny jumping movements, and after a few minutes switched to a slow hopping shuffle around the edges of the cell. No matter what else he accomplished, in the event his mother returned and tried to get him out, he had to be able to go. He couldn't be an impediment to the escape plan, whatever it might entail, and end up a liability that brought them both to their deaths. But the deep burn that shot through his stiff muscles with each movement sent spasms through his legs and into his back. This limited amount of movement did little to alleviate his discomfort.

Some drugs would help.

He squelched the thought. He'd been down that road and swore never to go back. Nor had he considered it—until now. But something to erase the burning aches in his shoulders and back would be nice.

As he scuffled his feet along the dirt floor, he allowed his thoughts to wander. When he'd been a child, he'd spent enough time in the homes of his friends to understand his mother harbored some inner drive other parents didn't have. She'd nurtured him, but pushed him—loved him, but never coddled him.

He'd wanted to do something special for her. So at the age of eight, he spent countless hours at the homes of neighbors—sweeping walks, washing cars, doing whatever he could to earn a few dollars. Then on Saturday, the day before Mother's Day, he'd ridden his bike to the jewelry store and bought her the gold ring. The mothers of all his friends wore a ring like that, and he wanted her to have one, too. The next morning, when he'd presented it to her, wrapped with far too much tape and an uncovered corner where the paper fell a hair too short, she'd opened it and started to cry. His mother had never cried—not in front of him. He thought he'd done something bad.

But she pulled him close and hugged him for a long time, until he wriggled away, tired of the mushy embrace. All she said was, "Thank you."

At the age of sixteen, however, he began to resent not having a father and blamed her for that absence. After years of badgering her for information about whoever the man was, and having her reticence remain steadfast, his anger at her and his own loss overwhelmed him. He went through a rebellious stage, fell into a bad crowd, and turned to drugs.

His experimenting began a destructive decline that he somehow managed to hide from the normally astute woman. Then two months before his seventeenth birthday, after an all-night party, he'd awakened in the morning, looked at the carnage around him, and been engulfed with the insanity of his activities. Beyond the lectures, beyond the verbal instructions, his mother's actions taught him more about life and growth than any of those so-called friends would ever recognize or appreciate.

In a flash flood of insight, the useless insanity of his actions gushed over him.

He crawled home to nothing more than a long look from her. No reprimands, no questions. But the haunting expression in her sleep-deprived, red-rimmed eyes sliced through him deeper than any knife could slash or words could describe. At that moment, more than any other, remorse consumed him. He said only, "I'm sorry, Mom," trudged to his room for the remainder of the weekend, and never faltered again.

When he graduated and asked her if he could travel with her and put off college, after some debate, she'd agreed. And as well as he knew her, she undoubtedly now cursed herself for that decision and blamed herself for his capture.

His breathing quickened as he kept moving. They'd argued Saturday night because the continuing encroachment by the Russians worried him. For them to stay any longer was too dangerous, and he hadn't been wrong in his assessment. And frankly, he'd tired of this trip and was anxious to get home. When she'd finally agreed, she'd tramped to Alexei's to tell him. Had she not, they'd both be dead right now. She was not to blame for this. If anything, that argument and her frustration had saved their lives.

His mother was the strongest—and best—person he'd ever known in his life. He could not let her down.

****

Chance stood in the corner, alternately watching Tempest when she turned on the light, and sensing her when the blackness enveloped them. After she'd developed the film, she left the red light on, working under its deep glow. It cast a sensual warmth throughout the small room, bathing her in crimson heat. But her methodical efficiency fascinated him. She wasted no energy, no movements.

She knew her job and did it well.

As her prints came out of the dryer, she set them aside. Chance moved around her, skimming against her back. "Mind if I take a look?"

She mumbled her consent, so he picked up a photo, holding it up to examine under the muted red light. As he studied each one, he pursed his lips. If Sloan could influence a person's thoughts with his written words, Tempest could rock them with her photos.

In the faces of his men were things he had never

91

noticed before. Intensity, determination, a desire to be the best. Traits he knew existed, had to exist, but had escaped his detection in such a concrete form. Other pictures showed them joking, smiling, processing out the remainder of the adrenaline rush from their jump and drill, preparing to tackle the next exercise.

He picked up another print and smiled. She hadn't lied—the preening she'd mentioned. Tempest had caught the men's actions with her lens, although it had soared right past him.

But at the time, he hadn't been focused on the troops.

She swished the last print in the chemicals, waiting for the images to form on the paper.

As her long elegant fingers grasped the tongs, a picture of her manipulating those hands on his body propelled though his mind. Would she graze her fingernails lightly across his chest, or dig them into his shoulders and back until she drew blood? And after—would they talk and cuddle, or drift into a satisfied sleep? A life with Tempest could—

He cut off the thought. A life with Tempest could never be. The physical draw was strong, but his desire to know her, to learn her habits, likes, and dislikes was what made him retreat and reconnoiter. Her hair fell around her face, obscuring much of her features. He reached out to tuck it behind her ear, skimming his fingers along her cheek.

With a slight hitch in her movement, she stuck the photo in a pan of water, then backed away. "That's all I'm going to do. I've got enough to work with here."

"Yes, I think there's more than enough to work with."

She stiffened, turned away from him, and started cleaning up.

He stepped behind her, ran his hands through her hair, and pulled it back over her shoulders, wrapping his fingers around it to make a ponytail. He spoke softly in her ear. "We've been locked up in here for hours. Aren't you hot?"

"No." Her voice cracked, and she cleared her throat. "It's cool enough in here."

He dragged his fingers over her neck. Her skin felt damp. "Then why are you sweating?" He leaned over, letting his lips sweep over her neck. "I take it back. You're covered with chill bumps. Maybe I should warm you up."

She made a tactical error then. She turned around. "Chance…"

Without hesitating, he slipped his arms around her and pulled her close. His mouth covered hers, controlling, taking, possessing. Husband or not, he wanted her, and she had given him no reason to think she didn't want him.

It took only a few seconds for her to grow slack in his arms. She met his kiss with an urgency of her own, accepting everything he offered. Her arms moved over his shoulders, clinging to him as if she would never let him go.

Slipping his fingers between the buttons on the front of her shirt, he brushed the smooth skin of her midriff. He popped open a button, and his fingers drifted up, stroking the cup of her bra. She whimpered, tightening her grip on him. He responded by kissing deeper, grazing her teeth with his tongue, exploring with a blinding hunger, savoring the taste of her.

He pulled back, and she opened her eyes. A guileless trust, eyes dark with desire, rushed across her face.

Chance swore and broke away. What the hell was he doing? The woman had more tricks than a well-trained pup. She switched it on and off faster than he could drop and insert a mag in his weapon. No matter how much she sucked him in, he couldn't allow himself to be duped by her seductive flattery.

Tired of the games and his muddled infatuation, he shifted his aggravation—again—to her. The tone in his voice said as much as his words. "Tell me something. Does Sloan love you?"

Chapter Eleven

Ghent Subdivision—Norfolk, Virginia
Friday, March 24—2:30 p.m.

Tempest swayed against the counter. The man's vacillating moods continued to keep her off-kilter. He kissed her as if he wanted nothing more in the world, then retreated as if repulsed. She lowered her head and pressed her fingers against her eyes. *What did he ask me? About Sloan. If he loves me.* "Of course he does. I…he says he does. How can you ever really know what someone else is thinking?"

Chance barked out a laugh. "I'd say that's a subject you're an expert on."

She frowned at him. "He's been traveling with me for two years. It was his choice to work with me. I didn't force him into leaving home."

He leaned closer to her. "Maybe he wants to keep an eye on you."

"He has said that on occasion."

"I can see why."

Fury flushed through her, tensing the muscles in her neck. She whipped around, gathering equipment. The manic activity let her work off the surge of anger. She couldn't afford to indulge in this irrational fantasy about Chance Adams. Far greater things had to be resolved first.

Like how to get to Sloan.

She drew in a deep breath. "He's alive."

"So you think."

"No. I know he is. I got a phone call this morning. From a friend. They found him."

"If they found him, why didn't they grab him?"

She glowered at him. "Oh, come on. You, of all people, should realize that's a stupid thing to ask."

"Okay, fine. He's alive. If your…*friends* didn't grab him, what else are you planning to do? Go back and do it yourself?"

She gave him a long, hard look.

"Oh, no. You tried that trick on Wednesday. Forget it. The Navy isn't going to get involved in this."

"I don't want the Navy involved. Just you. You've got the expertise. You've rescued hostages before—"

"Yeah—with a squad of SEALs behind me. Not alone."

"You wouldn't be alone. I'd be there."

He burst into laughter. "You've got to be kidding me. I was right. You *are* insane."

She grabbed his forearm and dug her nails into his muscles. "You're right. When it comes to Sloan, I am insane. I nearly lost him once, and it's not going to happen again. I *will* do whatever it takes to get him back."

He raked his fingers through his hair. "You are some piece of work. You can stand there ranting and raving about rescuing Sloan, not sixty seconds after you laid a kiss on me—"

She released her grip on him. "On you! You ki—" She stopped. "I don't see what one has to do with the other."

His jaw went slack. "What the hell kind of relationship do you two have anyway?"

His interrogation grated on her conscience. She'd flogged herself enough over this situation—she didn't need more recriminations from someone she barely knew—who didn't even remember her. She planted her hands on her hips. "Our relationship is fine. Not that it's any of your business." She glared at him.

"Yeah? It certainly works to your benefit, doesn't it?"

Her jaw tightened until she gritted her teeth. "Since you found it so repugnant, *I* will certainly refrain from kissing *you* again. Now are you going to help me or not?"

"Not."

She tossed the rest of her belongings in a box, laying the photos carefully on top. "Let's go."

He reached for the crate. "Here. I'll carry that."

She angled away from him. "I can manage." She didn't need this man, or any man, treating her like a helpless female.

His gaze bored through her. "Good. Since you're so capable, you shouldn't have any trouble getting your hands on your adoring Sloan." He yanked open the door.

They headed out of the darkroom in silence. As they passed through the store, Dan looked up with a smile that rapidly disappeared. She dropped the box on the counter and skirted behind the structure to give him a hug.

"You get everything done?"

"Yes. Thanks, Dan. I'll call you."

Before she could make her way back to pick up her

box, Chance grabbed it and headed out the door. She spat out an extended grunt.

"Tempest?" Dan's voice cut through the quiet store. "What's going on? Are you okay?"

She drew her hands into fists and held them behind her back as she turned. "It's fine, Dan."

His tone changed. "That guy messing with you? Because if he is—"

"Stop." She went back to give him another hug. "He's okay. Just aggravating."

He bellowed a laugh. "So that's how it is. In that case, good luck." He winked and scooted her out the door.

Chance had already cleared the corner, and she dashed behind him. Crape myrtle trees with tiny green budding leaves crowded the wide median strip of the side street. In front of one home, a plum tree filled with pink blossoms brought some early color to the yard. Another yard had a dogwood just starting to bloom. Beds of yellow daffodils in front of a group of apartment buildings waved in the slight breeze. The signs of emerging life gave her hope.

She hurried to close the gap between her and Chance and reached the Blazer just as he closed the hatch. He glanced at her and went around to open the passenger door for her. The cryptic expression on his face gave her no hints as to his thoughts.

Before she climbed in, he said, "We seem to have missed the lunch hour. Would you like to get something to eat?"

The question stopped her dead. "Why?"

His lips curled in, and he scraped his teeth over them. Voice tight, he said, "Goddamn it. Because I'm a fucking gentleman." He glared at her. "I thought you might be hungry."

Memories from the past exploded in her mind. Until now, he hadn't regressed to using profanity. She'd managed to anger him, nearly as much as Ginny did on that fateful night. She dropped her head and squeezed her eyes to stem the threatening tears. If he walked away, the odds of saving Sloan took a nosedive. And while she didn't relish the thought of engaging in any more verbal duels with this man, she still had to, somehow, convince him to help her. She couldn't accomplish that locked in her apartment.

Avoiding his gaze, she drew in a breath and struggled to keep her tone neutral. She had to back off, so she used the only tactic she could devise—honesty. "I'm sorry. I...I'm running out of options." Tears spilled from her eyes, and she swiped at them.

A deep sigh came from him. He took her elbow. "Have you been eating anything at all?"

"Not very much."

He shook his head. "Come on. Get in the car. You need something to eat."

He closed the door behind her and moved to the driver's side, slipping behind the wheel. When he stuck the key in the ignition, he glanced at the dashboard. "It's almost fifteen-hundred. By the time we get back to the base..." He paused, staring out the windshield. "Where do you live?"

"Sandbridge."

He chuckled. "Figures. Ends of the earth. Tell you what. I'd like to change—I'd rather not wear my uniform. Let's go get your car, and if you can hang on for another thirty or forty minutes, I'll take you someplace decent." He slipped his hand across the console to grasp hers. "Okay?"

Still unable to look at him, she nodded her head. "Okay. I should probably change, too."

He put the car in reverse and backed out of the space, giving her a quick once-over. "You're fine."

A tiny laugh caught in her throat. If he deemed her attire of blue jeans and a long-sleeved work shirt appropriate for dinner, then their definitions of someplace *decent* differed vastly. Still, he was being—a *fucking* gentleman. She huffed out an amused breath and turned her attention to the passing scenery.

When they reached the base and pulled up by her car, he started to speak, then stopped, scanning her face. "If you want to change clothes, why don't you go on home, and I'll pick you up?"

She knitted her brow. "Chance, it's a long drive out to the south end of Virginia Beach—at least forty minutes. You've already taken me all over town today. Are you sure you want to do that?"

He shrugged. "We can eat out there. You know the Little Italy?"

"Of course I do. They have the best Italian food in Tidewater."

"Good. At least we agree on something. I haven't been there in a while. What's your address?"

She scribbled it on the back of a business card and handed it to him.

He slipped it in his pocket without reading the address. "I need to run into the office for a few minutes, so I'll be about an hour behind you." He waited until she got in her car and started the engine, then headed inside the building.

Chapter Twelve

Sandbridge, Virginia Beach, Virginia
Friday, March 24—5:00 p.m.

As Chance maneuvered the Blazer toward her building, he let out a low whistle. Little Miss Photographer lived in one of the most luxurious oceanfront condominiums in Virginia Beach. He turned into the drive, pulling up to a tiny booth housing a security guard. The man monitored the parking lot, warding off the tourists and sun-seekers looking for a convenient place to leave their vehicles.

"I'm here to pick up Tempest Raines. Chance Adams."

The man checked his list, then handed Chance a guest pass. "We have some empty spaces along the side there, sir."

Chance thanked him and tossed the pass on the dashboard, then found a space and backed the Blazer in. He didn't bother to lock the doors.

Inside the building, a pristine whiteness assaulted him. Mirrored walls and white marble floors made the lobby seem even larger. Huge potted palms accented the room, but the area held little seating. Apparently, the homeowners' association didn't want people loitering on the building's ground floor.

"May I help you?"

Another checkpoint. He approached the hotel-like desk. "I have an *appointment* with Tempest Raines."

The man overlooked Chance's sarcastic tone and checked his list. "Commander Adams? Do you have some form of identification?"

Chance pulled out his military ID card and tossed it over the counter. It landed squarely on top of the guard's paperwork.

The guard picked it up, examined it, and passed it back. "Thank you. Miss Raines's apartment is on the fifth floor. She left word that you could go on up. The elevators are straight ahead."

Chance started moving toward the back of the lobby.

"I'll let her know you're on your way."

Without bothering to express any thanks, Chance entered the elevator and pressed five, but not before he noticed another guard lingering in the corner of the room. Shaking his head, he watched the doors slide shut, then focused on the silent numbers indicating the climb to the fifth floor.

He exited the lift and walked down the hall to Tempest's apartment. The strategically-placed security cameras didn't escape him. With a quick press on the bell, he lounged against the doorframe, arms crossed.

When she opened the door, he forgot his irritation. She wore a short suede skirt with a hip-hugging sweater. Soft leather boots wrapped around her calves. Everything matched in a deep shade of forest green, but with her dark auburn hair falling on her shoulders, the outfit did anything but camouflage her.

"I need to get my purse."

Chance sauntered inside and closed the door

behind him. Ahead and to his left, he glimpsed a living room stacked with piles of mail and newspapers. Amused, he asked, "Do you ever read your mail?"

She reappeared carrying a small clutch. "I'm still sorting through everything that collected while we were gone. And I had a choice. I could either clean the apartment or get dressed."

His gaze fell to her chest. "You didn't have to dress on my account." He snaked his arms around her waist, dipping his head to speak in her ear. "In fact, undressed sounds like a much better idea."

She wriggled from his grasp, shaking her head. "I wish you'd make up your mind," she muttered.

"I made up my mind a long time ago. I just haven't decided what to do with you yet." He appraised the long lines of her body. "Or when."

He watched her stiffen. Had she been a cat, her back would have been arched and her fur bristled. He backed off. Teasing might be acceptable, but not touching. His impulsive action in the darkroom this afternoon ate at his conscience already. A wave of frustration flowed over him, but Chance shrugged it off.

"I'm surprised a building with so many amenities doesn't offer a maid service."

"It does. I only use it when I'm gone. It's expensive."

He cocked an eyebrow. "What price fame. The security in this place is as good as the base's."

"I value my privacy. I don't get much time for myself. It's worth it to me to live in a building with some protection."

As they turned to leave, he faced a dining room. Diagrams, atlases, and papers littered the area, strewn across the tabletop. Out of curiosity, he left her standing and stepped over to examine the charts. Heavy markings all but obliterated maps of Georgia, Russia, Turkey, and the Black Sea. Different colors of marker encircled cities. Airports had stars on them, highlighted paths ran over the Caucasus Mountains. Some magazines, opened to the classifieds, sat at the table's end, with ads for mercenaries highlighted in bright yellow marker. He pursed his lips.

"Chance, can we go? I'm hungry."

He looked over at her. "You're really serious about this."

"Please."

He surveyed her for a minute more, then followed her into the corridor as she locked her door.

They went downstairs in silence, proceeding through the lobby. Both guards spoke to Tempest, calling her by name. Her grave demeanor vanished, and she addressed them with cheerful greetings.

Chance waited until they were in his car before he spoke. "How the hell do you do that?"

She shot him a questioning look.

"You change moods faster than rumors spread in a small town."

"I told you. I value my privacy. I don't care to have everyone around me know what I'm thinking."

"You don't do it with me."

She paused for a long time, staring out the window. "That's because I'm tired of games."

He started the car and pulled from the space. "I was enjoying them."

"That makes one of us," she mumbled.

He grinned and screeched from the lot into the

heavy afternoon traffic, gaining a scowl from the guard in the booth. The drive to the Little Italy only took a few minutes. Although early, the parking lot had already begun to fill. He found a spot at the far end and zipped in. As they walked up to the door, he slipped his arm around Tempest's waist. No reaction came from her.

The atmosphere inside the restaurant hummed with Friday happy hour patrons. The hostess seated them at a table in the middle of the noisy crowd, handing them menus and disappearing.

"Pizza okay with you?" Chance didn't bother to open the menu. Tempest nodded her agreement, then turned to stare across the room with a preoccupied look.

When the waitress returned, he ordered a loaded pizza and two beers, glancing at Tempest for her approval. Her attention remained elsewhere, so he handed the menus to the waitress and let her depart.

He rested his arms on the table, watching Tempest. Under the dim light, her green sweater looked darker, setting off her fair skin. Strands of hair curled under her chin. He laced his fingers together in a tight knot to keep from reaching over to push them back. As he examined her, his gaze returned to her eyes.

From the minute he'd gotten a good look at her in Marc's office, those eyes set off a series of memories he'd tried to forget. Until Wednesday, he hadn't thought of Ginny Randolph in years. Odd, considering the way he'd felt about her at the age of twenty.

But not so odd, considering how the relationship ended.

The mere fact she noticed him at all had sent his head reeling at the time. From a well-to-do family, she had it all. Looks, brains, and a Playboy bunny figure. A year younger than Chance, Ginny saw him one day in his ROTC uniform and made a pass at him that quickly blossomed into a full-fledged affair. He fell in love.

Although they dated for over three years, he realized early that he and Ginny came from different worlds. She would never deign to step down from her social class to marry a lowly sailor, officer or not. But with the optimism of youth, and the hope of winning her heart, he set out to be the best sailor he could become.

He decided to try out for the SEALs.

Soon after his grueling months of training, he showed up at her graduation party in full uniform with his shiny new Trident on his chest, only to discover she'd gotten engaged to some guy with three first names and a *third* tacked on the end. With a superior smile just shy of scorn, she flaunted the jerk in his face all night. Chance changed into the civvies he'd brought along, got drunk and made a fool of himself—and determined he would never again let a woman affect him that way.

Tempest hadn't lied. Even a SEAL could feel hurt.

His gaze swept over her. She held no such arrogance. Reputedly one of the best photographers in the country, if not the world, he suspected part of her success came from her ability to meld herself into her surroundings. Women like Ginny made a hobby out of being the center of attention. Tempest disdained the limelight.

More sensuality oozed from her than Ginny could ever dream of having. He studied her. The similarity between the two women ended at the eye color. Close, maybe, to Ginny's, but not the same. A deeper green, with eyelashes long enough to whisk against a pair of glasses if she wore them. Plus, Tempest's dark auburn tresses attracted him more than Ginny's hair color. Virginia Randolph was every bit the society bitch, right down to the perfect blonde hair.

At the time, he'd known, in his rational mind, he and Ginny didn't make an ideal match. He needed a woman with substance, intelligence, one who he could talk to. Not a social gadabout, only interested in social position and power. But in his besotted state, he reveled in her attention. Until she tired of him and cast him aside like an old sock with a hole in the toe. What had he thought? He could take a needle and thread and stitch up the sock every time it wore through? How many times could he do that before the sock held no yarn left to stitch?

Had he not sworn off women completely, he could almost...*almost*...envision a life with someone like Tempest.

Tempest period and no one else.

If she weren't married. His chest filled with a deep aching breath.

Their gazes locked, and she looked at him for a long moment. Then she leaned across the table. "Chance, you've got to help me."

Her demand made his nerves tingle. He'd jumped through enough hoops in the past for a woman. "I thought you could take care of yourself."

"Stop it," she hissed. "This isn't a joke. You're the only hope I have. I've got a plan, but I can't do it alone."

She isn't Ginny. Don't take it out on her. But the

past continued to haunt him. His tone blunt, he said, "You shouldn't have been messing around in the middle of a civil war. What about your Georgian friend?"

She hesitated. "He isn't Georgian. He's Russian."

He threw up his hands and let them land on the table with a thud. "What the hell are you doing making friends with a Russian? They're the ones who are invading Georgia. Who is this guy?"

The waitress appeared, balancing a huge round tray. With Tempest and Chance both leaning across the table, she had no place to set the heavy pizza.

"Umm, excuse me, sir?"

Chance looked up. "Could you put that in a box to go?"

With a shrug, the girl trotted off.

"Why are we leaving?"

"Because. We can't talk about this here. We're going back to your place."

Chapter Thirteen

Sandbridge, Virginia Beach, Virginia
Friday, March 24—6:00 p.m.

Tempest let out a huff. "My dining room table is covered with papers."

Earlier, he would have suggested they eat in the bedroom, but for once, he had no urge to tease her. The waitress came back with the boxed pizza and the check and placed them on the table. Chance glanced at the total, stuck some bills in the vinyl holder, and stood. He picked up the dinner. "Let's get out of here."

He stopped at a Wawa on the way to her condo and bought a six-pack of beer. As they pulled into the drive, the guard nodded and waved them through. In the lobby, the man behind the desk wordlessly watched them cross the room.

When they entered her apartment, she led him into the kitchen.

While she served their pizza, Chance uncapped two bottles of beer and put the rest in the refrigerator. She opened a cabinet and pulled out two foam drink holders, tossing one to him.

"I wouldn't have pictured you as the type to keep snuggies on hand."

"They're for company. I rarely drink beer unless I'm overseas."

"White wine, I imagine."

She picked up her plate and moved to a small table nestled in a nook overlooking the ocean. "Red."

He followed her over. "A born rebel. I'm surprised you don't down shots of Russian vodka with your Communist friends."

Her shoulders tensed. "I do." She scowled. "With my *Russian* friends."

He bit off a hunk of pizza and shook his head. She probably drank half of them under the table, too. The more time he spent with her, the less her revelations surprised him. "Why do you think you have to do this yourself? Have you talked to the government?"

"I tried. Since we went there of our own accord, they don't seem terribly inclined to do anything about the situation. The Ossetians haven't made any demands or declared him a hostage. In fact, I don't believe anyone outside their territory knows. I think our government is afraid of the possibility it could turn into an international incident."

Keeping his gaze on her, he took a swallow of beer. "That could be the case. What exactly do you think you're going to do?"

"Fly into Moscow. I can make my way down to Nal'Chik. It's only a hundred miles or so from where I think Sloan is being held."

He looked out the huge window at the ocean. Dark clouds clustered over the horizon. The setting sun reflected vivid shades of pink and purple on the gray shadows. "Where you *think* Sloan is? Isn't that a bit reckless?"

"Alexei said he's in a camp close to the foot of the mountains, near the Kura River." She lifted her bottle.

"At least I think that's what he said."

"Why? Wasn't he speaking English?"

"The connection had a lot of static. I couldn't hear him very well."

"Are you going to tell me who this guy is?"

She looked toward the window then returned her focus to Chance. "His name is Alexei Baranov. He's a friend. Sloan and I met him when we did the story on the oil pipeline."

While she spoke, he munched on his pizza. He set the slice down and drank some more beer. "And you trust this guy?"

She paused a little too long. "As much as I trust you."

Chance would have taken it as a compliment had it not been for her hesitation. For whatever reason, she didn't feel overly confident about this Alexei dude either. He let it slide. "How do you intend to hook up with this character?"

"He lives in Moscow. He'll pick me up at the airport, and we'll go together down to Nal'Chik."

"And then?"

"It gets a little…fuzzy."

He grimaced and shook his head.

"Alexei has access to a small plane. He plans to fly me over the mountains, and I'll parachute out near the camp and try to get Sloan."

He laughed. "You've been on one tandem jump, and you think you're qualified to jump from an airplane, alone, in the middle of a civil war." As he studied her, a distinct indignation skimmed across her face. Her lips tightened, and she started to speak, but clamped her mouth shut. Simply watching her could provide him entertainment for hours, but he only let out a deep breath. "You really are insane. If the jump doesn't kill you, the Russians probably will. And how do you intend to get out of there after you nab him? Walk?"

"That's where I start running into a little problem."

He rubbed his forehead. Beer in hand, he pushed from the table and went into the dining room.

Tempest followed him. When he bent over the map, she pointed. "I thought about going over the Black Sea and trying to go up the river, but I don't have access to a boat. And it would take too long. I'm afraid the longer I hang around, the more likely I am to get caught."

"You got that part right." He scanned the map. "Why are the Ossetians holding him anyway?"

She pulled out a chair and sat. "I'm not sure."

He propped his hands on the arms of her chair, leaning over her. "Bull."

Tempest combed her fingers through her hair. "I'm not sure it's the Ossetians who took him. I think it was the Russians."

Chance arched his brows, compelling her to continue.

"We went to Georgia to visit a family we met last year. They live very close to the border. While we were there, Russian soldiers broke into their home, as well as the ones surrounding it, and forced the families out. They're building a fence through Georgia, south of the pipeline, so they can control the oil flow. I took photographs of the soldiers beating the homeowners and killing one of them." She let her head drop back, staring at the ceiling. "Before I left, his captors used his phone to call me. They agreed to release Sloan if I would turn over all my film."

He dragged a chair over and sat in front of her, their knees almost touching. Arms resting along his thighs, he leaned toward her. "So why didn't you agree?"

"I didn't have it anymore. We mailed all the rolls home that afternoon."

Expelling a whoosh, he ran his hand behind his neck. "What did they say when you told them?"

A deep sigh streamed from her, and she closed her eyes for a second. Then blinking several times, she said, "I didn't talk to them. Alexei grabbed my phone when it rang."

That one admission crawled through him with an unsettling disquiet. "How do you know what was said?"

She shrugged. "I don't. Only his side because I was standing right there."

This entire thing made no sense. "Was he speaking English? To these supposed captors?"

"No. Russian." When he leaned back and studied her, she said, "I'm fluent." She tapped her fingers on the chair's arm. "But…" she trailed off.

"What? What are you not telling me?"

"Alexei never would say who they were or where they were from, but he was speaking to them in Russian, and most Ossetians don't speak that language."

Chance ran his hand across his mouth, the stubble on his chin scraping against his fingers. When she'd blurted out her demand in his office, he'd had no idea how serious the problem was…or how determined Tempest Raines could be. At the time, she was just some loony friend of Marc's. If what her pictures showed were that damning, this could cause the *international incident* the White House wanted to avoid. "Are you going to take the film back? It won't stop Sloan from writing the story when he gets home. Is that your plan?"

"Without the pictures, the story doesn't have the same impact. The photos are proof. The story could easily be dismissed as biased lies. Do you really think the current administration is going to stand up to Russia?"

He straightened, glancing at an eclectic array of keepsakes and relics from all over the world on display in a china cabinet. The woman had a point. Still, the needs of the many did not always outweigh the needs of the few. "Is this worth Sloan's life?"

Her head snapped up, and her gaze scraped over him. "No. What do you think I've been telling myself for the last week? Unfortunately, I developed it when I got home. I could take them the negatives, but I wouldn't be able to prove I didn't have prints." She focused on him. "Which I do. Two sets." Her voice lowered to a whisper. "And the minute they have the film, they'll probably kill him anyway."

"True."

Her lips tightened, and she rolled them in. "The Georgians have very little voice. Someone needs to let people know what the Russians are doing."

"And what do you think our government is going to do? Start funneling weapons their way? Pull our troops from Afghanistan and send them to Georgia to train them?"

In a tight voice, she said, "I'm only trying to

present the story."

He propped his elbow on the chair's arm. Admiration for her doused him. In the midst of her anguish, she still had concern for others. In his world, he fought against the same things she did—he just had different methods. Were they both right? Or both wrong? A fleeting sense of futility skipped through him. "I'm not sure any of our efforts will make a damn bit of difference," he muttered.

Her eyes flashed, and she gripped the arms of the chair. "We'll never know if no one tries, will we?" The anger in her voice lodged in the air. "I take pictures. I don't pose them or set them up. Anyone who looks at my work can make his own judgments."

He leaned back in the chair and crossed his arms. "What about Sloan? You can't tell me his stories aren't prejudiced."

"Sloan is an idealist. He doesn't always see the gray."

"Idealists are dangerous."

"I'm sure he'll grow out of the stage. He's only been in this business for a couple of years. He hasn't gotten as cynical as I...or you...have."

He expelled a deep sigh and left the dining room, then wandered down the hall toward the kitchen. From the refrigerator, he grabbed another beer and strolled back into the corridor. At the archway to the living room he paused, surveying the light floral fabrics covering the sofa and chairs. The comfortable, but elegant, room had a definite feminine feel to the decor.

He sensed Tempest come up behind him. Walking through the room, he stopped at the patio doors and looked again at the ocean. Black clouds loomed nearer.

Bolts of lightning seared through them. "Bad storm coming."

She opened the doors and stepped onto the balcony. He followed her, and they stood by the railing. The approaching storm made the ocean restless. Tall waves, unusual for Virginia Beach, crashed on the shore. No screeching gulls swooped over the breakers in the wind, and only a smattering of brave souls challenged the cold air and frigid surf by walking along the white sand.

He let out a breath and dropped into a chair. "Regardless of whether I agree with you or not, I can't help you."

A dejected, heartsick expression swept across her face. "Why not?" Her tone sounded desperate.

Tightness crawled through his chest. This woman needed him—his help and his expertise. But he simply couldn't do this. "I'd be risking everything I've worked for and everything I've done for the last twenty years. I can't just take off and fly into a foreign country, especially Russia. Even when I take leave, I have paperwork to fill out. People know where I am and where I'm going. They have to be able to reach me."

"Not if you lie."

He shot out a laugh. "Great. Then when I get caught, I'll be in twice as much trouble." He gave her a pointed look. "And there's not much hope we wouldn't get caught."

Her fists clenched, then she wrapped her arms around herself and shivered. "I thought SEALs thrived on accepting challenges and taking risks."

"Calculated risks. Not suicidal ones." He changed the subject. "Doesn't Sloan get tired of all that flowery stuff in the living room?"

Head cocked, she gave him an odd look. "He's never mentioned it either way. He isn't here all that much."

"Why? You two aren't gone year-round."

"No, but even when we're home, it's not like he's here constantly." She frowned, then her expression showed awareness, as if the reasoning behind his confusion had become clear. "Chance, Sloan doesn't live here anymore. He moved out last year."

The mist floating in his head dissolved, as if a gust of wind had blown it away. Now he understood— everything became clear. They were married—the plain gold band on her finger was evidence of that, but they were separated. Maybe she still cared for him, or felt obligated to save him, even if they no longer lived as husband and wife. It explained her vacillating moods and reactions. It also lowered his self-imposed abstinence from pursuing her.

Lowered his objections, but didn't completely erase the complications involved.

"Unh uh." His assessment that Tempest Raines would cause him misery hadn't changed. If anything, he believed it more now than ever. Her foolhardy and dangerous proposal proved him right. At best, if he helped her, it would end his career.

At worst...

She sat next to him, pulling the chair a little closer. Reaching over, she laid her hand on his leg. "You said *unh uh.* What is it?"

He regarded her, unable to keep from looking at her eyes. Damn it. After all these years of dismissing his past, of trying to forget the incident that molded him into what he had become, this woman showed up with eyes that reminded him of those events all over again.

He had no intention of throwing aside all the things he had earned for love—or even lust for a woman. One fiasco in that area per lifetime allotted him one more than he allowed. With a deep sigh, he stood, forcing her to move her hand. "I'm sorry, Tempest. I wish I could help you, but I just can't. It's too risky."

He set his beer bottle on a small table and left her apartment without another word.

****

Tempest stayed on the balcony, watching the clouds edge nearer until the sky overhead turned black. The darkness couldn't come close to the gloom squeezing her heart.

She had presented her case to Chance logically and without emotion, hoping to convince him to go with her. Marc's comment about the man having a heart had given her renewed hope but had garnered her nothing. Without his help, she had no idea how to proceed or what to do. With her less-than-thorough plan, her odds of success added up to something less than zero.

A bolt of lightning branded the sky, followed by a deep rumble of thunder. A jerking shudder ran through her as the light momentarily blinded her. Not unlike what being around Chance did to her senses.

She had one guaranteed way of persuading him to help her. Tell him the truth about Sloan.

A brisk wind swept over the patio. She shivered. Telling Chance he had a son might have the opposite effect. She might lose him forever.

"You fool." She stood and went inside, slid the door in its track, and locked it behind her. Losing

Chance forever implied she had him to begin with. Nothing could be further from the truth. She held no interest for him. His advances toward her came from a place solely sexual in nature. Her naiveté didn't stretch that far.

But he has a right to know.

She shook her head with fierce movements. If logic didn't work to win him over, resorting to emotions was a cheap shot. Besides, he would never believe her. At times in her life, even she wondered if she was indeed insane. Maybe time had warped her recollections and the way she wanted things to be. Not memories of the events as they actually happened.

No. Disclosing the truth to Chance now could only damage her cause. And her self-respect. No good could rise from the flighty idea. And even if she could convince him, knowing Sloan was his son would change the dynamics. Like a doctor operating on a family member, a SEAL involved in a rescue of someone close might skew his judgment. And should things go wrong, why burden him with the knowledge he'd had a child and lost him before he even had a chance to know him?

Her confession had to wait until after the rescue.

Still, she had to do something. The Russians wouldn't keep Sloan alive forever. Her only option now rested in Alexei and his desire to help her. He didn't have the resources Chance Adams did, but his connections and skills could not be dismissed. He had managed to get her safely up to Nal'Chik and on her way to Turkey.

A chill started at the base of her neck and ran down her spine. His interest in her film the night of Sloan's abduction hadn't escaped her. She had spent hours going back in her mind, trying to recall any other indications Alexei might not be who or what he seemed...but nothing untoward came forward. Plus, his actions since that night refuted whatever paranoia trickled through her thoughts. He'd only wanted to ensure the photos made it back to Georgia so Sloan would be released.

Right?

She shook off her anxiety. She had no reason to doubt his motives—he'd been nothing but solicitous since they met last spring. In fact, on more than one occasion she'd sensed a desire from him to take their relationship further, but she'd managed to keep him at bay. The friendship they forged provided enough to suit her.

But since Chance had refused to help, she needed Alexei. They must refine their own plan. Even if Chance's damning evaluation of their scheme was accurate, she fully believed in the adage that determination could overcome obstacles. Failure did not come to her mind as an option.

She could fly to Moscow Sunday and meet Alexei. With a deep sigh, she moved to the sofa to call the airline and book a flight. Then she checked the time. Three a.m. in Moscow, but Alexei wouldn't mind. He cared for her and had genuine concern over Sloan's abduction.

Didn't he?

Tempest dialed his number.

Chapter Fourteen

Breezy Point Officers' Club, Norfolk, Virginia
Friday, March 24—2130 hours

Chance snagged a table in a secluded corner of the Officers' Club, sipping a Chivas on the rocks. A young woman stood on a raised platform, singing some Madonna song along with the Karaoke machine. When she finished, a round of hoots and hollers went up from the Friday night crowd, and the next sacrifice hopped up to try his hand at pleasing the rowdy group.

He twisted his glass, setting the amber liquid in a swirling motion, deep in thought. Tempest's pleas continued to rattle through his mind, but with her harebrained scheme, she didn't stand a chance in hell of getting Sloan out of Georgia. She needed help—help he was qualified to give.

But why should he? She popped—make that *exploded*—into his life a mere three days ago. He owed her nothing. The fact he could hardly get her off his mind these last few days only frustrated him more. Whatever the hell her warped relationship with her husband involved, the fact remained the woman wore a ring. He had no business pursuing her, even if she and Sloan were separated.

It didn't make him want her any less.

And what about Sloan? The guy may have moved

out of their condo, but he still worked with her. They must not be completely estranged. He saw the look on her face every time she thought about him. Her love for him ran deep. Chance couldn't dismiss that intensity.

Sloan's articles showed the man possessed a talent and depth he himself could never hope to achieve. Chance's SEAL training and experiences had led him to be suspicious and wary of everything and everyone around him. Sloan Raines still saw good in the world.

Tempest called him an idealist and said he would grow out of it—as if he were still a child. She couldn't be more than early thirties herself. Maybe Sloan was younger than she was. It would explain some of her odd comments and possibly even why he wanted to break up with her. Maybe the man had tired of being married to an older woman. He lifted his glass, then stiffened in the chair. Without taking a swallow, he set the drink down.

Sloan might be her brother.

His gaze flitted around the room as he considered the idea. Then he slumped slightly in his seat and picked up his glass with a grimace. The thin gold ring she wore blew that explanation out of the ocean like a ballistic missile from a submarine. Unless her husband had died—but then who was Sloan? A brother-in-law? He shook his head in disgust. *You're grasping at straws.*

Chance drew a deep breath and leaned back, toying with his whisky. Somewhere in his mind, a kernel of skepticism niggled at him. Why would someone like Tempest Raines be interested in him at all, unless solely for what he could provide? For all of her self-righteousness, she couldn't have achieved such heights without using people. He twisted his neck, then took a sip of the Chivas.

Her actions and personality didn't support that theory, either. She didn't dissemble. An aura of honesty and authenticity floated around her. The photos she took of his men held a genuine frankness coupled with a sense of honor. Conscientiousness showed in her work. The woman, as she presented herself, did not strike him as a liar or a cheat, regardless of his reflexes and suspicions. He had yet to meet anyone he couldn't read with a fair amount of accuracy. A sudden unease that she might be the first slinked under his skin.

No. Not this one. Her genuineness was real.

A long sigh blew from his mouth, and he downed his drink in one swallow then set the glass on the table. Over the years, he'd sworn he would never allow a woman to undermine his self-confidence again. With his training and his missions, he'd been to hell and back, and could do it again. No one could take that away from him.

He dismissed the notion that in the past twenty years, he never let a woman get close enough to risk a repeat of that pain.

The waitress swept by his table, picked up his empty glass, and asked if he wanted another. Rather than try to speak above the din, he shook his head and stood. Nearly 2200. He needed to spend some time in the office tomorrow and catch up on the paperwork his two days with Tempest cost him, and his bed—his *empty* bed—beckoned. *Shit.*

A chill breeze surrounded him as soon as he stepped outside, so he zipped up his parka and took off in a fast walk. The rain had hit a lull, but large beads of water dripped from trees and overhangs, falling on the ground with distinct splats. He hurried to his Blazer, anxious to get out of the damp air.

When he arrived at his apartment, he went up to his quarters and let the door swing shut behind him. Melancholy assaulted him. Tempest had questioned his lack of personal items in his office. As he looked around the living room, he saw the same scenario here.

The walls closed in on him like never before. He trudged into his bedroom and plopped on the side of the bed, then pulled out his cell phone. A serious dose of common sense was in order, and who could do that better than his brother? He punched his speed dial.

The line clicked. "You realize it's almost midnight."

Chance smiled at the sound of Troy's voice. "It's barely eleven, big bro. And don't even try to tell me you were asleep, you lying sack of shit."

A chuckle came across the connection. "What's up your ass? You never call unless something's wrong."

Hell. Why had he done this? Now he had to go into details even he could barely untangle. "I met someone…interesting."

He could almost visualize his brother straightening in his leather chair. "No shit? That's—"

"She's married."

Dead silence assaulted him. Then a sigh, and "Don't do it, little bro." When Chance didn't respond, Troy said, "Please tell me you didn't."

"No, but I've been thinking about it. Too much."

"She must be some hot effing babe to suck you in."

The insinuation grated on him. "She's not—it's not—shit. Never mind. It's okay. What's new with you?"

"Oh, no. You're not pulling that subject change shit on me. It didn't work when you were sixteen, and it ain't working now. What's going on?"

With a sigh, Chance launched into details, ending with, "So it's like they're married, but not together."

"Fine. Then wait until the *married* part isn't a factor anymore." Ice cubes rattling in a glass filtered through the line, followed by a pause as Troy presumably took a swallow of whatever liquor struck his fancy tonight. "We've got two possibilities here. Either she's flirting with you to get your help, or she's leaving the guy but feels obligated to get him out of this mess before she cuts him loose. Either way, you can wait. If she's really interested in you, she'll still be around when he's not."

Troy's sound logic, as usual, gave him the reality check he needed.

"Besides, the woman's got a screw loose. She can't possibly think you would, or could, do this. You said she's a friend of Dickey's...she's got to have some inkling of how the military works."

"Unless Marc suggested the idea."

No sound, then a spurt of air winnowed through the line. "I thought Dickey had reined himself in."

"He has, but he hasn't changed. If they're as close as it seems, he'd want to help her."

"Fine. Let him haul his ass to god-forsaken Russia."

Chance chortled a grunted laugh. "Right." They chatted for a few more minutes and then started their goodbyes. Right before they hung up, Troy said, "Don't do it, little bro." His warning didn't refer to a rescue attempt.

He set down the receiver and muttered a curse, then went over to a closet to pull out a box of *National Geographics*. He'd intended to drop them off at the library last week but hadn't gotten around to it yet. His small, cramped apartment didn't allow for collecting magazines.

Ruffling through them, he forced his mind to recall. He'd seen an article by the Raineses recently. They'd been someplace in eastern Europe. He glimpsed each cover as he sifted through the pile, until one issue caught his eye.

Last fall. A cover story on the oil pipelines out of Baku, Azerbaijan. That was where they'd gone. Those lines cut across the country—one went up through Russia, another dissected Georgia, and a third went through Georgia and then down into Turkey. He pulled the yellow magazine from the box and flipped it open, settling on his sofa.

Twenty minutes later, he dropped the thick periodical back into the box and stood, stretched out his cramped muscles, and wandered over to the window. On the street below, an eerie fluorescent glow from the streetlights bathed the lines of cars in the parking lot, creating ethereal flickering glimmers from the dampness in the air.

However old Sloan Raines might be, the man had a gift. Someone like him had the capability to make a difference in the world, as preposterous a notion as that seemed to Chance.

The man deserved the opportunity to live.

Chance had the ability to keep the man's life from being cut short. In turn, it could very well end his own life as he knew it, but sometimes one's own needs had to be sacrificed for the good of others.

Still, the odds of him succeeding with a rescue attempt far exceeded those of Tempest and this Russian—*friend*—of hers. He shook his head. The determined woman intended to go through with her crazy scheme, whatever it entailed.

Regardless of the personal torment she caused him, using it as an excuse to refuse her went against not only his training, but his principles as a human being.

He had no death-wish, nor any desire to spend the remainder of his days in the brig, but if he planned carefully, maybe Sloan could be nabbed without serious repercussions. He doubted it, but he had to try. Otherwise he might never see Tempest again.

"Aw, hell." With a deep sigh and his brother's words hanging over his head, he grabbed his parka and headed out.

****

Chance strode through the sterile lobby, bypassing the desk. The night watchman looked up and shot from his chair. "Sir!"

He didn't slow his pace. At the elevators, the other guard slipped from the shadows, his hand resting on the butt of his gun. "Sir, may I help you?"

"I'm going to Tempest Raines's apartment."

"Is she expecting you?"

"Maybe."

The guard didn't budge. "We have to call upstairs. If you'll wait just a moment, please."

Chance considered the request. He could easily subdue this guy, but the guard at the desk undoubtedly had a gun, too. He didn't need to cause her another problem—she already had enough.

The man at the desk spoke feverishly into the receiver. "Miss Raines, I'm so sorry to wake you, but there's a man in the lobby who wants to see you." He lowered his voice and held his hand over his mouth, but his words cut through the quiet lobby. "I'm afraid he may be…intoxicated."

He listened for a minute, then covered the receiver with his hand. "Your name, sir?"

An urge to be a smart-ass swirled through him, but he curbed the impulse. "Chance Adams."

The man spoke into the phone and then hung up before shooting a glance in Chance's direction. "You can go up."

Chance tried not to sneer. The guy was just doing his job. "Thank you so much." He stepped onto the elevator, keeping his gaze on them until the doors closed.

On the fifth floor, Tempest stood at her door, waiting for him. Her voice came out in a whispered hiss. "Why are you here? It's after midnight."

Without answering, he pushed on her door and swept inside. As soon as he entered the hallway, strains of Tchaikovsky's *Capriccio Italien* crashed over him. "Isn't that kind of loud?"

"Listening to a little music before I go to bed helps me fall asleep."

"Can't you find something a little less…rousing than this? Bach or Brahms or something?"

"I like the Russian composers."

He hiked an eyebrow. "Yeah. I bet you do. While you drink your vodka." Turning his attention away from the music, he took a minute to examine Tempest.

Hair swirled around her head in a tangled disarray. Devoid of makeup, rather than being pale, her skin glowed. She wore a long ivory satin and lace robe, its neckline plunging between her breasts.

A dim glow of strategically placed nightlights shone throughout the dark apartment. The dangerous combination of shadows and her alluring attire presented too much temptation. He moved closer to her.

Tempest took a step back. "Are you drunk?"

"Hardly." He tugged on the tie wrapped around her waist. "But I may be intoxicated." The robe fell open, revealing a short silky gown in a leopard print. Uncluttered by any lace or accents, it hugged her slender frame in sensuality. Thin straps ran over her smooth shoulders, holding the negligée in place. It dipped low on her chest, barely covering the soft mounds he yearned to touch. He reached up and pushed the robe off her shoulders. The satiny garment dropped to the ground, and she didn't reach down to pull it back up.

A burst of light shot through the apartment's large windows. A stinging crack of thunder erupted through the air. Tempest jumped and let out a small scream, then started to tremble.

He slipped his arms around her and drew her to him, but she continued to shake. He smoothed her hair. "Tempest, it's okay. It's just thunder." He leaned back and saw the anguish on her face. Skin as pale as the ivory robe, lips quivering as panic, horror, and revulsion swept through her eyes. She melted in his arms. He pulled her closer, running his hands down her back. Her smooth skin stirred him, but right now he only wanted to calm her. Her trembling began to subside, and he brought his hands to her face, stroking his thumbs along her cheeks. Genuine desire simmered in her green eyes, begging him to kiss her.

She ran her fingers along the stubble on his chin. He caved in to his craving. No man could resist this much temptation. He leaned down and settled his lips on hers. God—and Troy—forgive him, but this wanting decimated his resolve. All of his brother's warnings flew from his mind. He wanted—*needed*—this woman.

She clutched his arms, digging into his muscles. When he pulled away, she found him again and nibbled at his lower lip. He dove back inside her mouth.

Chance traced his fingers along her neck, edging a strap off her shoulder. Her gown dropped an inch. He slid his hand across her skin, stroking along the edge of the soft fabric. Slipping underneath it, he fanned over her nipple with his thumb.

She sucked in a breath, leaned into him, and moved her hand down his arm, over his hip, brushing across the front of his jeans.

He grabbed her hand and lifted it to his lips, kissing her fingers.

She looked at him with her smoldering green eyes, and with his hand in hers, led him through the living room to the bedroom. As they stood by the bed, she tugged his shirt out of his jeans. He pulled it over his head.

Her hands on his chest, she skimmed her nails through his matted hair. He slipped his fingers under the other strap, and the gown slid off her shoulders. She wriggled, and the garment dropped, puddling into a pile around her feet.

He swept his gaze over her naked body and

moaned. "Tempest." His voice sounded strained, whispered, even in his own ears. Her skin felt as silky as the gown she'd worn. He ran his hands up her sides, cupping her breasts, then leaned down to flick his tongue over a nipple. She sucked in a breath and pressed harder against him, pulling his head up to kiss him again. They locked together, exploring, savoring, sensing each other's desperate need.

The shrill ring of a phone rocked through his brain.

She broke away with a gasp, as if she had awakened from a dream and found herself someplace distasteful. The phone rang again. "I have to answer it." Her voice was weak.

He moved away and wiped his hand over his forehead, dragging his fingers through his cropped hair. He'd accused Tempest of being insane. Apparently, that particular affliction had spread to him.

Her hand pressed against her chest as if to still her heart, and she dropped on the edge of the bed and picked up the phone.

Chance stood by, trying to placate his disrupted faculties. Had he lost his mind? Gazing at her sitting naked, he'd say that assessment hit the mark. He skimmed his hand across his face and started to turn.

"Alexei—thank you for calling me back— No, I wasn't asleep. In fact…" She glanced at Chance before continuing, "I was going over some advice I got from my Navy friend. No. He's given me some information, but he can't come out there. We've got to figure out something else. I'm flying to Moscow—I'll be there Monday night. Can you meet me at the airport?"

Chance stopped and stared at her. She met his gaze then looked away. After a few seconds, she broke into

Russian. Chance listened for a minute and understanding more of the conversation than he wanted to know, he shook his head and left the room.

He wandered into the kitchen, rummaged through all the cabinets until he found coffee and filters. He busied himself making a pot, then sat at the kitchen table, staring out the window at the blackness. Her reflex to the thunder continued to prickle. She'd been in war zones, and her reaction seemed far too close to servicemen he'd known. Years later, loud noises like thunder brought forth memories of artillery fire, friends being killed...nightmares that haunted them. Her admission—she'd seen some disturbing things in Libya—nudged his brain. He didn't doubt the truth of her statement.

The coffee finished brewing as Tempest reappeared—wearing only an oversized button-down shirt. The sight made his stomach tighten. In the man's shirt, she emanated more sexuality than she did in the negligée. With effort, he dragged his gaze away. What the hell had he just done? Or tried to do? Troy's warnings launched though him. "I thought Sloan moved out. That has to be one of his shirts."

"It is, but he left a few things here in case he wants to sleep over." Her shoulders hiked in dismissal. "I like wearing men's shirts. They're comfortable. And this one doesn't fit him anymore, anyway." She moved to a cabinet and pulled out two mugs. "Thank you for making coffee. May I assume you intend to stay for a while?"

As she poured the black brew, he twisted the end of his mouth. "I came over here to talk to you."

Tempest's eyebrows hiked, and a hint of a smile

creased her eyes. "One of the more interesting conversations I've had recently." She set the two mugs on the counter, then pulled some cream from the refrigerator and a sugar bowl from the cabinet. She brought it all over and sat, doctoring the black brew in her cup.

He dumped some sugar and cream in his mug. "Why are you flying to Moscow?"

She frowned. "Why do you think?"

"Let me guess. Because you're suicidal?"

She tapped a fingernail against her cup. "I'm not going to get killed in Moscow."

"You might, if the Russians want your film that badly. And Sloan, too. And maybe this Alexei friend of yours, also. What do you think you're going to do once you get to Nal'Chik?"

Tempest lifted her cup, held it to her lips, and took some short sips. Eyes closed, she'd either gone deep into thought or wanted to shut him out. Finally, she said, "I don't know. Alexei says he has a plan."

Silence settled over them. He drank his coffee, staring at the window, alternately looking at his own reflection and Tempest's in the glass. She kept her gaze on the table, lost in some world of her own, probably considering her choices, weighing the feasibility of her ideas.

That's what he would be doing.

He rose to refill his cup. The scent of the strong Colombian blend filled the large kitchen. The shot of caffeine had him fully awake, despite his long day and the late hour. Mug in hand, he strolled from the kitchen, wandered down the hall to the dining room, and flipped the light switch. She had been going over these maps again tonight. Their order differed from earlier this evening.

Chance bent over the table, examining the layout of Georgia and the Caucasus Mountains. He shook his head. Trying to fly over those peaks in a small plane would be foolhardy. A better way to get in had to be available.

He studied the charts closely. These maps didn't come out of an issue of *National Geographic.* She must have brought them home with her. Another facet of this Alexei's expertise? Still, although their detail helped, they didn't provide enough information to suit him.

He needed satellite data. A possibility popped into his mind—something that would be even easier to come by. He smiled. Shuffling through the pile, he pulled out a map of Georgia. He scanned the table and grabbed a small ruler, checking the mileage key and measuring. A shadow caught his attention.

Tempest stood at the doorway, watching him. "What are you doing?"

"Saving your ass."

She drifted over to him. "My ass is just fine, thank you."

He let his gaze drop to the edge of the long shirt. "Yes, I'd say it is."

She flushed and scowled at him.

Her scent rose over the smell of the coffee, momentarily distracting him. "Shouldn't you put on some jeans or something?"

She set down her mug, crossing her arms. "Why, Commander? Is something wrong? Is the mighty SEAL having trouble concentrating?"

He turned on her so rapidly she planted her hands

on his chest to stop him. "I'm trying to help you. Push me, and I'll walk out that door. Then you and your precious Sloan can fend for yourselves."

Myriad emotions raced through her eyes. She looked down and dropped her arms. Her voice hoarse and ragged, she said, "I'll go get dressed."

When she returned, she handed him his shirt. He glanced at her, then twisted his mouth into a smile. "What's wrong? Is the little photographer having trouble concentrating?"

She ignored him and snatched her mug to take a sip of coffee. "Have you come up with any ideas?"

He slipped the shirt over his head, unzipped his jeans, and shoved them down slightly to tuck the shirttail in. As he zipped them back up and buckled his belt, he looked over at her. "The first thing you're going to do is cancel that ticket to Moscow."

"Why? I've got to get out there—Alexei is expecting me. He's already making arrangements."

Chance moved close to her. "Then you'll just have to call him back. You're not going to Russia." He turned to inspect to the maps. "We'll go in across the Black Sea."

Chapter Fifteen

Saturday, March 25—1:00 a.m.

Tempest blinked and a spasm of hope pulsed through her. Hands shaking, she set her cup on the table. "We?"

"That's what I said."

"As in *you and I*?"

His features eased into a hint of amusement as he glanced her way. "That's usually what *we* means. We'll fly into Athens on Monday."

Chance's declaration rocked her, and a lump lodged in her throat. She almost took a step closer to throw her arms around his neck but held back. "Why?"

Focused again on the maps, he said, "Because I need time to set things up. I can do it more efficiently from here."

"I didn't mean that. Why did you change your mind?"

He looked up and surveyed her for a long minute, scanning her as if trying to read her mind. "Because you need help or you're going to get yourself killed. Besides, a SEAL never backs down from a challenge."

She pulled over a chair and sat, trying to stop her quivering. "Chance, if something goes wrong, it could ruin your career."

A tiny laugh puffed from him. "The odds of

nothing going wrong are very slim."

"That's what I mean."

His gaze settled on her eyes. "Do you care?"

"Yes. I do." More than he realized or would understand.

He reached for her, then stopped. "Would you mind getting me some more coffee?" He handed her his cup.

She hesitated, but then took their mugs and went into the kitchen. As soon as she returned, he spoke. "I have a friend in Athens who has some deep connections. Not to mention a yacht and a jet." He paused, his mouth twisted in a small smile. "And a vacation home on an island off the coast of Turkey. All of those may come in handy.

"We can stay with him in Athens and then take his yacht to the Georgia coast. I want to do some reconnaissance before we go in. We won't have any problems along the Turkish coastline—we can fly to his island. When we're ready, I'll drop near wherever they've got Sloan."

Much of his plan rested on this friend. She cocked her head. "How can you be so sure he'll agree?"

He glanced up, eyes narrowed, and studied her. "Because he owes me a favor." His expression told her not to ask any further questions. He perched against the edge of the table, sipping his coffee. "Where were you when they took Sloan?"

She looked down as she set her mug on the table. "I…umm…in another cottage down the road."

"Why? What were you doing?"

Her mind flashed to that evening—and her argument with her son. "Talking to Alexei."

The expression on his face changed. Lips pursed slightly, he peered at her. "Convenient."

The comment hit her wrong, and she tensed. "What are you implying?"

"I'm not implying anything. Just trying to figure things out. How did you meet Alexei?"

"We met while Sloan and I were in Russia last year doing our story on the oil pipeline. Our research and article intrigued him. He's made most of his money from oil."

He paused, watching her. "But you criticized the people who took advantage of the capitalistic influx. You defended the rights of the poor."

She hiked a shoulder a tic in a dismissive gesture. "Alexei didn't always have wealth. He doesn't hold any grudges or illusions about his rise. He's smart and saw the possibilities during glasnost. He took advantage of it and climbed in authority and wealth because of the new openness and freedom."

Chance snorted. "Right. Until it didn't work. What's his interest in a free Georgia?"

"His family used to vacation along the coastline when he was a child. He wants to build a hotel and turn the area into a resort."

A pronounced skepticism colored the huff that escaped from his throat. "A true capitalist. How charming."

She planted her fists on her hips. "Now who's being a cynic?"

"I don't trust the Russians. I didn't trust them when they were Communists, and I trust them even less now the country is being run by an ex-KGB agent."

"You can trust Alexei. He saved my life. I never

would have gotten through South Ossetia without his help."

Chance's brow furrowed into a deep V as he studied her. "Through South Ossetia? Why did you go that way? Why didn't you just go through Georgia?"

She hesitated. "I—it was the shortest distance to Nal'Chik."

His eyes narrowed, and he peered at her. "That was risky as hell. Why didn't Alexei take you to T'Bilisi? It's no farther than Nal'Chik."

The questions had never occurred to her. She blinked. "It's...he knew the route better." Tempest swallowed against the lump in her throat. "I don't know."

Quiet, his brow still creased, he continued to scan the map. After a minute, he went into the kitchen to get some more coffee. In the fridge, he spotted the box of pizza, and he pulled out a cold slice and then grabbed the carton of cream.

Tempest tagged behind him. "Do you want me to warm that up?"

His eyes glinted, and a smirk lightened his serious expression.

Lips tight, she shot a stream of air through her nose, then returned to the subject. "Alexei says Sloan's captors are still willing to make a trade for my film."

He chewed and swallowed. "Did you tell him you'd already developed the rolls?"

She looked down. "No."

He pulled a paper towel from a roll and wiped grease from his fingers, not taking his gaze from her. "You don't trust him, either."

Her focus shifted to the window by the table, and

139

she hesitated. In a soft voice, she finally said, "Of course I do. We got very close while Sloan and I worked on that story in Russia. We've kept in touch over the months."

"Oh? How close? Did you sleep with him?"

She shot her hand through the air to slap him.

Chance grabbed her hand, catching it inches from his face. "Don't *ever* do that again." Spoken in a cold, quiet tone, his words resonated with a warning.

She pulled her arm back to massage her wrist. For a second, his eyes revealed a look that clearly defined his dangerous side. Those who dared to cross Chance Adams would regret their actions. Marc Dickey hadn't exaggerated about Chance's attitudes. Whatever happened behind the scenes between him and Ginny wavered close to his surface.

Tempest turned to refill her mug, but her hand shook too much. She replaced the pot and hugged herself. From behind her, Chance set his cup on the counter and ran his hands along her arms, holding her against his chest.

His mouth close to her ear, he said, "I'm trying to help you. But I've got to know exactly what's going on. Information is power. The more I have, the better job I can do."

She croaked out an "Okay."

He slipped his hands up and pulled her hair back.

As his fingers grazed across her neck, the hairs on her nape tickled her skin. She shivered and started to turn.

With a quick move, he dropped his hands and backed away. "Stop fighting me and let me do my job. Would you like some more coffee?"

She nodded, so he moved beside her and filled her cup. She picked it up to drink, but he took it from her hand.

"You forgot your cream and sugar." He poured in a dollop of cream, scooped out a spoonful of sugar and dropped it in her cup, stirring the contents before handing the brew back to her. "I want you to do something for me."

Silently, she looked up at him.

"Don't call Alexei. Let him think you're still on schedule."

"I can't do that. He'll be worried. If I don't show up, he'll probably try to call me. Besides, how will we find the camp without him? He knows exactly where it is."

Casting a look toward the window, he didn't respond right away. Then, "Has he seen Sloan? Is he sure he's alive?"

"He's been to the camp, trying to negotiate with the soldiers. That's why he knows they're still willing to exchange Sloan for my photos. He said Sloan is tied up, but he's being fed and seems to be holding up."

"How is Sloan's health? Is he in good physical condition?"

"Yes. Very good."

Chance shook his head slightly, drinking his coffee. "This guy seems mighty chummy with these soldiers. Why would they even talk to him?"

"He's well-known. He has a position in the Russian government."

He puffed out a grunt and drew his mouth into a thin line. "What a surprise. Their government has more committees and commissions than all of our states combined."

His tone unsettled her. She took a sip of coffee then set down the cup, reaching out to place her hand on his arm.

"What's bothering you so much?"

Chance pulled away. "I haven't met this guy, and I don't trust him. Something about this whole situation doesn't feel right to me." He crossed his arms and studied her. "And you don't trust him, either. That doesn't help. What's got you concerned?" He paused then added, "Tell me the truth. I need to know."

She drew in a breath and moved to the kitchen table to sit.

He followed and sat across from her, waiting.

"It's nothing, really." She met his gaze. "When they grabbed Sloan, Alexei asked me where my film was. It just hit me wrong. I thought Sloan had been killed, and he seemed more concerned about the film."

He stroked at his chin. "How does he know what the pictures show? Was he with you when you took them?"

"A couple of times. I let him know we'd returned, and he came down from Moscow to visit with us. He drove us around to some of the places during our stay but didn't always follow us once we stopped. Sloan and I went into most of them alone. He wasn't there the morning we saw the raid."

"Can you speak Georgian?"

"Fairly well. My Russian is better. Sloan's fluent in both."

Chance stood. "Okay. You're right about letting Alexei know, but wait until Monday. You can call him before we leave. And let him think you're coming alone."

She stalled. "I don't know, Chance. He's my friend."

He reached across the table and cupped her chin in his hand, forcing her to look at him. "Yeah. A friend you don't trust." His gaze skimmed her. "He may be your friend, but he isn't mine. Too many loose ends are flying around this situation, and I'm a very suspicious man. If you want my help, you'll do it my way. Or you won't get my help at all."

****

Chance waited. The woman had spent three days trying to convince him to help her. She could hardly dictate his methods now. She stalled, then finally acquiesced. "Okay."

"Good." He set down his cup. "I'd like to see your photos."

She led him into her converted darkroom. A sink and counter rested along one wall, covered with trays for chemicals, with an enlarger sitting at one end. The pictures she'd shot spread out over a long table.

They showed more than the usual atrocities of war. Somehow, she'd managed to capture the depth of emotion the people felt. The photos became three-dimensional. Armed soldiers aimed their weapons at the residents, shooting up little bits of dirt. They battered them with rifle butts. Vivid, graphic portrayals of a man being shot and killed jumped from the prints. Women drew their children close, trying to protect them. An anguished man peered at his home while he watched the fence encroach across Georgian land. A young boy sat on the ground, brown eyes wide, his hand on his bloody cheek. The fear in the eyes of the children made him want to hold them against his chest to reassure them. "How do you do this? How do you detach yourself enough to take these pictures without getting involved?"

Head tilted, she gave him a puzzled look. "How do you do the things you have to without feeling any remorse or emotions?"

"That's different."

A small chuckle came from her throat, but she didn't argue with him. "It used to get to me. I guess the camera acts as a shield for me now. It's not real. It's like watching a show on television. Sloan taught me how. He said, 'We can't help them if we fall prey to our emotions.'"

Chance nodded. He understood that mentality. "He sounds pretty smart. I'm looking forward to meeting him."

Her hand jerked.

"You just thought something. What is it?"

She hesitated. "Nothing. I…just want him home."

"Come here." He wrapped his arms around her. "I know. I'll figure out a way." He brushed his lips across her forehead. "You need to get some sleep, and I need to take care of some things. I'll see you in a few hours, okay?" When she nodded against him, he gave her a soft kiss and left her apartment. As he walked down the hall to the elevator, an odd sense of longing overcame him, one he hadn't experienced in years. But his brother's admonitions pinged in his brain. *Don't do it.*

He needed to distance himself from this woman before she sucked him in any deeper. Every time he touched her, he wanted her a little more, but his plans for the future did not include a serious relationship.

Especially if the liaison required stealing another man's wife.

A hollow feeling swept through his gut. After Ginny, he'd buried his feelings so deeply, even he couldn't be sure they existed anymore. He satisfied his sexual needs by making sure the women understood the transient nature of the tryst. But this unexpected pull toward Tempest Raines wasn't lessening—it seemed to grow stronger the more he stayed in her presence. Something about her made him feel as if he'd known her forever. As if she fit with him.

And that revelation terrified him.

Chapter Sixteen

Joint Expeditionary Base—Little Creek, Virginia Beach, Virginia
Saturday, March 25—0800 hours

Chance threw down his pen and rubbed his hands over his face. Unlike the quiet he loved so much when he jumped, the weekend silence in the office building closed around him in a suffocating embrace.

Or maybe his mood contributed to this feeling.

Somewhere in his mind the notion lurked that whether or not he got caught up wouldn't make a damn bit of difference. But the training infused in his character repudiated the negativity. He didn't take his life lightly. If this mad rescue attempt held no chance of success, he wouldn't try it at all. Something about suicide missions went against his temperament.

Still, the odds did not favor them, and that knowledge stalked his thoughts. Cockiness bore as sure a death sentence as doubt.

The whole ordeal might be easier if he could push aside the picture he had of Tempest's naked body. In her presence, he seemed unable to keep from touching her. The deep auburn hair that skimmed her shoulders always had strands flying across her face. The wisps begged him to brush them back and caress her soft skin.

When the time came, he could focus on his work.

As they reviewed the maps and his mind flew through their options with the speed of an F/A-18 Hornet, no thought of her invaded his consciousness. But as soon as he had time to stop and reflect, she entered his musings again, pressing her body against him in a caress that betrayed her desire. And he accepted those caresses with a hunger of his own.

"Damn it." He stood to stretch, stacked his papers in an imprecise semblance of order, and scooped several quarters from his desk drawer. The phone call he needed to make shouldn't be done from his office or his cell phone. He took the elevator downstairs and ran into Marc in the lobby. "Sir. What brings you in on a Saturday morning?"

"Probably the same thing as you. Paperwork." The captain's gaze scanned him. "No uniform today?"

Chance cringed. "No, sir. I didn't plan to stay very long."

"Then I guess I'm messing up your plans. Come on upstairs with me."

Hell. Another delay. Such comprised the world of best-laid plans. Exactly why he didn't want Tempest going off on this witch-hunt alone.

They reached the captain's office, Marc grabbed some papers from his desk, and they settled into two chairs in a corner of the room.

Before his boss could speak, Chance jumped in with his question. "Actually, Marc, I'm glad I ran into you. That leave request you approved for Monday—I was hoping to extend it to a week."

The captain glanced up. His normally serious expression lightened. "Is that so? Where are you off to?"

Did the man just hide a smile? "Nowhere in particular. I thought I'd take my bike and head west. Ride for a few days, see where I end up, and then head back. The same plan I had before, just a few more days."

"Going alone?"

Chance studied him for a long moment. "Yes, sir."

His brows hiked such a minute fleeting amount, most people wouldn't have noticed. "Heading for the mountains?"

"I'm not sure yet. Wherever the mood strikes me, I guess. Just a ride."

"Huh. Sarah would never let me get away with that. Every trip has to be planned to the pit stops. I envy you that freedom."

"I suppose being unattached has its advantages."

His boss continued to observe him, his gaze settling on Chance's unshaven chin. "I seem to recall you once telling me you hated having a beard when you rode your bike. Said the facial hair made things too hot and scratchy with the helmet."

Chance nearly choked. The man had the memory retention of a damned dolphin. Did he ever forget anything? An unsettling reflex pitted his stomach as he searched for a response.

But Marc moved on. "Didn't you plan to leave today?"

"I decided to get through some of my paperwork first. I'm hoping for Monday now."

With a nod, the captain shuffled the papers on his lap. "Sounds fine. Things are quiet right now. Bring me the chit before you take off, and I'll get your leave squared away." He turned his attention back to work. "I need to go over this with you." They began reviewing some papers, but after a few minutes, Marc pulled all the sheets together and gave him a long look. "Did you ever meet Tempest Raines before last week?"

He frowned and looked up from the papers he held, shaking his head in thought. "Not that I recall. I suppose it's possible we met at some function years ago. She looks a little familiar, but I haven't been able to place her." He studied his boss. "Why do you ask?"

"No reason. I've known her for several years. I thought maybe your paths had crossed." He straightened in his chair. "You probably need to take care of some things before you head off on your trip. Go on. Get out of here. This shit can wait a week."

Chance shot him a sideways glance. What was up with him? "Yes, sir." He stood, but Marc remained seated. Chance started toward the door.

"Just leave the request on Lieutenant Ottman's desk. I'll find it and get the paperwork through the channel." Marc held his gaze for a minute. "Chance, be careful on your…ride." He stood and moved across the office.

He knows. Damned if he doesn't know. Has he talked to Tempest again? "Thank you, sir." He headed toward the door, opened it, and then turned around. "I'll see you next Monday, Marc."

His commanding officer drew in a breath and nodded, but a fleeting glimpse of concern flashed in his eyes. "I expect you back at your desk in a week, Commander."

With his boss's words ringing in his ears, Chance jogged downstairs to retrieve his paperwork, then locked his office and went back up, dropped the request in the yeoman's inbox, and shot a final look at his captain's door. Something outside the norm transpired in that office this morning. Marc Dickey never acted that obtuse. He said what he meant and made his expectations undeniably clear. This job harbored no room for innuendos. Somehow, his boss had recommended, or at least suggested, some kind of plan to Tempest Raines to help her, without getting the Navy or the government involved.

And apparently, that suggestion included him.

He took the elevator down while his mind and mood plummeted with the car's descent. He would take orders from Marc and follow him to hell if necessary, but he detested being manipulated, and this entire scenario felt as if he were a marionette on strings.

The image of a hangman's noose swung in his head.

However, at the same time, Chance understood Marc's reasoning, if not his motive. No one else in the teams had his precise unique situation. Unattached, his retirement looming, he had less to lose than his teammates. He had the ability and experience to pull this off—with a lot of planning, a hell of a lot of luck, and not a little divine intervention. He let out a breath and shrugged. What the hell. Might as well go out with a bang.

When he hit the parking lot, he climbed in his Blazer and drove to the Navy Exchange. Wandering to a pay phone nestled in a quiet corridor, he dropped in some coins and dialed a number in Washington. The barked greeting he received gave his spirits an immediate lift and brought a smile to his lips. "It's always a pleasure to call you, Leon."

"Hooyah! Where yo' at, C'mander? Y'all in town?"

"No, but I need to come see you. You going to be around this afternoon?"

"Ah always be 'round. Get yo' ass on up here. Whassa occasion?"

Chance hesitated, his voice lowered a notch. "I need to borrow one of your babies."

A lengthy pause halted the conversation. "They's all growed up, Chance. Gones off ta college and making they's own babies."

"I'm not joking, Leon. I need a plane."

Leon lost his uneducated accent. "What kind of plane?"

"Depends. What've you got?"

His friend didn't give him a direct answer. "When are you going to be here?"

"As soon as I can get to the airport and catch a flight. Three, four hours?"

"I'll have Hattie leave the gate unlocked."

Chance clicked down the receiver and dialed Tempest. When she answered, she sounded groggy. He wasted no time with greetings. "How fast can you get to the airport?"

Instantly, her voice became alert. "An hour."

"Meet me at the Air Commute ticket counter. You don't need to pack anything. We'll be back tonight." He hung up, hurried from the building, and rushed to the airport.

****

Chance stood near the TSA checkpoint, watching the crowd intently. As soon as he spotted Tempest, he strode up to her and grabbed her arm. "Let's go.

They're already boarding."

She hurried to keep up with him. "Where are we going?"

"D.C."

His manner precluded further discussion, and she remained silent until they boarded. Within ten minutes, the plane taxied down the runway, en route to Washington.

He looked over at her, his brow creasing. Her disheveled hair evoked an image of her in bed, after some long and passionate love-making. He reached over and combed his fingers through the mass, trying to tame the riotous locks. "Your hair looks different." *And damned sexy. God, he wanted this woman.*

"I didn't have time to mess with the curling iron." She dragged her purse in her lap and dug inside. Extracting a fabric-covered band, she pulled her hair back and twisted it into a semblance of a bun.

The stewardess droned on with her instructions as Chance continued to study Tempest. "It looks nice like that. I like the bun." He brushed back a few strands from her face.

A deep flush colored her cheeks.

A deep yearning tightened his chest. "Did I wake you?"

"No. I haven't been to bed. I dozed on the sofa for a while."

"Don't do that. You've got to get some rest. These next couple of days are going to be hectic, and then… Who knows when you'll get to sleep? I need you alert."

"What about you?"

He shrugged.

A grimace twisted her mouth. "Ye olde double

standard."

Chance turned on her and lowered his voice to a hissed whisper. "This isn't a game, Tempest. It's deadly serious. And I emphasize *deadly*."

She paled and settled her gaze on the stewardess. Then she refocused and changed the subject. "Why are we going to Washington?"

"To visit a friend."

"Do you care to elaborate?"

"No."

With an exasperated grunt, she faced the window.

He let her stew, then hit her with his nagging question. "Did you ask Marc Dickey to help you find Sloan? Did he concoct that whole photo op idea?" He watched her.

Her shoulders twitched, the movement barely discernible.

That tiny action and his years of studying human behavior told him the answer before she opened her mouth.

"Of course not."

"You just happened to be in his office the day after you got home from Turkey." He let his gaze rake over her. "Three days after Sloan's abduction."

Her expression tightened. "We've been through this before. Marc is a close friend. I was on the base for…other reasons, so I thought I'd stop in and say hello. Our chat turned into me doing a story on the teams." She twisted a little to face him. "He told you why. Do you think he would lie?"

He ran his hand behind his head. He had to give her credit. She might not be the best liar—although she was good enough most people wouldn't be able to tell—but she could keep her mouth shut. His opinion of her elevated another half-notch. Or three.

She turned to look out the tiny window, and he turned his mind to refining his game plan.

Chapter Seventeen

Outside Washington, D.C.
Saturday, March 25—1:00 p.m.

When they arrived in Washington, a rental car awaited. Tempest climbed in, and Chance had them speeding down the beltway before she could catch her breath.

He zipped around the traffic. "Did you get our tickets to Athens?"

"Right before you called. The flight leaves JFK Monday at noon and arrives in Athens Tuesday morning. I found a flight from Norfolk to New York that gives us about a three-hour gap, but it leaves early." She paused, twisting her mouth. "I guess I owe you for this little side-trip, too."

He grinned. "Don't worry. I'll put it on your bill when this is all over."

She shook her head and watched the fleeting scenery. "We're not headed for the city. Where are you going?"

"I told you. A friend's place." He maneuvered the car through the heavy traffic, finally exiting and traversing highways that held fewer and fewer vehicles until they traveled over a nearly-deserted country road. Slowing, he peered at the road's shoulders, eventually turning right onto a dirt drive. A hundred yards from the entrance, a rickety wire gate blocked the path. "Push that open, would you?"

Tempest climbed out and opened the unlocked gate, reclosing it after Chance pulled through. As she hoisted it back into place, her attention fell to her left. A tall chain-link fence topped with barbed wire loops zigzagged through the thick, tangled undergrowth. Where had he brought her? To some top-secret military compound? But with no guards?

As she hopped back in the car, she spotted a tiny infrared light searing across the drive. She threw out her hand to stop him from pulling forward. "Is that laser beam going to set off an explosion?"

He laughed. "If it was, our body parts would already be in the trees right now. Up there with the cameras." He pointed up. "It's just keeping an eye on things."

Nestled in the tall, dense trees hanging over the road, two cameras, one on each side of the drive, perched securely on respective tree branches. She scrutinized the thick forest. "What is this place? Camp Peary is easier to find than this."

He peered at Tempest. "You've gotten into Camp Peary?"

"Ha. I don't think the president could get into that spy training ground. Or whatever it is." She turned to study him. "I suppose you have."

Chance didn't answer, but his mouth curled up in a smile. He continued along the dirt road until, without warning, the forest ended and they arrived at a clearing. Huge ancient oak trees dotted the landscape. An enormous old house stood to the right. Once stately, the home looked ready to crumble at the slightest movement. Peeling paint and boarded up windows created a forlorn look.

To the left of the house rested a small bungalow. A woman sat on the front porch, slowly rocking back and forth. A huge bowl of green beans nestled in her lap. Methodically, she snapped off the ends, discarding them into a bucket at her feet. She watched their approach, nodding as Chance drove by. Tempest almost raised her hand in acknowledgement, but the woman's stern expression stopped her. Whatever her role on these grounds, this woman did not suffer foolishness, nor superficial niceties.

He pulled up to a barn in nearly as much disrepair as the house. "Well, honey, we're home."

Without comment, she emerged from the car, waiting for Chance to lead. Going up to the huge doors, he yanked on one, heaving it up a little to drag it over the dirt. She stepped inside, then stopped short.

They stood in a pristine, white corridor, faced by another set of double doors. Before Chance had the opportunity to knock, it opened and a tall, lithe man bellowed out a "Hoo-yah!"

Chance grinned, and they shared back-slaps and a man hug. "It's good to see you, old buddy. You up to any good?"

"Me? Yo's the man what's always got me in trouble." He faced Tempest. "Now yo's bringing a pretty lady wit' ya? Yo' didn't tell me I needed to clean misself up." He whooped out a laugh. "Come on into my little la-bor-atory." He laughed again, pushing open the door to let them enter.

Tempest glanced around the large space and blinked. The brightly illuminated finished room had a modern sterile appearance. Everywhere, model airplanes in various stages of assembly sat on long tables. She glimpsed three computers, all with aeronautic schematics on their screens. She nudged Chance and spoke in a low voice. "Is he a drone developer?"

The man heard her and barked out another laugh. "Yes'm. I makes the big boy toys. These little babies all be some a' my unmanned aerial vehicles—what you peoples call UAVs." He continued to chuckle, speaking to Chance. "I's got holda some good moonshine, C'mander. Yo' and your ladyfriend want yo'selves a slug or two?" With a pronounced limp, he moved to a built-in cabinet and opened its doors, revealing a wet bar stocked with the most expensive brands of alcohol legally available, and a few that fell outside that sphere. He eyed Tempest.

Chance stepped up to the bar. "She only drinks vodka."

She scowled at him.

"Got dat, too. So when yo' gonna introduce me to yo' ladyfriend?"

Chance hesitated and glanced between them, finally saying, "Tempest Raines, Leon Jackson."

Leon had started to pull out a bottle of Zyr vodka, but his manner changed abruptly. He approached her, and although he continued to favor his right leg, his posture straightened. He extended his hand. "It's a pleasure to meet you. You are a true artist. Your photographs are stunning." He lifted her hand and brushed a light kiss across the knuckles.

The chivalrous action had become so uncommon in the United States, heat flashed across her face. As he lowered her hand, he continued to grasp her fingers in his. An intelligence shone in his dark eyes, appraising everything and everyone around him. His sinewy body moved gracefully, despite his limp. She smiled. "Thank you. You're terribly kind."

Still holding her hand and without taking his gaze from her, he addressed Chance. "So, my friend, you need a UAV. What for?" Leon released her and faced him.

Chance peered across the room, scanning the tables before he brought his gaze back to Leon. "Surveillance. Depending on its size and how quiet it is, four- to five-thousand-foot altitude should do. A hundred-mile range, maybe two."

Leon examined him for a long time, as if assessing the seriousness of the request. He perched against the edge of the wet bar's countertop and crossed his arms. "Chance, there's no one in the industry with a UAV that can stay in the air more than forty-five minutes. That's forty miles. Tops. If I had something like that, the damn Pentagon would be knocking down my door."

A hint of a smile tinged Chance's face, and his eyebrows ticked up. "Okay." The single word held a tiny intonation, imploring Leon to continue.

He observed Chance for a minute more, then pushed himself away from the bar, looked down at the floor, and shook his head. "It isn't ready."

"How not ready?"

"It hasn't been tested."

With a grin, Chance moved over and slapped him on the shoulder. "Leon, my man, have I got a test situation for you."

"Shit. I know about your *test situations*. You'll

send my baby over some godless place like Iraq, and I'll never see her again."

"I wouldn't dream of putting one of your babies in jeopardy. We just need to do a little picture-taking over Georgia."

Leon grimaced. "I assume we're not talking about the United States, annual St.-Patrick's-Day-bash-in-Savannah, Georgia."

Chance started wandering around the room, looking at the varying-sized devices. "It's just a little run to the edge of the Caucasus Mountains in South Ossetia. What could be easier?"

Leon glanced at Tempest. The whites of his eyes gleamed under the blinding light. "Is this for some kind of magazine story?"

Tempest threw a look at Chance. He shook his head imperceptibly. She turned back to Leon. "No."

"Something for the teams?"

Chance answered. "No."

"Chance—"

"Don't ask, Leon."

He hobbled over to a table covered with a sheet. "I guess you do need my help." With a flourish, he yanked the white cover off the table, revealing a UAV with a two-foot wingspan.

Chance let out an appreciative whistle. "I'll be damned. You got it this small?"

He indicated another table with a plane half the size. "No. I got it that small. But it doesn't have the endurance."

Chance walked around the table, surveying the machine from all sides. "But not with this one."

Leon shrugged. "I told you. It hasn't been on a full-scale test."

"Will it hold a camera?"

"That's what it's designed for. There's one on each of the wings."

"Range?"

Leon scratched the back of his head. "Five hundred miles at about fifty miles an hour. Or two hundred miles at a hundred miles an hour. If it holds up."

Chance didn't bother to disguise his admiration. "Can we take it for a spin?" Without waiting for Leon to agree, he picked up the hundred-pound drone with a slight grunt and headed for a door at the back of the room.

"Wait a minute. I've got to set things up. Tempest, would you grab that case with the laptop on the counter over there?" Leon shuffled over to the table to pick up a control box, then the three of them went outside.

"Set it on the pad and stand back. Over there. Tempest, you can sit on the bench." He pointed to a spot about ten feet away, then he played with the controls on the box until the UAV lifted and started across the sky.

He handed the box to Chance. "Watch the radar. It's high enough. Let's take a look on the laptop." The two men moved to the bench and sat on either side of Tempest.

Leon reached forward and ran his fingers over the laptop's touch pad to manipulate the image. "There. Take it up higher, C'mander." Pointing out the buttons, he explained to Chance how to manipulate the UAV.

Chance played with the controls, sending the UAV over the landscape and circling around.

"Take it up some more. You've got it at about three

thousand feet now."

The images on the screen remained sharp. The plane flew over the bungalow. Leon smiled. "See that? Fresh green beans for dinner tonight. Hattie's counting on you staying."

"Fried chicken?"

"Hell, no. Damn best blackened snapper north of New Orleans."

Chance grinned. "We wouldn't miss an invitation for Hattie's cooking, no matter what's on the menu. Let's bring her down and see how low it is before we can hear the motor."

Tempest spoke first. "I can hear it now."

"Good. It's at two thousand feet. We'll keep it above that. Show me how to land the baby."

While Leon instructed him, Chance maneuvered the UAV. "That's it. Now bring it down."

Chance played with the remote, bringing the device down smoothly and turning it off. Leon went out to retrieve it, giving Tempest a wink on his way. "Cute little thing, ain't she?"

Tempest smiled, and they went back inside. Chance headed straight for the cabinets and started to rummage.

Leon came in with the plane. "Hey. What yo' doin' in my shit?"

"Calm down, Leon. I'm just looking for some infrared lenses for the cameras."

Tempest spoke up. "Why? The pictures from these cameras were good and clear."

Chance pulled a box from a cabinet and glanced at her. "Yeah. In the daylight. But this won't show us what's going on inside the buildings, and it's going to be dark. The thermal imaging will tell me how many people are in the area and where they are, even if they're asleep."

Leon let out a long, deep sigh. "You're taking my baby."

"Got to." He looked at his friend. "I wouldn't ask if it weren't important."

Leon closed his eyes for a second, and then sighed. He shook his head. "Yeah. I figured. Let me show you the finer points."

They spent the next hour listening, watching, and learning. Finally, Chance said, "Let's box it up. I need you to FedEx it overnight to Athens for me. Get a Sunday pickup so it'll be out there by Tuesday—I don't want it to get held up in customs."

The man's eyes widened. "Athens? Where? To Dimitris?" Chance nodded, and after a long look, Leon disappeared behind a partition. His muffled voice floated across the room. "Overseas overnight FedEx? What'd you do, win a high-stakes poker game?" He reappeared with two flattened boxes under his arm. As he approached Chance, he tossed a tape gun to him.

Chance nabbed it out of the air, shooting a leer at Tempest. "Better than that."

Her mouth tight, she let out a low huff.

Leon watched the exchange with his lips pursed. "Miss Tempest, there be's a box a' packin' peanuts b'hind that wall. Yo' wanna haul it out here fo' me?" When she was out of sight, he cut Chance a smirk. "You got something going here?"

"No."

Leon hooted. "You're a hardass if ever I saw one. You wouldn't know a good thing if it got crammed down your throat. Or better yet, up your ass."

Tempest's return ended the conversation. She dragged a cardboard box over to them.

"Let's get her packed up. Grab a sheet of that plastic over there. You don't want any of this Styrofoam shit getting into the plane."

They worked together, packaging up the UAV and control in the two boxes. While Tempest sealed them with tape, Chance put the laptop in a case. "We'll take this with us."

Leon bent over slightly, rubbing his thigh. He looked tired. "Let's go see Hattie and eat. I'll call FedEx from the house."

As they made the short walk to the bungalow, Tempest examined its frame. The primitive cottage looked like it had been plucked from the corner of a poor small Mississippi town, but when they went inside, for the second time, the contrast between exterior and interior surprised her. The little four-room house gleamed. Its modern kitchen far exceeded her condo's gourmet kitchen. Leon introduced her to Hattie, who promptly shooed them all from her domain.

"Aw, hell," he muttered. "Might as well go back to the la-bor-atory and get ourselves a drink. You two go on. I'll make the call and be right there. I need to talk to Hattie for a minute, too."

Chance took Tempest's hand and led her across the back yard. Dragging open the barn door, he let her enter first. She passed through the false front into the lab.

The track lighting along the perimeter of the ceiling had been dimmed and suffused the walls with a serene warmth. In the center of the room, the model planes looked small and benign, like the play toys of a child. They walked over to the bar. Chance started rummaging through the bottles. "Vodka?"

"I really don't feel like drinking."

He set down the bottle of Zyr and backed her against the wall. "What do you feel like doing?"

She tried to slip away, but his arms pinned her. "Stop it, Chance."

He traced a finger down her cheek, sweeping a wisp of loose hair from her face.

A burning need surged though her, but she forced herself to shove at his chest. "The only thing I want is Sloan back alive. Then I can worry—"

In a quick move, he stepped back, as if scalded by her touch. A fleeting expression of uneasiness flashed across his eyes.

His sudden shift startled her. With a strength of will she'd believed lost, she kept her hands steady, and despite her refusal, poured a shot of the Zyr. Unwilling to acknowledge her actions or validate his with any kind of explanation or excuses, she met his gaze and held it until he turned away. "How did you meet Leon?"

As he examined the rows of liquor, he spoke over his shoulder. "ROTC in college, at Virginia. Neither of us could afford tuition, and it gave us a way to go to school for free. And we went through BUD/S together."

She dropped two ice cubes in her glass and took a swallow of the vodka. "He's a SEAL? You were in training together?"

Sifting through the bottles, he pulled out some Chivas. "Yeah, but he was only in for eight years. He went on a mission and got his leg blown off trying to save a teammate. Nearly killed him, and our teammate didn't make it, either. He's got a prosthetic, but I think he's in a lot of pain. He'll never admit it, though."

She shuddered. "I'm sorry."

"Yeah. Me, too. He was a damn good teammate." His voice softened, and he stared into his glass of whisky. "I'm the one who talked him into trying out for the teams. It's my fault."

She set her hand on his arm. "Chance, you can't—"

He shifted his gaze to Tempest. His expression told her he didn't need, or want, to be mollified. "He's never said a word to me about the accident, but it took him a while to get through the rehab. He got pretty bitter. I've always thought if he'd been able to save Barkley, it would've helped. But he got a medal and an honorable discharge and got out."

"He seems to have a good sense of humor."

"Yeah. Now. Hattie's a big reason for him getting through all the rough times. They got married right after we finished BUD/S. When he got out of the Navy, he went back to school for his masters. Now he's got a couple of Ph.D.s from M.I.T. He's rolling in dough. The Pentagon is already knocking down his door, so he hides in this hell-hole." He chuckled. "The man's a damn genius."

"You already got your UAV, Chance. You can skip the flattery." Leon came up behind them.

They spent another hour in the lab. Tempest's obvious interest in Leon's work spurred him to take her on a detailed guided tour, but she remained fully aware of Chance standing nearby, watching her quietly.

When Hattie called them to dinner, Leon hustled them back to the house. "Don't want to cross that woman. I'd hear about it for six months."

Well after dark and the best blackened snapper north of New Orleans, Chance begged off. "We need to get home. We still have a lot to do. Let me hit the head before we go."

Chapter Eighteen

Saturday, March 25—9:00 p.m.

When Chance disappeared around the corner, Tempest saw Leon staring at her.

His gaze didn't waver. "When are you leaving for Athens?"

She paused. "Chance is going out Monday."

He scratched at the back of his neck, glanced toward the hallway, then came back to her. "And you?"

She didn't respond.

"He's going out there because of you."

She drew in a deep breath and exhaled. "I…I don't know all his plans."

His focus steady, he stared her down. Even Hattie gave her a stern look. "Tempest," Leon continued, "I've known Chance Adams for almost twenty-five years. Whatever you've gotten him into, he's worried, and I can't remember ever seeing him like this. Not to this extent." He leaned forward, his voice tight with concern. "He doesn't expect to make it back from this trip…to whatever hell-hole it is you've got him heading to."

His glaring expression drilled through her, and she looked away. Leon's harsh prediction made her skin crawl. Her shoulders sagged.

He waited for her to answer, but she only shook her

head. "What's going on in Georgia? Or is he headed to Russia?"

"Leon…"

A controlled anger tinged his previous easy-going manner. "This better be some shittin' important reason. And not some damned magazine story you're concocting."

Her voice so faint she barely heard it herself, she said, "This isn't a story, Leon. It's life and de—" She choked and covered her mouth.

He drummed his fingers on the table. "Does Dickey—does his CO know he's doing this?"

She squeezed her eyes shut to keep her tears at bay. Her chest rose and fell with each deep breath.

The man looked over at his wife. "I gotta go to Athens. He needs help."

Hattie nodded and reached over to grasp his hand.

Tempest shook her head. "I'm not sure that's such a good idea. He…He's very…stubborn."

Hattie laughed. "Honey, Chance Adams isn't just stubborn. He's the definition of stubborn." Her mirth vanished in a blink however, and she gave Tempest a long, hard look. "You make sure my men come back to me, Tempest Raines. Both of them."

All she could do was squeak, "Yes, ma'am."

Leon kept his gaze on her. "Don't tell him I'm going out there, Tempest. He'll hit the roof."

Chance's reappearance kept her from acknowledging his comment.

"The three of you look like you're heading to a funeral. I know you missed me, but I only went to the bathroom." Chance came to the table and held out his hand for Tempest. "Come on. We need to get back to

Norfolk."

They went outside, and Leon limped up to the rental car with them, Hattie by his side. "Miz Tempest, yo' take care o' this boy. He needs some lookin' after."

His return to the playful jive didn't delude her. If anything happened to Chance, he would hold her responsible. But she managed to keep her tone light. "I'll do my best, Leon. Thank you for everything. We'll take care of your plane." She moved up and kissed him on the cheek.

He shrugged. "I can always build another one."

She got it. A plane, yes. Chance, no.

Then Hattie moved over to embrace her.

Surprised by the gesture, Tempest spoke in her ear. "I don't want them to get hurt, either, Hattie."

"I can see that." She turned slightly to angle away from the men, and pushed Tempest back a bit, speaking in a soft tone. "I've known Chance almost as long as Leon has. That man cares for you. Don't hurt him—he's been through that once already."

In opposition to Leon's comments, Hattie's didn't address the physical danger, but peeled away another layer of Chance's history. One even though Tempest knew, she'd never heard from his perspective. She observed Hattie for a moment, trying to read her. "I don't think so. This is just a mission to him."

Her eyes twinkled under the yard's floodlights. "We'll see." Hattie moved over to embrace Chance.

Tempest slipped into the car to let them say their goodbyes.

****

Chance shut the door behind Tempest, then gave Hattie a hug.

"That woman cares about you, Chance Adams. Don't you make her another one of your conquests."

Aggravation shot through him, but with Hattie he could never stay angry. "You matchmaking again, Miz Jackson?"

"Just makin' an observation." She turned to go inside.

Leon gave him a long look. His voice low, he said, "I can't guarantee the UAV will hold up."

"It better, Leon." He shot a glance at Tempest, staring out the windshield. "It's all I've got."

The two men inspected each other for a minute. Leon let out a breath. "Chance..." He shook his head. "Be careful, my friend."

Hell. The second time I've heard that today. Without speaking, he shook Leon's hand, drew him into a quick one-arm-hug, then climbed in the car and left.

****

Chance watched Tempest fall into the airplane seat in exhaustion. They had barely spoken since they left Leon's. Hattie's comment continued to rattle around in his head. Where Leon's intelligence fell into Mensa levels, Hattie's intellect reached into understanding people and what made them tick. Her mystifying ability had unnerved him more than once.

This time included.

Regardless of her pronouncement, she and Leon both knew of the Raineses. Why would Hattie make a declaration for him not to hurt Tempest? What purpose did it serve? She must have noticed the ring on Tempest's finger. He glanced at her, shifting in the seat next to him. Was it true? Did she have feelings for him?

Chance reached over and stroked Tempest's cheek,

turning her face him. "I want you to get some sleep tonight. I'll come over early in the morning."

She nodded, leaning her head against his shoulder. She looked up at him. "Thank you." Then she snuggled against his arm. Before the plane left the ground, she had fallen asleep.

He adjusted his position to give her head some support. Gently, he swept the loose strands of hair behind her ear. Regardless of her intelligence and competence, she exuded a childlike trust that kept eroding his resolve.

No wonder Sloan cared for her. The question was, would he let her go? The self-inflicted debate flirting with his mind, he closed his eyes and nodded off.

****

A sense of comfort flowed over Tempest as she leaned against Chance. Sloan's father—the words she avoided for so many years, trying to deny the past, her history, her son's ancestry. How could she explain this to Sloan, much less to Chance? Marc's warning about Chance's ideas on family ate at her. If he felt that strongly, would he ever forgive her for keeping his son away? Would he understand?

When she learned she was pregnant, two months after Ginny's party, her parents had all but disowned her. After refusing her mother's insistence she have an abortion, they had determined to send her to a home for unwed mothers in South Carolina. A home that provided medical care throughout the pregnancy, and then whisked the babies off for adoption as soon as they were born. This was for the best, they had claimed. As it stood, this *dilemma* would delay her entry into the University of Virginia by a year. And as she was too immature to take the necessary precautions to avoid pregnancy, she certainly wasn't capable of caring for a child.

In their minds, this *indiscretion* would undoubtedly taint the family name, and although the message remained unverbalized, the essence was clear.

They'd allowed her enough time to pack a few clothes and a toothbrush and plopped her on the Greyhound to Columbia. But when the bus stopped in Richmond, she hopped off and called her father's sister in Colonial Heights. Aunt Mary came to get her, took her in, and never betrayed her whereabouts to anyone. Her aunt had cut ties with the family when her brother, Tempest's father, had married Patricia, claiming the woman was a social, money-grabbing elitist.

Exactly what Ginny had become.

As soon as Tempest learned she carried Chance's child, she'd tried to find him. But at eighteen, with no understanding of the military and no resources, she'd never been able to learn where he was stationed. The SEALs were a secretive, exclusive group, and outsiders simply couldn't break through their walls. When Aunt Mary asked who the father was, Tempest told her he was a boy she'd met, they'd dated for a while, and he'd been killed in a car accident.

She'd always thought Mary didn't quite believe her, but the woman had never questioned her further.

Once more, Marc's declarations about Chance spun in her mind. If she had only been more forthright, if she'd pushed a little more, maybe Marc would have helped her get in touch with Chance. Had she given up too easily? Waves of regret swelled over her. She swallowed hard and rested her hand on Chance's arm, nuzzling deeper against his shoulder. Beyond saving her—*their*—son, she could foresee no happy outcome from this quagmire.

****

When they arrived in Norfolk, Chance woke her up, giving Tempest a few minutes to orient herself. As they disembarked, she held his arm. The glazed look in her eyes concerned him. "I'm going to take you home. We can get your car tomorrow."

She protested. "That's too much trouble. I'm fine. Really."

He studied her for a few seconds. "Okay, but I'm following you home. I want to make sure you get there without any problems."

As they headed down the escalator on their way to the parking garage, she pulled the band from her hair, running her fingers through the wayward curls.

"Do you usually need a lot of sleep?"

"Not really. Five or six hours. I just haven't been getting that much this week."

"Try to get some tonight. You look terrible."

"Thanks a lot." She reached over and skimmed his cheek with her fingers, sending a static charge through his nerves. "You could use a shave yourself."

"Not now. Not until this is over." He tilted his head away from her touch and escorted her through the doors into the night. Keeping some distance between them comprised the only safety net he could devise. He had one purpose, one goal. To save Sloan's life without getting them both killed. Then he could occupy himself with what to do about Tempest Raines.

****

When they reached her condo, she took him

upstairs and gave him a key to her apartment. Back downstairs, she cleared his access with security and secured a vehicle pass for him. They walked together through the lobby toward the exit.

"You didn't have to get me all these passes. It's no big deal."

"I was tired of them calling me every time you showed up. You can return the key when we get back from Greece."

They stopped near the exit. He crossed his arms. "Or maybe I won't. Do you trust me?"

She spat an annoyed huff. "I guess I must. Not that you deserve any."

A brazen smile tugged at the corners of his mouth. "The guards might think we're having an affair."

"I don't give a damn what they think. It certainly isn't true."

"But you wish it was."

Expelling another burst of air, she spun on her heels. He caught her arm, forcing her back around.

"Let me go."

A voice echoed across the lobby. "Is everything all right, Miss Raines?"

"It's fine, Wade." Through clenched teeth, she whispered, "I think it would be a good idea if we stuck to business. I don't need help from someone who can't separate his brain from his..." She looked down at his pants.

In a flash, he wrapped his arms around her and kissed her hard and deep. His hands ran over her back with a detectable gentleness that concealed the strength of his grip on her. Powerless to stop him lest it arouse the suspicion of the guards, she could do nothing but let him take her.

After he ravaged her for a full thirty seconds, his mouth left hers, moving to her ear. "Might as well give the poor bastards something to think about."

"You're repulsive. Let me go."

He loosened his grip, kissing her on the cheek. "Goodnight, *lover*. I'll see you in the morning." Shrugging on his parka, he ambled through the doors into the cool air.

Tempest watched him cross the parking lot. Her lips were swollen from his kiss. She curled them in to keep from running her tongue over the tender flesh and tried to erase the memory of his touch. Why couldn't he just leave her alone? Every time he claimed her in one of his indisputable rites of ownership, it brought her a little closer to blurting out the truth. She had to tell him.

But it could wait until Sloan had been rescued.

Struggling to assume a grace far surpassing the confusion in her heart, she strolled back to the elevator and stepped inside, keeping her gaze everywhere, anywhere, to keep from making eye contact with the guards.

Upstairs, fueled with an anger directed at herself as much as at Chance, she slammed the door to her apartment, insensitive to the late hour and her fellow residents. Stomping into her bedroom, she stripped and fell onto the bed.

The torment of the last week encased her, committing her to a mental and emotional collapse. She eventually drifted into an uneasy sleep, images of Chance and Sloan parading behind her eyes. They butted together, clashing against each other in a wordless struggle, until finally their faces overlapped, merging together as one.

Her subconscious mind accepted and embraced the repercussions of having Chance and Sloan meet, even if her rational mind could not.

Chapter Nineteen

Norfolk, Virginia
Sunday, March 26—0030 hours.

The penetrating ring of his landline hit Chance's ears when he opened the door to his apartment. Only one person would be calling him at this hour. He dashed through the living room and snatched up the receiver. "Is something wrong?"

"You tell me." The terse tone of his brother's voice assaulted him.

Shit. No words, no fabrications came to his mind. Troy knew him too well.

"You're doing it, aren't you?"

He dropped onto the sofa. "She needs help."

"Doesn't have to come from you. You know people—there are plenty of guys who are out and would love something to do. Send her to one of them." Frustration rankled his tone. "Do you have any clue how bad things are in Georgia?"

The question hurtled through Chance's gut. "Of cours—"

"No. No, you don't. The information you have isn't close to what I know."

He couldn't argue the point. Troy subcontracted to both the government and private concerns as a political analyst, had a slew of security clearances, and access to far more than Chance could find, even with his own clearances. "Fine. Fill me in."

An extended pause ensued. Chance waited. Finally, Troy warned, "I swear to God, if you get yourself killed doing this, I'll come after you in Hell."

The abrupt, loud click blistered his mind. A sick feeling dripped through his veins, every nerve in his body prickled with a biting frost. Eyes closed, he wiped his hand over his face and dropped his head.

He had made Tempest a promise, and he never went back on his word.

****

The dazzling, rising sun poured through the plate glass of the bedroom's sliding door, flooding the room with pale pink light. Tempest turned over in bed, stretching her arms above her head. Feeling a chill, she ran her hands over her body with a start. She'd fallen into bed naked last night. She couldn't remember ever sleeping in the nude—certainly not with Sloan in residence.

Worse than that, the slight dampness of her sheets provided a glaring reminder of her disturbing dreams. Rolling off the mattress, she stripped the bed in haste, as if by stuffing the linens in the washer the action would cleanse not only them, but her thoughts as well.

After she tossed them through the door into the hallway, Tempest dressed in a ragged sweatshirt and running shorts. Reaching under the bed, she pulled out a pair of Reeboks and slipped them on, tying the laces tightly.

After a few minutes of stretching, she jogged down the five flights of stairs to the lobby. The guard posted near the elevators greeted her in surprise—it had only been six hours since she passed by him last night.

"Morning, Wade," she called out, her voice cheery. She headed through the building's back door and down to the beach, working her way through the soft white dunes to the ocean's edge. The ebbing tide left a wide strip of hard-packed sand. She stretched a bit more, then took off in a slow run, increasing her pace as her muscles warmed up. The cool morning air slapped at her skin as her feet pounded the sand until her endorphin level increased and her mood lightened. The anxieties of the last week slid away, skimming off her body in currents. The ache in her legs and joints disappeared, and she glided over the sand, immersed in an unconcerned oblivion.

An hour later, back in front of her building, she slowed down, pacing in a circle while she tried to catch her breath. Sweat drenched her clothes even with a sixty-degree temperature. After a few minutes, she trudged through the yielding sand and entered the condominium, panting a greeting to the new shift of security men.

When she stepped into the elevator, she leaned against the wall until reaching her floor. Sunday papers dotted her neighbors' thresholds, but her doorway was bare. Great. It would take a couple of hours for the circulation department to deliver the missing copy.

Muttering a curse under her breath, she entered her apartment, inhaling deeply. The scent of freshly brewed coffee reached her, but before she had time to consider why, a voice called something from the dining room.

She yelped and flattened herself against the wall.

A bare second later, Chance moved into the hall, giving her an amused look. "I asked, 'How far did you run?' "

She rested her hand against her pounding heart. "What are you doing here?"

He dangled her key in the air. "How soon they forget."

With a scowl, she pushed herself from the wall and tromped into the kitchen. "I wasn't expecting you to show up at the crack of dawn."

He ambled down the passageway behind her. "You went running at the crack of dawn. It's well beyond that now. It's almost seven o'clock." Crossing the kitchen, he opened a cabinet and pulled out a mug. "Coffee?"

The ease with which he proceeded through *her* apartment, readily handling *her* things, impinged on her sense of privacy. Still, she had willingly given him a key, and not at his prompting. She could hardly fault him for making a pot of coffee.

"I threw your sheets in the washing machine for you." He poured her a cup, dropped in a spoonful of sugar and some cream, stirred, and handed it to her. The corners of his eyes creased, teasing her. "But I draw the line at making your bed. Especially if I'm not sleeping in said bed."

She slammed the mug down on the counter. Hot coffee sloshed over the rim, scalding her hand. She winced and wiped the liquid on her shirt. "What did you do? Snoop through my whole apartment while you were waiting?"

He shrugged. "No. Just parts. I saw you leave the building when I came in. Wade said you usually run for an hour, so I came up here and watched you from the balcony till you were out of sight. I made some coffee and took care of the sheets. Then I sat on the balcony and read the paper until I saw you coming back. You keep up a pretty good pace. How far did you run?"

She blinked. The barrage of information glutted her mind. She tried to assimilate the details, but one thought kept returning. "Wade? You're on a first-name basis with the guards now?"

"I'm a friendly guy." The slight teasing smile in his eyes vexed her as his gaze roved over her. "Maybe you should take a shower. We've got a lot to do."

She whirled and headed for the bedroom. "I'd appreciate it if you'd keep your hands off my laundry."

"If you insist. I can think of several of your things I'd rather keep my hands on."

She slammed the door, but his chuckle still crept into the room. She started yanking off her clothes, stopped, then went back and turned the lock on the doorknob. The flimsy device wouldn't serve to keep him out if he wanted to gain access to her room, but it helped her retain some control over the situation before he forced her to surrender.

When she emerged from the bedroom, she found Chance standing by the built-in bookcase, examining a photograph of her and Sloan, her arm across his shoulders.

"Who is this with you?"

"Sloan."

His brow furrowed. "He looks like he's about fourteen years old."

She cocked her head at his odd comment. "Close. A friend took it a couple of months before his birthday."

He shook his head in wonder. "I've thought a lot of things about you, but I sure as hell never thought you would resort to…" He blinked. "Huh. Brings a whole new meaning to *boy toy*," he muttered. Eyebrows hiked, he looked at her. "I hope you at least waited until he hit eighteen."

She frowned. "Boy toy? What are you…" She stopped and stared at him. "Oh, my God. You think he's my husband." She stared at him, blinked, then broke into laughter. "Chance, I'm not *married* to him. Sloan is my *son*."

The expression on his face shifted from confusion to disbelief to understanding. In a flash, his inconsistent attitude toward her became clear. His deep-seated morality wouldn't allow him to be with another man's wife. For whatever acts he might be required to commit in the line of duty, in his personal life, he held to certain boundaries and would never cross them.

Chance traversed the room and now stood by her. He took her left hand. "What's this ring? Did his father die?"

"Chance, you—" She coughed. "I…no…I never married his father. Sloan gave me this ring when he was eight years old. He said all of his friends' mothers had a ring, and he wanted me to, also. He saved his money for weeks and gave it to me for Mother's Day." The last words from her lips choked her. She covered her mouth with her hand, squeezed her eyes shut, and bit at her lip. A tear escaped and ran down her cheek.

"Hell." Gently, he wrapped his arms around her waist and pulled her to him. With his thumb, he wiped the tear from her face and then trailed his tongue along the track, settling on her lips with a soft kiss. He moved to her ear and whispered, "I'm going to do my best to get him out of there, Tempest. I promise."

She nodded against his chest and sucked in a ragged breath. Then a thought hit her, and she pushed him back. "Wait a minute. Did you—do you—actually think so little of me you believe I would…have *sex* with a child?"

"I—well—no, of course not—"

"You do." She knotted her hands into fists and whacked them against his chest, breaking his hold on her. Then she whirled and stomped into her bedroom, slamming the door.

****

"Oh, shit." Chance dropped onto the arm of a chair. For the second time in less than a week she'd caused him to forget his training, lose his bearing, ignore his focus…*fail*. Dangerous didn't begin to describe Tempest Raines.

And none of that mattered.

The damned fact remained—he cared about the woman, and now nothing stood in his way. Except his own stupidity. He shoved away from the chair and went to the bedroom, tapping lightly on the door. "Tempest?"

No answer. He tried the handle, and the door opened. No answer, but the bathroom door sat slightly ajar. He went over and heard water running. He knocked and raised his voice. "Tempest!"

"Go away." Her voice streamed through the sound of the shower.

He pushed open the door and stepped into the steamy room. "Tempest."

Her voice tight, she said, "Get out of my bathroom, Commander. Now."

"No. We're going to talk." He grabbed the curtain and scraped it across the rod.

She shrieked and reached up to pull it back.

He kept his hand on the bar, kicked off his shoes, and climbed into the tub. Water splashed over him, drenching his clothes. He ran his hands down her sides, then slipped his arms around her back and pulled her closer. "You already took a shower."

She shoved at his chest.

He kept his grip, sliding his hands along her slick, soaped body. Water cascaded over her, her hair drooped against her shoulders in wet bunches. He leaned near her ear, resisting the urge to nibble, as the continuous stream pelted his head. "I'm sorry. It just surprised me. I don't believe you would do that." The tension slinked from her muscles.

She shifted her hands on his chest, but no longer pushed. "You need to go. Please."

He didn't move. "We still have a lot to do."

"In the shower?"

He pressed against her. "I'm comfortable here."

She bunched up a bit of his shirt in her hand and squeezed out water from the material. "Your clothes are soaking wet."

He slid his hand to her shoulder, then behind her neck. His lips close to her ear, he whispered, "Then I guess I'll have to walk around here naked until they dry."

She slapped at his chest, forcing him away. "You are an insufferable jackass. Get out of my tub." She reached behind her and turned off the water.

He let his hands slide off her body, but took his time, lingering on her hips. "I've had a lot of insults hurled at me, but I don't believe anyone has ever called me an *insufferable jackass*."

A growl spurted from her, and she yanked a towel from the rack, wrapping it around her curves. Without comment, she climbed over the edge of the tub and tromped into her bedroom.

He chuckled and took another towel from the bar, blotting at his wet clothes. His rash action created a bit of a problem, but what the hell. He enjoyed toying with her. *And she's not married.* He stripped down to his underwear and draped the wet clothes over his arm, moving into the bedroom. "Mind if I put these in the dryer?"

Tempest waved a hand at him, which he assumed meant okay, but before he left her room, he took the time to study her. She stood by a dresser, now wearing black lace panties and a black bra, with her hair bundled up in a blue towel. Her comfort in her own skin intrigued him even more. He'd seen her naked twice, and neither time did she try to cover herself. Yet, her lack of modesty didn't make him think of her as a tramp. Sexy, sensual, seductive…yes.

Oh. Hell. Yes.

He had to get out of her bedroom, so he went down the hall, stripped off his undershorts, and tossed the wet clothes in the dryer. He ran the towel over his body, dried off, and called out to her. "What size shorts does Sloan wear?"

"Thirty-four." Her voice floated through the air.

"Can I borrow a pair, or some swim trunks or something?"

Now dressed in sweats and a T-shirt, she came down the hall, disappeared into another bedroom, then popped up at the laundry room door. "I think that would be a very good idea." Her gaze flickered over him, dropped, then darted up to remain steady on his eyes. She handed him a pair of baggy running shorts and departed. "I need to dry my hair," she called out, then shut her door with a firm thud.

He slipped on the shorts and went to the kitchen to refill his coffee. Maybe a shot of caffeine would help expunge his thoughts. Single or not, he needed to get her out of his head. This lunacy couldn't continue.

Then a disturbing notion struck him. He might not have the willpower—or the desire—to stop.

Chapter Twenty

Sunday, March 26—9:00 a.m.

Tempest wandered into the living room. Chance was on his cell phone. He wore his T-shirt and Sloan's shorts, but hadn't put on his jeans. They must still be in the dryer. A vision of him naked skittered through her mind, and her skin tingled before she buried the image. She passed by and went into the kitchen, pouring herself some coffee. His cup sat nearby, so she filled it and took it into the living room.

As she handed it to him, he winked at her. Twisting her mouth into a grimace, she dropped into a chair, observing him. His amiable conversation with whoever was on the other end of the line didn't conceal the professional undertones in his words. A tautness permeated the air around him. In his element now, everything about him connoted self-confidence and a belief in his mission.

The comic interlude from the shower had evaporated with the steam from the hot water.

A sudden calm infused her. If anyone could succeed at this foolhardy attempt, it had to be Chance Adams.

When she'd initially gone to see Marc, thoughts of Chance had already pervaded her brain. Since she'd never mentioned him to Marc again, she hadn't known if Chance was still on active duty at all, but the fact remained, in the romanticized fantasies of her imagination, she'd pictured him as the one to help rescue Sloan. Her rational mind knew Marc could not, would not, officially help her. Her rational mind expected him to provide her with contact information for some retired SEAL in the area who might be willing to take on this challenge.

She didn't really expect to see Chance. Ever again. In fact, with his dangerous job, she couldn't be sure he hadn't been killed in a mission. Like his teammate Barkley.

Tempest needed to push aside her feelings for the man and focus on the real issue. Whether or not she ever saw Chance again after this exhaustive rescue attempt bore no consequence to the goal. As she spent more time with him, it became apparent he would never forgive her transgressions or her past. He wouldn't understand her reasons or motivations for doing what she had done. For all of his sexual overtones and trifling with her, he held an integrity so deeply ingrained she couldn't pretend to grasp the concept.

Once she told him the truth, whatever hopes she had would be splintered into more pieces than any bonding could repair. He would never be hers.

And what about Sloan? Once she confessed her deeds to Chance, Sloan would learn the truth also. What would that do to their relationship? Her son's one rebellious period in high school had only strengthened his own deep-seated morality. What if he rejected her? She closed her eyes. She could foresee no outcome for this situation short of tragedy. Because of her failings, they would all be hurt. After years of hiding the past, it had returned and could not be denied.

Considering her limited options, if she wanted Chance, she would have to satisfy herself with one sexual liaison and spend another twenty years living in the memories.

The thought splintered through her, and she dropped her cup. Coffee spilled on the carpet, spreading in a toffee-colored pool across the thick pile. She dashed to the laundry room and grabbed a towel, coming back to blot up the mess. In the recesses of her mind, she heard Chance say a sentence or two in Greek and hang up the phone. He disappeared then came back with a damp sponge.

He knelt beside her, pressing the sponge onto the stain. "Are you okay?"

Unable to speak, she nodded.

He took the towel from her, laying it on the floor. Framing her face with his hands, he instilled her with his own reassurances. "I'm working on a plan. We have a good shot at getting him out."

Tears flooded her eyes. He slipped his arms around her, holding her against his chest, stroking her hair, until she finally pulled away, wiping across her eyes.

If only she could have them both.

****

Tempest's eyes still felt puffy, even after time spent with a cold washcloth pressed against them before she put on her makeup. She returned to the living room and dropped onto the loveseat.

Chance emerged from the dining room and sat next to her. "How old is Sloan now?"

"He turned twenty last month."

He stared at her. "How old were you when you had

him? Twelve?"

"Eighteen."

"Geez. I thought you were in your early thirties. So what happened to the guy? Some high school sweetheart who bailed on you? Or did the guy's parents put the skids on things?"

Eyes closed, she twisted her neck to ease the tension. "Neither. Just a…mistake."

With a frown, he settled against the arm of the loveseat and faced her. His tone gentle and quiet, but steady, he asked, "Did you get raped?"

She studied him for a long moment. "No. I didn't get raped."

Silence fell between them. He didn't pursue his interrogation, but instead, changed the subject. "You said Sloan speaks Georgian and Russian fluently. How did he learn them?"

Tempest drew in a long breath, burying the memories. "He's quick with languages. His Spanish is fluent, too. He took a class in high school and enjoyed the challenge, so when we started working together, he made an effort to learn the language wherever we went."

A small *huh* emerged from him. "That's impressive. Isn't he interested in college?"

"He's starting this fall. He wanted to travel with me for a couple of years, and I thought it was a good idea." Her eyes began to blur. "Until now." When Chance didn't respond, she countered with a question of her own. She needed to get off this topic. "Who were you talking to on the phone?"

"Dimitris Thalassinos. My friend in Athens. And I'm glad you mentioned that. You need to call Alexei."

A hollow feeling pressed against her chest. Calling Alexei meant more half-truths and deceit. The notion began to repel her. Hadn't she told enough lies? She stared toward the sliding patio doors. "What do you want me to tell him?"

He straightened and took her hand, but the action held no nuances. His demeanor emanated nothing but business. "We need a better idea of where the camp is. Will he tell you?"

She lifted her shoulders. "I don't see why not." She paused to pull her hand from his, flexing her fingers. A red burn blanketed it from her thumb across the back of her hand to her knuckles. "I have to come up with an excuse for not needing his help, though."

Chance ran his thumb over her hand, examining the burn. "You should put something on this."

She snatched it back. "It's fine."

His anger surged forth. He grasped her shoulders and turned her to face him. "Listen to me. You asked for my help. Stop working against me. I need you rested and in good physical and mental condition, or you'll get Sloan killed. And us, too. Is that what you want?"

The fierceness of his declaration plunged through her. Without Chance, they would more than likely die. They might die regardless. She closed her eyes for a second to shut out his piercing glare. "No."

He released her, and she picked up the phone to call Alexei.

Chance stood. "Do you have anything to drink besides coffee? I think we've both had enough caffeine."

She managed a smile. "Vodka."

The ends of his mouth creased.

"There should be some soda in the pantry."

She watched him disappear into the hall while she punched in some numbers on the phone. He still loitered in the kitchen when Alexei answered. With a hasty greeting, she leapt into her story. "I couldn't get on the plane to New York, Alexei. I got to the airport late, and they had overbooked the flight. I wouldn't have made the connection to Moscow."

Chance wandered back in with two glasses of 7-Up and sat next to her, setting their drinks on the coffee table. The cushions shifted under his weight, and she straightened, pushing herself closer to the arm of the loveseat. He grabbed a piece of paper, scribbled a few words, and handed it to her.

She scanned it before speaking again. "I can't get there until Wednesday. Is Sloan all right?" She paused, squeezing her eyes shut. "Yes, I'm bringing the film. Do you really think they'll let him go?"

****

Chance continued writing, passing notes to her as she talked to Alexei. He watched her closely. He'd never known a woman with so many layers. An hour ago, he'd been drawn in by her sensuality…now, a palpable anxiety showed on her face, yet her voice remained even and calm. The things she had seen and captured on film had toughened her. He didn't doubt she could hold her own in a crisis.

He also had a good grasp of what her reaction would be once she realized he planned to go into the camp alone.

"Can you give me an idea of where the camp is? No, but Commander Adams said he could give me some advice on how to proceed if he knew more about the location and the terrain. It might be helpful."

Chance raised an eyebrow. The lies spilled forth so easily from her lips. How much practice did she have? Although not close to Hattie's insight, for years he'd prided himself on his ability to read people, but Tempest stretched him to new heights. He couldn't swear he'd ever figure the woman out.

Another notch attesting to his fascination with her.

She snatched the pen from his hand and started writing. "Yes, I'm sure that will be enough. The commander said he can give me some suggestions." The expression on her face changed. "Well, of course, we should try to get him peacefully first. You're right… Yes. I'll see you on Wednesday. Assure them I'm on my way. Don't let them hurt him."

She hung up the phone and leaned back, closing her eyes.

"Well?"

Wresting herself to attention, she shoved the paper at him. "This is about where the camp is. He wasn't very specific. I couldn't exactly ask for the precise coordinates."

He examined her notes. "This will do. At least I'll have an idea where to send the UAV. Once we do that, we'll know where the camp is located and its layout. If we're lucky, we might even see Sloan or be able to figure out which building he's being held in."

Banishing his brother's damning threat from the night before from his mind, Chance spent the rest of the morning with Tempest, mapping out their plans.

Chapter Twenty-One

Sunday, March 26—1300 hours

Finally, Chance stood and stretched. "We need to take a break. Does anyone around here deliver, or should I run out for something?"

"I can see if I have anything in the freezer."

He chuckled. "You cook?"

She planted her hands on her hips. "I raised a boy. Of course I cook. Do you think I let him grow up on nothing but Tostitos and Mountain Dew?" She started toward the kitchen. "Do you want a bologna sandwich? I can throw some grit in it if it'll make you feel more at home."

He pulled her close and slipped his arms around her. "You don't have to cook. I can think of other rooms I'd rather see you in besides the kitchen."

She jerked back. "What is it with you? Do you want to just go into my bedroom and screw? Fine. Let's go." She spun.

He grabbed her arm and moved back in front of her. "I annoy you, don't I?"

She pursed her lips and crossed her arms. Sarcasm laced her tone. "Whatever makes you think that?"

"My uncanny astuteness and ability to read people." With a soft touch, he ran his fingers across her cheek then brushed his lips over hers.

She didn't budge.

He tried again. This time, he settled on her lips and teased until her mouth parted and he could dive inside. When the stiffness eased from her, he tightened his grip, reveling in the scent, the taste, the softness of this woman.

Her hands on his shoulders, Tempest ran her fingers behind his neck and scraped lightly through his untrimmed hair. Then she slipped a hand down his chest to the bottom of his T-shirt and inside, dragging her nails up his back.

Her touch sent waves of sensation through his skin. He still wore Sloan's shorts—he'd never pulled his jeans from the dryer. Without the thick denim and zipper between them, a new awareness bolted through him. He tugged at her T-shirt and began to pull it up, but she took his hand and started to turn. He held back, twisted, and plucked up the phone's receiver, tossing it on the loveseat. No phone call would interrupt them this time.

She led him into her bedroom and reached down to grasp the edge of her shirt.

He stopped her. "No. Let me." His hands pushed the shirt up, relishing the soft satin of her skin, finally lifting the barrier over her head. Then he repeated the action in reverse, pushing down her sweatpants.

Tempest stepped out of them, and he drank her in, his gaze sweeping over her figure adorned in black lace. He yanked off his shirt and pulled her close. A faint scent of vanilla came from her skin…the soap in her tub. He inhaled as he ran his lips across her shoulder and slid his hands behind her to unhook the bra then slip down her panties.

"Chance."

The slight huskiness in her sultry voice infused every pore in his skin, every cell in his body. His own voice deepened as he whispered in her ear. "Do you want me?"

In response, she nodded and pressed against him, skimming her tongue across his chest.

He took her face in his hands and tipped it up. "I just need to hear you say it." He stroked her cheeks with his fingers. "Please."

Her green eyes bright with desire, she brushed the stubble on his chin with a delicate touch, dancing her fingertips across his lips. "Yes. I want you, Chance."

A low groan came from his throat. God, he hadn't wanted a woman this much in years.

Ever.

He shoved down his shorts and led her to the bed, needing nothing more than to bring her to heights she'd never experienced. To torment her until she screamed his name, crying for more. Begging to have him inside her. He trailed his tongue down her belly and barely brushed against her tender flesh before she sucked in a breath.

Her responses stroked his senses like a feather on his skin. A woman so strong, so vital—yet, so delicate and soft. He caressed her sensitive skin with his tongue, gently sucking, then tracing with slow strokes. She moaned and arched her back to press against him, and he dove deeper until she clutched his shoulders, tugging on him to bring his mouth to hers. She took his kisses greedily, then in a quick move, rolled him on his back and straddled him.

With a deep groan, he sank into her folds, feeling

their heat mingle as she slowly stroked him. He played with her breasts, teasing and gently squeezing her taut nipples, watching her rear her head back while she moved on him. He shifted his hand to caress her until her muscles began to tighten around him.

The sensations were sheer, glorious torture. He flipped her on her back and sank deep inside, thrusting, plunging, until she dug her nails into his back and called out—her shuddering body pulsing against him, drawing him into his own release.

Spent, he lowered himself and nestled against her. His hand cupped her breast as her heartbeat slowed. Unwilling to break the connection, he kissed her on the neck, running his tongue across the slight saltiness on her skin. If he stayed here much longer, he'd be ready to take her again.

No one had ever consumed him like she did. How could he consider letting her go?

****

Tempest awoke with a start and raised up to look past Chance at the clock. After two o'clock. They'd both dozed off. Elbow on the pillow, she propped her head against her hand, watching him sleep. A deep longing surged through her.

Without opening his eyes, he inched closer and nuzzled his lips against her chest. "Ready for another round?" he mumbled into her skin.

A tingle rippled in her veins. She let her fingers drift down his arm and kissed the top of his head. "Shouldn't we get something to eat?"

"Mm hmm." He took her breast in his mouth.

She sucked in a tiny breath and moved her hand down to his hip.

Chance caught her hand, kissed her fingers, and then pulled away. "As much as I'm enjoying this, it's not the best time." He sat up. "We could take a shower together, though." He leered at her.

"Didn't we try that this morning?"

He leaned over her. "Yeah, but I have something different in mind this time. No clothes, for one thing."

A burst of heat ran through her.

His gaze teased her. Eyes twinkling, he watched her for a few seconds, then rolled over and stood.

She surveyed the lean, strong lines of his body. How did a forty-two-year-old man stay in that kind of shape? She felt another tingling, from a different spot. No man had affected her like this since—

She stopped that thought and sprang from the bed. "Do you like Chinese? I can order some delivery."

"How long do they take?"

"It's between lunch and dinnertime. Probably twenty minutes."

"Good. Anything with chicken works for me. Why don't you call and then join me in the shower?" He jiggled his eyebrows.

Skeptical, she peered at him, but saw no dissembling in his expression. He wanted her. The tingle returned, so she grabbed her robe from a chair and trotted into the living room.

He stuck his head out the door and called behind her. "I don't suppose you have an extra toothbrush."

"Check the bottom drawer of the bathroom vanity."

****

Chance entered the spacious bathroom and found a toothbrush and some toothpaste. This interlude had served several purposes. He felt more relaxed, and apparently, so did Tempest. But the break had also brought forth a small complication. He'd wanted her before they made love—now he never wanted to let her go. His mind floated back to their jump, when he'd compared her to Charybdis. And like Odysseus, he'd sailed right into her whirlpool.

Recognizing the truth did nothing to dispel his desire.

She came into the bathroom and shed her robe, hanging it on the door hook.

The vixen looked just as good from the back as she did from the front. He reached into the tub to turn on the water, resisting his urge to keep the water temperature on cold. "Hell."

She heard him. "What's wrong? Did you forget something?"

He shook his head, his gaze scanning her. "No. I haven't forgotten a damn thing."

She flushed.

And every time that rush of pink ran over her, his desire multiplied. Exponentially. He climbed in the tub, took her hand to help her in, and wasted no time. He switched places to let the water run over her and moved her arms over his shoulders, then set his hands under her rear to hoist her up.

She wrapped her legs around him and let him take her.

****

Chance tipped the delivery guy, carried the bag to the kitchen, and started to unload the contents.

Tempest came in, her hair combed, but still wet.

Damn if every time he saw her in a different light, he didn't get sucked in more. What the hell was it with her? No woman had ever pervaded his thoughts this way.

He scowled and grabbed one of the square white boxes without opening it before moving to the kitchen table. Then he went back to the refrigerator and pulled out one of the beers he'd left Friday night. Tempest gave him an odd look, but he ignored the questioning glance.

She drew two plates from a cabinet, got some silverware, and brought everything to the table. Then she went back and retrieved the rest of the takeout boxes. She sat across from him.

Keeping his focus elsewhere, he sensed her gaze on him. He ate in silence.

"Chance, what's going on? You're acting strangely. Have you thought of something we missed?"

He had no urge to tease or cajole her. With a burst of brutal honesty rushing through his mind, he conceded she'd done nothing to deserve his harsh treatment of her. No matter what she'd done to enlist his aid, she'd never lied about her motives.

Nor did she lie when they made love. Her desire for him flowed through her as surely as the air in her lungs. Could he walk away? He turned toward the window. "No. I'm just thinking. I need to get home and pack. I've got a fair amount of gear I need to round up—I might need to run to the base. We have to be at the airport early, so I'll swing by here and pick you up at five." He stood. "Do you mind if I take some of this with me? I can eat it later."

"Of course not." She got the takeout bag and set half of the white boxes inside.

When they got to the front door, he stroked her

cheek, then gave her a brief kiss. But even as he pulled away, a parching thirst for her made his mouth dry. His tongue heavy, he said, "It's going to be okay. We're in good shape." He left her apartment, hoping to God he hadn't lied.

And praying his brother was wrong.

****

Tempest leaned against the wall in concern. Everything had been going well. With the plan in place, Chance had instilled within her a sense of confidence. He could do this. Plus, he still didn't know Leon would be there. His teammate's presence could only help.

When they'd made love, it seemed real. He didn't fake his desire for her—she had a better grip on people than to misread his actions. And yet, his mood changed in a flash. Only two suppositions came to mind. Either he found something wrong with his plan, or he regretted their liaison. Given those choices, as much as it hurt, she prayed for the latter.

With a long, deep breath, she forced herself upright and headed toward the bedroom to prepare for the trip. She could eat later.

Once the suitcase was packed, she rummaged through the closet for her jumpsuit and parachute and carefully set them in a tote, along with her helmet and goggles. She hadn't told Chance her grasp of languages nearly matched her son's. She knew enough Greek to pick up him making far too many references to "I" and not "we" when he spoke to this friend of his. He planned to go on this rescue alone.

However noble of him that might be, she had other plans.

Regardless of their afternoon together, and her

feelings for him, she doubted whether she would ever see him again after this week. So whether or not she pissed him off made no difference. As long as Sloan came home, she could deal with the rest of her life—with or without Chance Adams.

With would be nice, though.

Her packing almost complete, she wandered into the kitchen for something to drink and to eat some of the lunch they'd abandoned. As she poured herself a ginger ale, her gaze fell on her fortune cookie. She cracked it open and popped half in her mouth, untangling the small strip of paper to read what the stars predicted.

A dream you have will come true.

An ache spasmed in her chest, and the meal once again deserted, she carried her glass into her bedroom to gather the few remaining things on her list. Then she strolled into Sloan's old room and pulled out some clothes. He would need them—*when* they got him out of there.

****

Chance entered his apartment and dropped the takeout bag in the kitchen. Food could wait. He went into the bedroom to retrieve his pre-packed duffle and started to roll up the few additional things he needed for any trip. With the number of times he'd gone through this routine, he barely needed to think beyond whether to pack for cool or warm weather.

In fifteen minutes, the bag sat in a corner, ready to go.

He settled in a chair by a small desk and started to make a list. Once finished, he checked it over, added a couple of items, and stood to stretch. His stomach growled, so he strolled into the kitchen and pulled out the containers of food and then smiled. Tempest had included two fortune cookies.

After he'd spooned some chicken and rice onto a plate and stuck it in the microwave, he broke open one of the cookies while his dinner heated.

If you have something good in your life, don't let it go.

He scowled and crushed the other cookie in his hand.

The greatest risk is not taking one.

His scowl deepened, and he tossed the crumbs and tiny slips of paper in the trash as the oven beeped. Why did he bother with that crap? Generally, the recipient of those morsels of insight twisted them to fit whatever their own situation warranted or needed.

What he needed couldn't be predicted or solved by an obtuse saying generated from some factory in China. What he needed was to get Sloan Raines out of Georgia and home safely, finish his last few months in the Navy, and take off.

Right?

He plucked his dinner from the oven, moved to the table, and shoveled some food into his mouth. For months, he'd looked forward to his retirement and finally having some time to enjoy life. Not having to follow the orders of the people above him. Being able to do what he wanted, when he wanted, without any lingering *I-should-be's* haunting him.

Freedom from his self-inflicted prison.

He loved his job. He'd thrown himself into it and had no regrets. It didn't mean he couldn't now move on and try something different.

Right?

He pushed from the table, took his plate to the sink, washed, and stacked it in the cabinet. He threw out the bag, then wiped down the counter. Where did this sense of discontent come from? He hadn't felt this restless in years.

Not since his fiasco—he stopped the thought. Far too much time recently had revolved around the unwanted memories.

But the reason for those reminders couldn't be ignored. Another woman had popped into his life, causing those feelings to resurface. Therein lay the problem. Women. Whenever they got into the mix, things got muddled, complicated...turned into piles of crap. He'd gotten over the caustic relationship, and in the long run had been better off. Did he want to go through the pain again?

Then his traitorous mind turned to an image of Tempest, lying next to him in bed, pressed against him in the shower. *But those pictures don't tell the whole story, do they...jackass*? He chuckled. This burning physical desire notwithstanding, the woman kept him from getting mentally lazy. Wouldn't that be preferable to a future alone, on a bike until he couldn't ride anymore? Then what?

Submerged in the feelings of discontent, he straightened and left the kitchen to complete his packing. Tomorrow morning loomed too near.

Chapter Twenty-Two

A small compound in South Ossetia
Monday, March 27—5:00 pm

Sloan stretched out on the dirt, his mind wandering. The interminable repetition of these past days, with no information or contact, stretched into a mass of protracted, endless monotony. The bar on the cell door scraped, and he huddled back against the wall. Had the guard come to beat him again?

The shadowy silhouettes entered and crossed over to him. "Guess what, Sloan." Alexei stopped. "That is how you Americans phrase it, is it not? When you have a joyous surprise for your comrade?"

Foreboding caused his empty stomach to tighten.

"Our Storm will be here, I believe, on Thursday. She is due to arrive in Moscow Wednesday. She could not find any assistance, but she returns with her film to negotiate your release with your captors." He let out a *tsk*. "How unfortunate that it will only end in both of your deaths."

The declaration ate through Sloan's weakening grip on hope. "You don't have to kill us, Alexei. All you want is her film. Get it and let us go."

"Ah, my dear Sloan. You are such a child still. If I were to release you, do you not think our Storm would retaliate? She would go to your government, or worse, your media, and tell them of your experiences." He drew an exaggerated breath, causing his shoulders to rise. "No, you cannot live."

Sloan shifted on the hard-packed dirt. "Then will you at least untie my legs? I'd like to walk again if I'm going to die in a few days."

Alexei shook his head. "Such defeat. I am disappointed in you. But such is the way with you Americans. Your lives are so easy, you are unable to cope with adversity." He turned to the guard. "Cut the ropes around his legs." As the man approached, Alexei reached over and grabbed Sloan's chin, clamping it so tightly pain shot through his face. "Do not use this as an attempt to escape, Sloan. You will not survive. At least let your mother see you one last time before you both leave this Earth." With a rough move, he released Sloan's face, causing his head to snap sideways.

Struggling against stiff muscles, Sloan stretched out his legs to allow the man to cut the ties. Blood begin to flow freely, back to his feet. The sensation almost made him giddy, until the pins and needles crawled over his limbs.

"With your legs now unbound, perhaps you can scrape some dirt over your excrement in the corner. The stench in here is becoming quite unpleasant. It is good we are not in the middle of summer." The Russian watched him for a moment, then turned on his heels, and the two men left. The bar slipped back across the door with an almost death-impending clunk.

Sloan took a deep breath and rolled on his side, then spread his legs, lifted them individually, and tried to get rid of the tingling. He rolled on his back and started doing bicycles. This exercise, this effort, might be futile.

But it might not.

For days he had rubbed the rope around his wrists against the stone walls. He could find no rough edges in the cell to aid in his task. But the friction helped. The ropes had loosened some. If he could get his hands free…

He didn't intend to make a break for it now, but when his mother arrived, he would be ready. Sloan rose and began a slow jog around the small area. So much easier than the hopping motion he'd done for the past several days. But his legs remained weak. He needed to get some strength back.

Alexei insisted Tempest had no help, but Sloan didn't believe him. He knew his mother too well. If Captain Dickey couldn't help her, she would not give up.

His mother never gave up.

She would find someone even if it meant going to a mercenary before she hit that point. No, Tempest Raines did not quit. She had a plan. He was certain.

His pace quickened.

****

Athens, Greece
Tuesday, March 28—10:00 a.m.

As the plane neared Athens, Chance studied Tempest, dozing, nestled against his shoulder. Having her in that familiar position had become far too comfortable. They'd spent hours talking during the flight, and his assessment about her intelligence had been accurate.

Her intense sensuality aside, he could spend a lifetime just talking, debating, playing with her. The great sex almost seemed like a bonus.

Chance shook his head. It wouldn't work. His plans had been mapped out. She had a son and a life and intended to keep working—if they'd met twenty years ago, maybe. Not now. That window had closed and been nailed shut. A tightness clutched at his chest and throat, threatening to choke him. He needed to get Sloan out of Ossetia so they could all return to life as it should be.

Lives that held no room for each other.

He tapped on her arm gently. "Tempest. We're about to land."

She snuggled deeper into his shoulder, then stretched her legs as far as the tight seats would allow. After the plane coasted to a stop, they gathered their things in silence and debarked. Customs checked their identification and all but waved them through. She cocked an eyebrow at him.

"What?"

"Do you always get through customs that fast?"

"Depends on the country. Here, yeah, usually. It's all in who you know." He winked at her.

She twisted her kissable mouth. "Maybe I should travel with you more often."

Without response, he grabbed their large totes while she picked up the smaller ones, then he led her outside. A car and driver waited for them, and Chance dropped their things in the trunk. Once they were settled in the back seat, the man took off.

A bit later, they drove through a gate and up a long drive to what, in Tempest's eyes, constituted a mansion. She'd been in homes this large, but not in recent years, and never overseas. The three-story white stucco house gleamed against the clear cerulean sky, in striking contrast to the lush green lawn and burst of colors from the flowers. Before they climbed from the car, a short man with graying hair and a slight paunch around his midsection burst through the door and threw out his arms. "Chance Adams! What a delight it is to see you again!" He embraced Chance before turning to Tempest. "And your beautiful young woman." He took Tempest's hand and kissed it lightly. "A true privilege," he said.

Heat rushed into her face. She felt spent and ragged and hardly anything approaching beautiful. But she mustered a smile for the charming Greek gentleman. "Chance speaks so highly of you, Mr. Thalassinos—"

"Dimitris! We have no such formalities here among friends!" He placed his hand on the small of her back and steered her toward the house. "Giorgos will bring in your things. Leon and Troy have already arrived."

Walking by Dimitris's other side, Chance grabbed his arm, bringing the man to an abrupt halt. "What?"

"Yes. Leon called Sunday, and they came in last night. It is wonderful to see him again, and to finally meet your brother."

Tempest held her breath during Dimitris's declarations as her gaze riveted on Chance. His face creased in anger then eased as he nodded. Apparently, Leon's assessment over his temper only held partially true. Maybe he recognized his former teammate's assistance could prove helpful. But why was his brother here? Chance had mentioned him when they talked during the flight but said little about the man's profession. Was he also a military man?

Dimitris continued toward the house. "Come. I will show you your rooms and give you the afternoon to rest and freshen up." He winked at Chance. "This evening we will dine on the covered patio. It is a bit chilly to be outside by the pool. Dinner will be at seven, but feel free to explore as you wish."

"Dimitris. This isn't a pleasure trip," Chance warned.

"Nonsense. Without pleasure there is no life. You must relax tonight and sleep off your jet lag. Tomorrow we will fly to the island and take the yacht out. I have had it left there for us."

Tempest glanced at Chance, and he shrugged. Her nerves prickled. As kind as this man acted, he didn't seem to understand the urgency of their mission. Every day—every hour—marked a critical point. Had everyone but she forgotten the enemy held Sloan? Men who might kill him at any time?

Their host led them to an elevator that took them to the third floor. They followed him down a hallway where he opened the doors to two adjacent rooms. "Giorgos, place Ms. Raines's things in the blue room, please, and the commander's in the gray room." He turned to Chance. "As soon as you are ready, feel free to relax in the solarium and help yourselves to the beverages. I believe Leon has rekindled his liking to that area. We will join you after a bit. Elini is most anxious to see you again." He disappeared down the hall.

Chance faced Tempest but didn't give her the opportunity to speak. "I know what you're going to say, but it's too late in the day to leave now. We'll leave early, before dawn." He backed Tempest into her room a few steps, taking her into his arms. He smoothed back her hair, still disheveled from the long trip. "Trust me, Tempest. We're going to get him out of there."

Even though her mind told her otherwise, Chance managed to fill her with a sense of calm. She let him hold her, as if his closeness would somehow filter into her through some version of osmosis.

He leaned down to kiss her, gently touching her lips with his.

Despite her fatigue and nagging worry, she melded against him.

His grip tightened, and he kissed her with an urgency of his own, but before she surrendered, he backed away. "I've got to take care of some things. Why don't you lie down for a while and get some rest?"

She wanted to argue with him, but the sight of the comfortable-looking bed pulled at her. Yet she said, "I should help you."

"Leon and Troy are here. We've got this." He led her across the roomy space to the king-sized bed and nudged her enough to plop her down. "Need some help undressing?"

She shot her gaze toward the ceiling. "You're still an insufferable jackass."

With a smile, he leaned over to kiss her then left.

Chapter Twenty-Three

The Thalassinos estate on the Aegean Sea—Athens, Greece
Tuesday, March 28—Noon

Chance wound through the house to the sunroom and found Leon and Troy sitting in chairs near a window, chatting and gazing outside. "You sons of bitches. What the hell are you two doing here?"

Troy's expression impaled him. "It's good to see you, too, little bro."

Leon ignored them. "Helping your sorry white ass."

He dropped into a chair by his brother. "Leon, it's a fucking suicide mission."

"All the more reason you need help." The man eyed him. "Besides, the Chance Adams I know doesn't go on suicide missions."

Leon spoke the truth. He had to continue to believe in the feasibility of this fiasco, or they would all die. His glance fell on Troy, who continued to glare at him, arms crossed. "What's up your ass?"

Troy's expression hardened. "You've lost your mind."

He clenched his jaw until his teeth hurt. Had his brother flown all the way out here just because he feared Chance was going to get involved with a married woman? "Sloan isn't her husband. He's her son."

Leon hooted. "You dumbass. We know that."

The declaration made him jerk. "How the hell do you know that?"

"Because I read the damned bios at the end of the articles. Yo' should try it sometime, C'mander."

Shit. Way to make him feel like more of an ass. Chance stared at him until Troy broke his concentration. "Leon and I have pieced this thing together, bro—and I repeat, you've lost your mind. What the hell do you think you're doing?"

Impatience rattled through him. He had enough misgivings about this mission. Having his brother impress more upon him would do nothing to help him accomplish his goal. "Back off. We have a plan, and it's a good one. You can ream me after it's over."

His brother opened his mouth, then clamped it shut. Success relied on conviction, and Troy was aware of that.

Silence closed around them as their collective tension ebbed. "So why are you two here?"

Leon shifted in the chair, favoring his right leg. "I can keep an eye on you with the UAV." He tightened his lips, then ran his tongue over them. "If something goes wrong, we'll know where to look for you. At least I know how to get in touch with Dickey."

Troy set his coffee cup on an end table. "And I can fill you in on some items of interest I couldn't explain on the phone."

Chance drew a breath and focused on the gardens outside. Their ideas held merit and eased some of his foreboding. The outcome of this attempt might not be changed by Leon's and Troy's unexpected appearances, but should things not go as planned, at least their bodies wouldn't rot and be torn apart by wild dogs in the mountains. He turned his gaze to his friend. "I didn't bring any transmission gear. You can't talk to me."

"You're slippin', C'mander." His white teeth gleamed against his dark skin. "I brought a few things that might come in handy."

Chance turned half his mouth up in a smile. Damn, he missed his teammate. "Thanks."

Leon stood. "Don't thank me. I want to make sure I get my baby back."

Despite the circumstances, Chance shot out a laugh. "Yeah. You keep telling yourself that." He pushed from the chair. "Let's get everything loaded on the plane."

"FedEx showed up this morning. Troy and I carried most of the gear out there already. We just need the laptop and whatever else you brought."

Chance stared at him.

"Like I said, someone has to help your sorry ass."

He shook his head and chuckled. "Okay, then. The rest of it's in the car. Let's drive out to the airstrip."

They headed to the front of the house and found Dimitris in the entry. "Ah, gentlemen. May I accompany you to the plane? We can discuss your plans there, where we will have more privacy."

Chance agreed, and Dimitris drove to the airstrip. They unloaded the remainder of the gear and settled in a meeting area at the back of the small jet. Some refreshments had been set out by Dimitris's staff, so the men helped themselves, and after several minutes of chitchat, Chance turned to business. "Having Leon here has changed my thoughts, but this should work better.

He's more skilled with his UAVs. When we get to the island, we can take the yacht out at dusk." He paused to pull out his maps then directed his question at Dimitris. "Would you be able to dock in Anaklia Beach?"

The man hiked a shoulder. "It should pose no problem. I have done so many times at the private dock of a friend. Elini enjoys the area because it is quiet."

"Good. Perfect." He cleared a space and spread a map over the table. Your pilot can fly us inland on the 'copter—I'm thinking near Gori. We can do our reconnaissance from there. Then later he can take me near the camp, and I'll make the jump. Once—"

"Wait a minute, little bro. Why Gori?" Troy straightened in his chair and set down his drink.

Chance tapped on the map. "Because it's a straight shot to the South Ossetia border. It's close to where they were when Sloan got nabbed. Alexei said Sloan is at a camp near the Kura River."

Troy leaned back, crossed his arms, and stared at Chance for several seconds, then he ran his hand over his mouth. "That's not where he is."

"How do you—" He stopped. "You've heard something. Where is he?"

"Somewhere along the Qvirila River. At the foot of the mountains. You'd be better off using Chiatura as your base."

The three men stared at Troy, but his gaze fastened on a spot behind Dimitris. Deep creases edged their way across his brow. "Who is this Alexei? What's his last name?"

An uneasiness crept into Chance's gut. "Baranov."

Troy's gaze shot back to his brother. "Shit."

Dimitris spoke up. "You know this man, Troy?"

His expression became grim. "I've had an eye on him for a couple of years. He has connections to the KGB."

"But the KGB is no longer." The Greek twisted his hands together.

Troy spat a laugh. "Right. Now they call it the Federal Security Bureau. By any other name, it still stinks. And South Ossetia established their own KGB. Either way, Baranov is in deep with them."

The tidbit of information crawled over Chance. His instincts about Alexei were on target. He studied the map in search of alternatives. "Okay. The location has changed but not the plan." He glanced at Troy. "You're sure your information is accurate?"

His brother's eyebrows inched up, his expression unyielding.

Chance turned back to the map. "Then we'll land near Chiatura and fly the baby along the river until we find the camp. Then I'll drop in, make the grab, and get us out of there. The UAV should be able to find a place where the 'copter can land and pick us up. I don't know what kind of shape Sloan will be in, or if I can get both of us in a harness and hold on till we get back to the yacht, so it would help if we don't have to go that route. Leon can watch us with the UAV and direct us to our transport when we leave the camp."

Dimitris nodded. "That is good, Chance, my friend. My pilot is familiar with the terrain along the South Ossetia border and edge of the mountains. I believe this will work." He stopped to scoop up some olives, stuffing them in his mouth. "But I fear I may have muddled your plans a bit."

Chance suppressed a grimace. The plans had

already been muddled.

"I assumed Tempest would accompany us to the island, and Elini wishes to go as well. I thought Elini's presence might help Tempest remain more calm during the rescue."

A protracted sigh slipped from Chance, and he ran his hand over his forehead and down the back of his head, finally massaging the muscles in his neck.

"This is a problem?" Dimitris laced his fingers tightly once more, his expression stricken.

He focused on his friend. "I'm afraid she wants to jump in there with me. I can't let her do that. It's too dangerous. I hoped to get out of here in the morning before she's up." He shook his head. "How angry would Elini be if we left them both behind?"

Dimitris shrugged. "Elini always finds a reason to be angry with me, but I make it up to her. It is a game we play."

"Then we can still leave at five and tell the women we're leaving at six." His statement had a bit of a hike at the end, as if it were a question.

Dimitris nodded. "I will take Elini to the island when the weather has warmed a bit." He picked up another tidbit from the tray. "It will be fine. I am sorry if I have caused your plans to go awry."

"It's all right, Dimitris. We'll slip out early." He picked up a small tomato with a wedge of cheese. "You might want to warn Elini, though. Tempest can be…intense."

Dimitris slapped his knee. "Ah! What woman is not?"

The men laughed and spent another thirty minutes going over the plans before returning to the estate.

Dimitris walked with them to the solarium. "I must attend to some things, but please help yourselves to the bar." He made his way down the hall.

Chance moved to a paneled wall and spoke to Troy. "What're you drinking these days?"

"What's he got?"

He hit a button and the wood panels spread open to a restaurant-sized collection of bottles.

"Holy hell. Where does he get all this? Half of it's not even on the market."

Leon hitched over and gazed at the rows. "He had a pretty good stash fifteen years ago. I think it's grown. Gimme some a' dat Blanton's."

"That'll work for me, too, little bro."

Chance poured them each a glass of the bourbon and they went back to sit.

Leon sniffed the fine liquor and let a sip roll over his tongue. "I thought you swore off the bourbon, Chance. I haven't seen you drink any in twenty years. Since that party—"

He held up his hand to stop his friend. "I did. And I don't need any reminders about that party or that night." He hitched his shoulders up. "This week I've just had a taste for something besides scotch."

Leon fell silent then said, "I'll say one thing for your woman."

Chance clenched his jaw. "She's not my woman."

Leon eyeballed his friend while Troy choked out a laugh. "Uh huh. Well, she's got some steely nerves."

"What makes you say that?" Chance looked at him over the rim of the glass.

"Doesn't open her mouth. Wouldn't tell me a thing." He paused to sip his bourbon. "Dickey send you out here?"

Chance set his drink on a small table. "No. He doesn't know. At least I don't think he knows. Well, maybe he knows."

Leon's eyebrows shot up. "You're shittin' me. Where does he think you are?"

"On my bike, heading west."

"If he believes that, it's time for him to retire. He's losing his grip." Troy closed his eyes, held up his glass, and inhaled.

Leon shifted in the chair and lifted his drink. "Yo wanna start at the b'ginnin' and tells us this whole tale, C'mander?"

With a deep sigh, he related the story of his first encounter with Tempest Raines. "It's got to be why she was in his office," he finished. "But she won't own up."

Leon let out a tiny chuckle. "I repeat, the woman's got some steely nerves."

His old friend spoke the truth. The woman aggravated him, tantalized him, fascinated him— downright pissed him off. But when someone she cared for, like her son, was in trouble, she'd have their back. And he suspected her grit went deeper than family.

Another quality he couldn't easily overlook.

"Or she's a damn good liar." His face stoic, Troy sipped the bourbon.

Chance glared at him.

"So you two gonna hook up when y'all gets back to Nawf'k?"

He snapped his head up and scowled. "No. And I mean a big, fat, NO."

Leon snorted, and Troy rolled his eyes.

Tempest wandered into the room, and he clamped

his mouth shut. As she approached them, she appeared calm and rested, and a wave of relief washed over Chance.

Although he continued to sputter denials to Leon, his concern for the woman's welfare continued to engulf him. He wasted no time going over to her. "Would you like something to drink? Dimitris has just about everything and more. Vodka?"

"No, I don't think so. Not tonight. Maybe just some wine."

He opened the door of a large temperature-controlled wine cooler, pulled out a bottle of pinot noir with a questioning glance, and when she nodded, he poured her a glass. As they made their way back to the seating, he glanced at Leon's mocking expression. One hand behind Tempest's back and his glass of bourbon in the other, Chance scowled, raised his glass slightly and shot him the bird.

Leon hooted.

Tempest looked over at him. "What's so funny?"

"Aw, nuthin', Miz Tempest. I's jes' gets amused at pretty much anything what strikes me."

She laughed, and in a flash, the reasons why he'd never lost touch with Leon rushed over Chance. A better friend couldn't be found. Their gazes met in understanding—a bond from the teams. Whether Leon still wore a Trident or not, the man would always back him up.

He glanced at his brother, silently watching the proceedings, and introduced Tempest to him. With a reasonable amount of chivalry, Troy stood, shook her hand, then retreated to his seat in silence.

The evening served its purpose. Tempest became

more relaxed as the hours passed. She'd been wound tighter than a ball of rubber bands and seemed precariously close to bouncing off the walls.

Midway through the evening, Dimitris took him aside and referenced Tempest's mood. "Tempest seems distracted."

"She's worried, Dimitris."

"Then she does not know you as well as I. If any man can rescue this boy, it is you. Of this I am as sure as I am that you are in love with her."

Chance laughed. "Me? No, you're wrong. A diversion, maybe. That's all."

Dimitris slapped him lightly on the back with a chuckle. "Bring her back here. We will have a proper Greek wedding for you."

Chance continued to sputter denials as Dimitris returned to the small party.

The gathering ended early with apologies, since they would need to be rising in a few hours. He walked Tempest to her room and stopped in the hall. "I think it would be best if we stayed in our own rooms tonight."

She gave him an odd look but made no rebuttals. If she suspected he had any agenda of his own, she didn't voice any concerns or arguments. "I'll be ready to go at six. That's when we're leaving, right?" She cocked her head and continued to stare at him.

Chance twisted his neck to stretch the muscles. "Yeah. Six." He disappeared into his room without touching her. He had to start the weaning process now. He had no intention of taking her into this camp and certainly didn't plan to see her again once they found Sloan and returned to the States. He'd finally realized the absurdity of his fascination with the woman and made up his mind. He would finish up his last few months and then hit the trail on his bike. Travel across the country, see the sights, forget the last twenty years. That remained his goal. His plan included no room for a woman. Tempest Raines had her own life to live, and he didn't need to be a part of her future.

So why did that make his stomach churn?

****

Tempest closed her door and leaned against the polished wood. Chance intended to sneak out of here earlier than six a.m. She'd listened as the four men made random comments, and those remarks didn't add up. Her grasp of Greek helped, as did her newly forged friendship with Elini. She'd tried to question Dimitris, but he held true to Chance and sidestepped her interrogation. People who chose to follow Chance Adams did so as a pact, an alliance. They did it because Chance commanded that kind of respect—and friendship.

She couldn't dismiss that bond.

Chapter Twenty-Four

Athens, Greece
Wednesday, March 29—5:00 a.m.

Tempest was standing in the hallway when Chance emerged from his room. He looked ready—she saw no evidence of fatigue or lack of sleep. Apparently, this spelled nothing but another mission to him.

He did seem surprised to see her dressed and ready to go, however.

"Trying to sneak out, Commander?"

He gave her a hard look. "Did you get any sleep?"

"Yes. I slept. Quite well, in fact."

"More than fifteen minutes?"

"Are we leaving or not?" She hoisted her tote over her shoulder and started down the hall.

He grabbed her arm and turned her to face him. "I told you this once already. This is serious. It's not a game. If you aren't rested and alert, you could get us all killed."

She jerked her arm from his grasp. "I'm fine. Do you think I don't have at least a vested interest in this whole undertaking?"

"You two tryin' to wake up the whole house?" Leon emerged from his room and approached. Troy exited his room a second later.

"I'm trying to knock some sense into this woman."

His expression terse, Chance kept his gaze on her.

Leon drew his lips into a thin line, shot him a look, and took her arm. "Come on, Miz Tempest. If'n the C'mander won't escort you to this party, I will."

Fury flashed across Chance's face. She'd never seen him look quite this angry, not during their encounter at Marc's office, the brief burst after they were at Dan's shop, or even at the fateful party twenty years ago. She glanced at Troy, who merely studied her. His constant scrutiny made her uncomfortable. Leon pressed her down the hall. They went to the front of the house in silence, each lost in their own thoughts. Dimitris met them at the door but stopped when he saw Tempest. Forehead creased, he looked at Chance.

Chance threw up his hands. "She was in the hall."

Tempest ignored him and spoke to Dimitris. "I explained the situation to Elini last night, Dimitris. She won't be angry with you."

"Ha. She will find a way." He smiled and shrugged. "The car waits to take us to the airstrip. Let us go." He turned and faced his wife. She had slipped up behind him as he spoke.

"You are not leaving here without me." Elini crossed her arms, steadfast.

"Women," Chance muttered.

Tempest smiled and linked her arm through Elini's.

With the enormity of Dimitris's estate, it took nearly ten minutes to pull up to the jet at the airstrip. Chance used a small high intensity flashlight to guide them across the tarmac. The sliver of moon in the sky shed no light, and in the blackness, the area held a sense of emptiness. She glanced over at Chance. "Don't you have any gear?"

"We loaded everything up yesterday."

He seemed disinclined to elaborate, and they walked to the Lear in silence.

"Thanks for keeping me in the loop," she muttered.

Leon took her arm and lowered his voice. "It's okay, Tempest. Just let him do his job." They brought up the end of the procession, and he stopped her, turning her to face him. "He's the best. If anyone can get Sloan out of there, it's Chance."

She gave him a weak smile.

He took her hand. "Come on. I'm not very fast, and we don't want to fall behind."

When they reached the plane, Dimitris and Chance moved up front to sit with the pilot, leaving the four left to sit together. She made some small talk with Elini, but Leon and Troy said very little during the flight. When they neared Trabzon, the pilot veered the plane north until they reached a small island. Another car and driver waited for them at the airstrip. They transferred the gear and took off for Dimitris's vacation home.

Again, his hospitality surfaced. His staff showed them to their rooms, then they returned downstairs where a lunch of gyros and salad awaited them in a pleasant room overlooking the sea. She chatted with Dimitris, Elini, and Leon while Troy ate in silence and Chance scowled at her throughout the entire meal. As soon as she swallowed her last bite of the gyro, she rose. "Thank you, Dimitris, Elini. I think I'll rest a little before we go out on the yacht." She started to turn then looked at Leon, ignoring Chance. "About five o'clock, right? So we'll be there after dark?"

Leon nodded while he shot a look at Chance. His expression brooked no room for argument from the

SEAL.

Chance's eyes narrowed, his mouth tightened—anger seeping through the rugged angles of his face.

She watched the exchange then went to her room to organize her belongings.

****

Chance rose to follow her.

Dimitris stopped him, begging off as well. "Chance, we have not been out here in several months. Elini and I must check on some things. I will make sure we have adequate refreshments on board the yacht, since we will now be traveling overnight."

Chance smiled. Dimitris's *refreshments* generally constituted a full meal for most people. He turned toward the doorway.

"Where the hell do you think you're going, C'mander?"

He glared at his friend. "None of your business."

Troy leaned back in his chair with a smirk, but Leon stood and stalked over to Chance.

Chance watched him and frowned. "You're not limping."

"Because I'm pissed off. When I get pissed off, I don't think, and when I don't think, I forget the pain." He grabbed Chance's arm. "Why are you being such an ass?"

He jerked away. "What are you talking about?"

"You. Tempest. You're treating her like crap."

His jaw tensed, Chance stared at Leon for several seconds. "Because she disob—" He clamped his mouth shut. Was he about to say she disobeyed an order? Like she was one of his men? He took a step back and dropped onto a chair, running a hand over his mouth.

What the hell was wrong with him? Had his monastic personal life made him unable to allow anyone else in?

Arms crossed, Leon continued to stare at him. "For twenty years you've pushed away everyone who tried to get close to you. You need to forget that bitch and move on, brother."

Chance blinked. He didn't refer to Tempest. "I forgot about Ginny years ago." *Until Tempest showed up.*

"Yeah? Then how come every woman you've met that might actually be good for you has ended up running away?" He grunted and sank onto a loveseat, stretching his leg. "I tried to tell you not to get involved with that woman. She was a grade A, blue-nosed, stuck-up snot, but you wouldn't listen back then—not to me—not to Hattie—not to anyone." Leon shook his head. "You know, I don't give a shit whether you throw your life away or not. But don't drag Tempest down with you. She doesn't deserve it." He shoved himself up from the sofa and limped across the room.

Chance shot from the chair and followed him. He had to explain. "Wait, Leon."

His friend's shoulders drew up with his breath. He turned.

"You don't get why I'm upset. She's got this crazy idea about jumping into the camp with me. It's dangerous, Leon. Besides not knowing what she's doi—"

"Not knowing what she's doing? What're you talkin' about?"

He frowned. "Jumping. It takes a lot of practice and train—"

Leon shot out a laugh. "Is that what's got you all

228

up in a roar? Damn, Chance, the woman's got two or three hundred jumps behind her. Sloan's written at least a couple of stories about their experiences."

"No. You're wrong. Marc—" His thoughts reverted to that morning, a short week ago. The way she'd looked at Marc when he suggested the tandem jump, her comment about the insurance video, and saying the harness didn't need to be so tight...not asking, but telling him.

Son of a bitch. He stared at Leon for a minute, then spun around and left. He wasn't angry any longer.

He was livid.

Chapter Twenty-Five

The Thalassinos estate on the Aegean Sea—Athens, Greece
Wednesday, March 29—Noon

Leon shook his head as his friend stormed out. He couldn't help Chance with this problem he had. Nor could Hattie. They'd tried, for years, but Chance Adams took advice from no one. Orders, yes, but never advice.

A shadow fell across the floor, and he glanced behind him.

Troy had come over to stand by him. "That was fun."

Leon shot out a laugh.

"I don't suppose you know where the booze is stashed in this place."

"Never been here, but knowing Dimitris…" He scanned the room and shuffled toward a wall with a pair of pocket doors, sliding them open to reveal the well-stocked bar.

Troy wandered over and scanned the rows of bottles, pulling out a bottle of Macallan single malt scotch. "Join me?"

"Might as well." He hitched over to the chairs and lowered slowly into one.

Chance's brother handed him a glass of the whisky

and sat nearby. "He's got it bad for her."

Leon glanced at the man. "He could do worse." He paused to take a drink. "A lot worse." They sat in silence, each lost in their own musings. Leon spoke first. "Do you know anything more about Baranov?"

"His ties to the Kremlin are strong, but since the president is ex-KGB, that's no real surprise. He's wealthy—on paper, his money came from oil, but I suspect there's more. It's something I haven't been able to unearth yet. He's unmarried and always has a beautiful woman on his arm. Fancies himself a playboy. But he's ruthless. Seems like there's a trail of bodies in his wake, but the connections are too weak to make any moves against him. Yet." He snapped a fingernail against the Waterford crystal glass, and a clear ding rang through the room. "I can see why Tempest got his attention."

Leon didn't respond, instead sipping on his whisky and staring out the windows. Then he tipped the glass back, drained it, and stood. "It's going to be a long night. You coming with us?"

"Yeah. I need to talk to Chance."

Leon nodded and limped off.

****

Chance stalked through the house straight to Tempest's room and pounded on the door, then threw it open without waiting for a response.

She hovered over a tote on the bed. His sudden entrance made her twitch, but she stayed silent and focused on the bag, reaching inside.

"What the hell is going on, Tempest?"

After a pause and without looking up, she said, "We're trying to rescue my son."

He moved to the other side of the bed, next to her. "You lied to me. How long have you been jumping?"

Her head jerked up. Eyes narrowed, she tightened her hands into fists. "I did not lie to you. You made an assumption, and I didn't correct you."

"Oh, no. Don't play word games with me. You and Dickey hatched this whole scheme, didn't you?"

Her eyes closed and she slumped, blowing out a breath. She shook her head and then studied him with a tired expression. "I've told you this already. Marc thought the photo shoot would be some good publicity for the teams. I never mentioned Sloan to him. When you came down to his office, I realized you might be able to help me, or suggest someone who could."

He peered at her, assessing the honesty of her statements. Wasn't lying, his ass—but something else still didn't feel right. She'd deliberately left something out. He skipped over the obvious and went for his gut instincts. "Do you know me?"

Her gaze darted to the wall behind him then back. "I knew your name. Through other people."

Chance took a step closer. "What other people? Who?"

Irritation swept across her face. She stiffened and chewed her bottom lip. "Do you want a list? You're not the only SEAL I've met, Chance. I've known Marc for years. People talk, names come up, even in your secretive world." She picked up some folded men's clothing and stuffed the items in the tote.

Watching her chipped away at his anger. Those had to be clothes for Sloan. In the midst of her worry and fear, she continued to plan, to prepare, to hold onto hope. A desperate ache surged through him, a longing

232

for someone to care for him in that way. He swept his arm through the air to rid himself of the childish thought. But his hand came back and fell on her shoulder. He let his thumb skim her neck, and his voice softened. "Tempest, I'm not kidding. This is going to be dangerous. I don't know how many men will be there, or if I can even locate Sloan. Odds are whoever is there will have guns, and they won't hesitate to use them." He swept his gaze over her, slid his hands down her arms, and loosely grasped her wrists. "You must have watched too many movies. This isn't Kung Fu, where one guy can take out a half dozen bad guys who all happen to be bad shots with their guns. Real weapons, real bullets, and believe it or not, they can actually hit their targets."

She let out a tiny sound, and a slight quiver disrupted the flow of her voice. "I've been in combat zones before. I have a pretty good idea what it's like."

Her argument didn't sway him. He surged ahead. "I'll know more tonight, after we send out Leon's UAV. But this has nothing to do with whether you can jump or not." He continued to hold her hands, running his thumbs over them. "I don't want anything to happen to you, Tempest."

Chance's declaration brought tears to her eyes. She squeezed them shut, tugged one of her hands loose, and swiped at her face.

He drew her close, slipping his arms behind her back.

She spoke against his chest. "I need to see him. If…if something goes wrong and you don't get him back here…" She leaned back to look at him. "…I need to see him."

He drew in a deep breath then let it seep out, bracing himself for the hard question. "Do you need to see him dead?"

She lurched in his embrace and held his gaze. In a whisper, she said, "Yes. Otherwise I'll question it for the rest of my life."

He gathered her closer. Finally, he asked, "Do you have any experience with weapons?"

Against his chest, she nodded.

Chance chuckled. "Why doesn't that surprise me?" He stepped back and led her to a small sofa by the window, then sat, pulling her down with him. "It's not easy to shoot a person."

Her face paled, her gaze switched to something behind him. "I know."

Watching her, he waited. When she didn't speak, he said, "Tempest?"

"I…had to. In Libya."

Their conversations shot through him. She won her Pulitzer for her pictures there. But it brought back some bad memory, she told him. It could only be one thing. "You fired on someone?"

Her eyes closed, she nodded. A shudder ran through her as she visibly swallowed. She inhaled, and the breath caught in her throat. "I—killed him."

Would she always rattle him like this? He smoothed her hair. "How did you do? Afterward?"

She lifted one shoulder a minute amount. "Okay. Until I got out of there and started to rehash everything in my mind." Her gaze vacant, she stared across the room. "I'll never forget the look in his eyes. I still—sometimes I have nightmares."

Good. The people who claimed otherwise either

lied or were sociopaths. At least she had a grip on reality. But the pain on her face wrenched his heart. He continued to stroke her cheek and tried to draw her thoughts away. "What kinds of weapons can you handle?"

His question brought her focus back to him. "I've practiced with all of them, but I like 9mm the best. It's easy to handle."

He drew in a long breath. Dear God, this went against all of his good judgment, but if he refused, he didn't doubt she would find a way to go anyway. At least with this plan he could keep an eye on her. "Okay. I'll find something for you, and you can go." He took her hand. "But you've got to listen to me and stay out of the way. I'm going to be concentrating on finding Sloan, and I can't do that and protect you, too."

"I won't get in your way. I can take care of myself."

His mouth twisted in a smile. "Yeah. I know you can. But maybe I want to be the one to do that." He settled his lips on hers, even as his mind cursed him for falling into her trap. Again.

****

Tempest melted against his touch. She had to stop letting him affect her this way. As much as she wanted him, as much as she dreamed of a life with him, getting Sloan out of Georgia remained her only mission.

During the flight to Athens, they'd talked for hours. He had one goal, one desire…to retire and take off. Not once did his description of his plans include anyone else. He'd spent twenty years taking orders and wanted to spend the rest with no one dependent on him or making him feel obligated.

She refused to be the person who trapped him. She didn't do it twenty years ago, and she'd be damned if she would do it now. Still, she let him undress her while she unbuckled his belt.

With a new certainty, she understood she would not see Chance Adams again after they rescued their son.

Chapter Twenty-Six

A small island off the coast of Turkey
Wednesday, March 29—1700 hours

Chance sat in the front of the van with Dimitris driving. His friend maneuvered the vehicle to the sea where a yacht and sailboat sat at a pier. He parked, and as they transferred the equipment to the yacht, Dimitris released his captain and steward. When their gear had been squared away, Dimitris moved to the cabin and started up the engines, raising his voice to be heard above the rumble. "My crew does not need to know our destination or plans."

Without giving him a verbal response, Chance set his hand on the man's shoulder as a gesture of thanks.

The Greek navigated at a leisurely pace through the quiet waters until a mile from the shore, when he opened it up and took off. The yacht cut through the sea leaving a deep wake, bouncing over the swells as they cruised along. Every so often Chance would leave the bridge and go below to check on Tempest, Leon, and Troy. When he saw her sitting by Leon with the laptop and the three of them laughing at something, a pang stabbed at his chest. Was it jealousy? Had he become so caught up in himself he would begrudge his best friend—and his brother—assistance from a perfectly capable woman, just because he craved her attention

237

himself?

He went back up the stairs and stood on the deck for a while, oblivious to the cold sea air rushing over him, the occasional spray of frigid water spattering him. Was Leon right? Had he pushed everyone away because he feared a repeat of Ginny? If true, that bespoke of an insecurity he didn't care to admit. It showed weakness.

And it explained why he'd attacked his job with what amounted to a vengeance.

But the failure with Ginny didn't tell the entire story. His brother's calamitous marriage had played a large part in his attitude. That woman had nearly destroyed Troy. She'd cheated on him for years, then had gone to court and painted Troy as a child molester in order to get full custody of their two children. When the case didn't move quickly enough to suit her, she came after Troy with a baseball bat. It had taken two years for him to clear his name, and he still suffered from occasional depression. But he'd gotten custody of the boys, and she landed in a psychiatric ward. Chance's nephews, a couple of terrific kids, were now in college and doing well. And recently, Troy had met a good woman and planned to remarry.

Maybe the time had come for him to find that same happiness.

The chill wind began to cut through his parka, so he thrust his thoughts aside and turned to go inside but sensed Troy next to him.

He handed Chance a cup of coffee. "I'm sure you'd rather have a shot of scotch, but no booze before a mission."

"You know, it bugs the shit out of me that you

know more about my work than I do about yours."

Wind blew through Troy's hair, and the man pulled his jacket tighter. "Perks of being first born. After I got all the looks and all the brains, there wasn't much left in Mom and Dad's gene pool for you."

Chance laughed. "Don't forget humble."

"Nah. That would just sound conceited."

They both chuckled. Chance drank some coffee and turned his thoughts to serious matters. "Thanks for coming out here. Your intel helped. I wouldn't have had time to search every river in Russia to find the kid."

Troy brushed off the comment. "I still don't like what you're doing."

Chance propped his forearms on the railing, the mug nestled between his hands, and gazed over the black water. Still fifty miles from shore, nothing broke through the darkness except the stars and small white caps dotting the sea. "I don't either, but I'm in it now." He turned and leaned against the rail. "Being in it isn't the problem. Getting out is. This Baranov worries me."

"He should. He's a cold-blooded son of a bitch."

"If he's everything you say, I don't get why he let Tempest leave the country at all."

Troy took a swallow of coffee. "Could be orders from higher up. Someone at the Kremlin wants that film, but my guess is he's only after her."

The tone in his brother's voice made a knot form in his throat. Then Leon and Tempest came up from below, and they stopped their conversation.

Tempest stood by Troy, shivered, and zipped up her jacket.

Chance moved beside her and slipped his arm around her waist. "We've still got an hour before we get to Anaklia. Why don't you wait in the cabin where it's warm? Get something to eat."

"I don't trust you. You might leave me behind."

A small chuckle escaped him. "I've never known anyone who parachuted from a yacht."

"For all I know you've got some aircraft carrier out there, waiting to pick you up and fly you over the camp. I'll stay here."

The edges of his eyes crinkled in a smile. "An aircraft carrier. In the Black Sea." His gaze teased her. "Suit yourself." He started to turn but stopped and took her hand. "How about getting us something, then? At least some refills on the coffee. Okay?" He squeezed her fingers gently. "I'm not trying to keep anything from you."

With a glance at Troy and Leon, she went inside.

He expelled a deep sigh and stood between the two men. "I wish I had half the connections and skills she thinks I have."

Leon grimaced and shook his head. "You'd better have some. She's expecting this to work."

Chance gave his friend a long look. "You don't?"

"It's a mission. You gotta think it will work, or it won't. But I'd feel better if you weren't going in alone."

"Yeah. Me, too." He let out a mirthless chuckle. "And I'm not. Tempest is going with me."

Troy swore, and Leon cut him a glance.

He ignored his brother. "Having you here is helping. Don't kid yourself. I feel a hell of a lot better knowing I can talk to you while I'm out there. At least I'm not going in blind."

Leon acknowledged Chance's comment with a

nod.

"Bro." Troy waited until Chance glanced at him. "You can't have second thoughts about this. Not now."

They studied each other until Tempest returned with a tray, and they ate in silence for a while. When they were finished, she gathered up the plates to take back to the galley. Before she descended the stairs, she crooked a finger at Chance, asking him to come with her.

With a second's hesitation, he followed her below. "What's wrong?"

"I was going to ask you the same thing. The atmosphere up there was worse than bleak." Her gaze skimmed him as she set the tray on the granite countertop. "You don't think this is going to work, do you?"

How could he answer that? He moved closer and took her hands. "I wouldn't do it if I didn't think it could work."

She slipped her arms around Chance, and he held her tightly. "Tempest, I want you to go to one of the staterooms and get some sleep." Before she had a chance to object, he brushed her cheek then spoke close to her ear. "Please don't argue with me. We'll be docking soon, and nothing is going to happen between now and ten o'clock. When we do this, I may need your help. You've got to be alert."

"I don't think I could sleep now."

"Then you can at least get some rest. Please?"

"You won't leave without me?"

He let his gaze sweep over her. "I said you could go, and I don't break my promises. I don't like it, but I'm not going to leave you behind. Do you trust me?"

She nodded and relented. "Okay. It's a good idea." She gave him a crooked smile. "I've never gone five days without sleep, eating nothing but bologna sandwiches coated with sand."

He chuckled. "Five and a half." He let his gaze sweep over her. "Tempest, I lo—" He coughed then pulled her close and kissed her. Finally, she broke away and went to one of the staterooms to lie down.

When he emerged on the deck, his brother regarded him in silence for a long moment.

Hell.

Leon started moving toward the bridge. "Let's go inside. We should be docking soon." They joined Dimitris until they reached the Georgia coastline.

****

Tempest plopped on the bed. So far, everything had progressed smoothly, but at some point the ball would drop. She had seen too many times when perfect plans went awry.

Like in Libya.

An eruption of nerves exploded through her. She couldn't dwell on that now. Couldn't allow herself to envision the look on that young man's face when she shot him. She'd had no choice. He intended to kill her, but that surety did nothing to lessen her regret. Chance had brought the memory to the surface, and now she couldn't make it go away. She'd sooner go to Hell herself than have God retaliate by taking her son.

She curled up on the bed and prayed.

****

A small compound in South Ossetia
Wednesday, March 29—9:00 p.m.
Sloan's movements quickened. He rubbed the rope

binding his wrists furiously against the wall. If only he could see what went on behind him—but he'd swear the tension had loosened some more.

A sudden snap nearly made him lose his balance. His hands fell free, and expelling a whoof he brought them forward, inspecting the burns on his wrists. His shoulders ached from the unfamiliar movement. Stinging bursts of pain shot into his neck as he bent his elbows then rotated his arms in their sockets.

According to Alexei, his mother should have arrived in Moscow today, which meant she'd be here tomorrow. He had to keep his freedom hidden until then. This evening, when they'd brought his food, he'd stayed nestled in a corner, moaning and feigning a weakness he didn't feel. The man had approached and nudged him with his foot. Sloan had stayed silent, so the guard kicked him, hard, and Sloan groaned and slumped to the side. With a snort, the guard had set the cup and plate on the ground nearby and left without comment.

If Sloan could maintain that deception, maybe they wouldn't discover his missing ropes. He pressed his hand against his thigh where the guard had kicked him, massaging the bruised muscle. Then he scooped up the cords of flax and took them to the corner where he'd been relieving himself, covering them as much as he could without disturbing the stench of the pile. With the darkness in the cell, it should go unnoticed.

If only he had some accurate information about his mother's plans. Whether she came alone or arrived with help made a significant difference in what he would, or could, do to help them escape.

He had seen the layout of the camp when they

brought him here and fought to retain that memory. This structure where they'd put him had four barred doors along the front, with the same tiny window above each one. The spacing between them appeared to be about eight feet, but the window to this cell had a gap of several more feet from the one adjacent to it...this cell must be larger. He'd paced it off on his first day— about twelve by eighteen feet.

How kind of Alexei to give him the best room in the house.

Outside, four other buildings in various sizes dotted the landscape, with some temporary structures and tents dotting the grounds. A few men, some in Russian uniforms, had been entering and exiting the largest one—it must be the barracks. As they'd dragged Sloan across the grounds, he'd seen a man emerge from another building with some weapons and assumed it held their artillery. The two other buildings probably housed some kind of office and living quarters. Alexei Baranov would not bunk down with the common soldiers.

During the day, he could hear movement, talking, and vehicles coming and going. But at night, the compound stayed quiet. He would overhear several men conversing, then a rumbling truck would leave, and the noises ceased. Only a few soldiers stayed during those hours—three, perhaps as many as four. Alexei sometimes, but not every night.

They had a shot at getting out of here. Sloan had to try.

****

Lights from a sizeable seaside home glimmered in the distance. One mile offshore, Chance and Troy stood by as Dimitris slowed the engines, and the yacht glided through the calm waters to the pier. An enclosed slip held a large sailboat, tied up for the season. In an area to the side of the grounds, Chance glimpsed a helicopter through the trees. Dimitris maneuvered the yacht to the pier's adjacent side, and Chance and Troy tied it up as Dimitris killed the engines. An intense quiet surrounded them.

Chance studied the house and grounds. "I thought the owners weren't home, Dimitris."

"They are not. The lights are for security purposes only."

No movement or sounds invaded the stillness of the night, beyond the yacht bouncing against the wood pier. "Let's go below. We don't need to leave for a couple of hours." The four men went inside and spent the time rehashing, rechecking, and finding alternatives, but ultimately came back to the plan as it stood.

As it neared ten o'clock, Leon asked, "Shouldn't you wake Tempest?"

He cringed. Why the hell had he told her he wouldn't leave her behind? If anything happened to her during this rescue attempt, he'd never forgive himself. His gaze switched to Leon, and they studied each other for a long moment. Finally, he expelled a breath and his shoulders dropped. "Yeah." He stood.

Leon spoke before Chance reached the door. "If you don't want her to go, I'll cover for you."

He chuckled and shook his head. "I never thought you had a death-wish. What are you going to do? Tell her we forgot?"

Troy spoke up. "No. You leave, and I'll tell her it was my idea. That I insisted because I was afraid she would get in the way."

Leon's dark eyes narrowed into slits. "Or we'll tell her the truth. You love her and you don't want her to get hurt."

Anger flushed through him and just as quickly subsided. He could no longer deny his feelings for Tempest. But her plea to him echoed in his brain. *I need to see him.* This rescue held about a fifty-fifty chance of success, and if it fell into the side of failure, he couldn't deny her that one request. "No. I made a promise." He left for her room, praying they didn't all die because of his stubborn attitudes.

Chapter Twenty-Seven

Anaklia Beach, Republic of Georgia
Wednesday, March 29—2200 hours

A tender caress on her cheek made Tempest turn her face into the touch.

"Tempest. Wake up. We need to get ready to go." Chance's deep voice swirled through her semi-conscious.

She dragged her eyelids open.

"Are you sure I can't talk you out of this?"

She rose up on an elbow, then sat upright. "Yes."

He cradled her face in his hands. "I'll be able to concentrate better if you don't go."

She closed her eyes and drew a breath. "Please."

He let out a long sigh. "Come on. Put your jumpsuit on. I'll grab the parachutes."

"I have mine."

A laugh spurted from him. "The teal and purple one? We'll take the ones I brought."

"Who packed them?" When it came to packing a parachute, she trusted no one.

His mouth twisted into a smile. "I did."

"Oh." Except maybe Chance. "Okay." She watched him leave and dug through her tote for her jumpsuit. Five minutes later she met the men on the deck.

Chance surveyed her, his gaze landing on her high-topped hiking shoes.

"Did you think I was going to wear flip flops?"

His eyes creased in amusement, but he didn't answer. Instead he handed her a chute. "Tempest—I have to ask you this. Are you prepared to shoot to kill if you have to?"

A sudden revulsion swept through her, and a breath caught in her throat. Bile rose in her throat as she nodded, while all four of them continued to watch her. She straightened her posture. "Yes."

His gaze stayed riveted on her, until he finally opened a tote by his feet and reached inside. "Here's a Glock and a loaded magazine."

Hesitating for only a second, she took both, then unzipped her suit and tucked them securely into two inside pockets. "What else are you bringing?"

"Things I might need. You ready?"

She nodded.

Dimitris set his hand on Chance's shoulder. "Godspeed, my friends."

****

Chance gave his old friend a slight smile, took Tempest's hand, and they climbed off the yacht with Troy and Leon behind them, then hurried down the pier and across the grounds toward the waiting helicopter. As they approached, the pilot, smoking a cigarette, wandered from the edge of the opening. In English, the man said, "You are ready to go?"

Chance acknowledged him. "Pavel, do you know someplace outside Chiatura where we can land and survey the surroundings?"

"Yes. To the northwest—away from river. No people." He threw the butt on the dirt and ground it out.

Behind them, Leon and Tempest were in the helicopter, taking the equipment and stowing it as Troy handed it up to them. Chance and the pilot made their way to the bird, and Pavel climbed into the cockpit. Troy held his brother back.

Chance faced him. "Get in, bro."

He shook his head. "No. The 'copter only has five seats. When you get Sloan, there won't be room. I'm going back to the yacht to wait with Dimitris. I've given you all the information I know. I'd just be in the way."

Chance studied him then agreed. "Okay. You can keep Dimitris from getting too worried—and keep a lookout while he gets some sleep. It's going to be a long night. See you in a few hours."

They exchanged a hug a fraction longer than usual, and Troy squeezed his shoulder. Before he turned, Tempest leaned forward and peered at him through the door. She mouthed *thank you*, and Troy gave her a thumbs-up and winked, then jogged back to the pier. Chance slid the hatch in place and got into the cockpit with the pilot.

The 'copter lifted off and shot through the onyx sky, the rhythmic whump of the rotors lulling Tempest into a hypnotic state. But even with the calming monotone, nerves burned her skin from the inside. So many things could go wrong—they might be unable to find the camp—one of them could get hurt during the attempt—

Sloan could already be dead. The thought crawled through her and she gasped, unable to breathe. Leon reached over and squeezed her hand, and the small gesture gave her hope. These two men, as well as the pilot, Dimitris, and Troy—even Elini and Hattie—were all stretching far beyond friendship for this undertaking. None of them knew of her history with Chance—they only wished to help her.

The realization of the extraordinary kindness of these people immersed her with a gratitude she couldn't express. She glanced at Leon and smiled, and his deep brown eyes softened in understanding. He patted her hand with a final squeeze and turned his attention back toward the window.

Whatever transpired in the next few hours, she would never be able to repay them.

****

The forward motion of the aircraft stopped, and Chance leaned forward, gazing at the landscape. The 'copter began its descent, blades whipping the branches of the few nearby trees. It landed smoothly, and Pavel cut the engines quickly. Quiet surrounded them immediately. They sat for a few minutes, watching, then Chance moved from the front as Leon opened the door. Their tandem actions attested to years of training and working together, even after a twelve-year lapse.

Tempest and Pavel transferred the gear to them and then jumped outside. Cold winds from the nearby mountains cut across the field, and Tempest shivered.

Chance saw her. "Why don't you wait inside the 'copter until we get things set up?"

She shook her head. "I'd like to see what's going on."

Leon positioned the UAV and set up the laptop. The bright glow from the screen lit his face and reflected across the field. He started the plane and raised it into the air, and the camera sparked to life. He maneuvered and sent the aerial vehicle northward along the river. They watched as the UAV sped through the sky. After forty minutes, he said, "Here. This has got to be the camp."

Tempest hovered behind Chance and stared at the images. "I've never been able to figure out how you can tell anything from these thermal pictures. All I see are blobs of red and yellow."

Chance pointed at the screen. "It picks up heat. Look. See that movement? It looks like a truck. All the small images are probably people getting into the back." He pointed to another longer building at the rear of the camp. "Someone is crossing the road. Now he's disappeared into the building. It looks like three people are in there. That could be where Sloan is." He made some notes in a pocket-sized notepad and sketched the layout, then watched the images again. "The truck is leaving."

Leon let out a low whistle. "That could be a break."

"Yeah. As long as it doesn't come back with the second shift."

Tempest leaned forward, peering at the images. "What are all those little dots in the middle?"

Both men studied the screen, then Chance said, "Probably some tents or tarps of some sort. Might be protecting some supplies from the rain and snow."

Leon tapped on the screen. "Might be someone in that building on the right. Or it could be a heater. Hard to say. The structure looks larger. Some kind of barracks?"

"Could be. If they've got barracks, though, they might be bringing in more people. How much time do you think it would take for them to come back with another group?"

They watched as Leon punched in some numbers. "Dunno. Not much around here. They've got to be coming from pretty far away. You want to follow the truck and see?"

Chance shook his head then said, "No. If they were changing shifts, that crew would've come in with the truck. They're heading out for the night. I think this is all we've got to deal with for now."

"That's my thinking, too." He circled the plane around.

Tempest crossed her arms and tapped her fingers against her sleeves. "Why do they have this base here at all? It's nowhere near the pipeline and well inside the border."

"It could be set up as a stopover of some sort. It would explain why it's not well-manned." He paused. "Or it's strictly for prisoners."

Leon broke in. "Got two coming out of that building. One's still there. Not moving—wait a minute—now he is." He frowned. "It looks like he's jogging or something. Around the edge of the room." They exchanged a glance and then looked at Tempest.

She stared at the screen. "It can't be. Alexei told me they had Sloan tied up."

He studied the images. "If you look at the layout of this place, that's the only logical location for Sloan. If we're looking at the right camp. One of those two who left is just outside the building. He didn't go anywhere. He could be a guard. But who's the other one? He went into one of the smaller buildings."

They watched in silence for a few seconds, then

Tempest said, "It could be Alexei."

Chance drew in a slight breath. He'd said nothing to Tempest regarding Troy's information on Alexei. She didn't need any additional reasons to worry. "What makes you think that? He should be in Moscow. He thought you were coming in today."

"But I didn't. He would've gone to the airport to pick me up, and I didn't show up, and if he tried to call me, I didn't answer the phone. He might have flown his own plane down. It would only take about three hours." She looked at Chance. "He might suspect something. He isn't stupid."

"I thought you trusted this guy."

She paused. "I did. I'm not sure I do anymore. Some things don't make sense." She shuddered. "I can't believe he would do this, though. I don't understand why."

Chance had a pretty good idea why, but he didn't want to push her. "Leon, can you take the plane around the area? Maybe we can see if there's something that looks like an airstrip, or someplace that would work for a 'copter to land. And maybe see if there's a small plane around somewhere."

Leon swept the UAV in increasing circles around the camp. "There. Hard to say, but it looks flat. Big enough for a whirlybird, but not a plane." He brought the UAV back, and they watched for another thirty minutes.

Chance tapped on another spot, drawing a "yeah" from Leon, but none of the other structures appeared to have any people in them. He glanced at his watch. "You want to bring her back in?"

"You got the layout?"

Chance made a few more notes in his book and nodded. "Pretty much a U-shape."

"Okay. I'm pulling my baby in."

Tempest looked between them. "Does that mean there are only three people guarding Sloan? That's good, isn't it? It won't be too hard to get him from just three people, will it?"

"Could be as many as five, but yes. It helps. It depends on how alert they are. And whether that truck shows back up with reinforcements." He focused on her. "And whether one is Alexei. If he's there, he's going to be on alert. If we lose the element of surprise it makes it harder." He glanced at his watch. "It's after midnight. It'll take at least thirty minutes to get to the mountains and find a safe place for us to jump. That'll make it after one, maybe even close to two before we reach the camp. I don't want to drop too nearby." He cut his gaze to Tempest. "This is an honest question. Are you going to be able to keep up?"

"Yes."

No hesitation, no qualifying or quantifying.

Her quick and forceful response made him duck his head to hide his smile. "Okay. It's going to be fast and intense. Just be prepared."

Chance and Tempest slipped on their parachutes as Leon brought in his UAV for a landing, adjusted the cameras, and changed the batteries.

While they waited, Chance jogged over to Pavel. The pilot paced around the helicopter, checking it out.

Chance spoke to him in Greek. "We're almost ready to go. You'll be looking for a place to the east of the camp, right?"

"Yes. I believe I know of some areas within a mile

that should work for you to jump. Then I will find a closer place than this to wait. We will retrieve Leon after you are back on board. He says this is a field from which he can fly his toy."

Chance choked on a laugh. If Leon heard Pavel call his baby a *toy*, the resulting conflict would be entertaining at the least. He brought his mind back to the plan. "Okay. Good. After we jump, Leon will let you know when we're on our way out of the camp. Just stay in communication with him and he'll be able to tell us where you've landed."

The pilot nodded, made a final check around the 'copter, then climbed inside.

Tempest crossed over to them, carrying the extra tote. Chance grabbed it and helped her on board as Pavel started the engine and lifted off.

Chance shoved Tempest into a seat. "Buckle up," he shouted over the sound of the rotors. From his seat, he opened his tote and began sorting through it, extracting some night vision goggles and a headband with in-ear headphones and a small microphone. Tempest tucked her hair snugly inside her suit and checked her goggles. He leaned closer to her. "We're only going up about eight thousand feet. We won't be in free-fall as long as you're used to. I want you to jump out with me. When I let you go, open your chute." He set his hand on her leg. "Got it?"

She gave him a loose salute, and he smiled.

After twenty minutes, Pavel motioned to Chance, and he slipped from his seat and positioned himself at the door, sliding it open. Wind rushed through the helicopter, and Tempest adjusted her goggles and grabbed a bar to steady herself as she crouched beside

Chance. The pilot gave him a thumbs-up, and Chance grabbed Tempest's hand and pushed himself out, pulling her with him.

As they plummeted toward the earth, his grip on her stayed tight. After a minute in free-fall, he released her hand, and they fell away from each other. He pulled his cord and checked to make sure Tempest had done the same. She worked her lines to bring herself within feet of him. The dark chutes were barely visible against the midnight sky, but she stayed near and when they hit the ground, she landed just a few feet away from him.

As irritating as the woman could be, she continued to surprise him. Her jumping skills impressed him, and he'd seen the gamut when it came to parachuting techniques and abilities. He tore his thoughts away from her. He had one goal, and one goal only. To get Sloan out of this damned country—alive—and get back to the States. Without losing his job or his life. Tempest was on her own after this mission was over.

Yeah, right. Don't kid yourself.

He motioned for her to roll up her chute and hide the yards of fabric and goggles under some brush. The equipment bore no markings to indicate its origin, but the longer the evidence stayed hidden, the better. He slipped the earphones on and adjusted them, speaking in a low voice. "Leon. You with me?"

Static assaulted his ears, then Leon's voice crackled. He adjusted the volume.

"Roger. You're about half mile due east of the camp. How's the terrain?"

"Flat, but rocky. We're going to have to go slower than I'd like." He clicked off. "We're heading west. Be careful—I don't want you twisting your ankle on any loose rocks. This isn't beach running."

"I know. I've spent enough time hiking in these mountains."

With his finger on his lips to indicate silence, he set the NVGs over his face then motioned for her to follow him. They headed across the field toward the edge of the woods and ducked into the brush. He sensed her close behind him and had a fleeting admiration for her skill, but set it aside and refocused. He couldn't let her distract him.

"Open flat area to your south. About thirty feet. Looks like a road." Leon's voice echoed in his ears.

Probably the road the vehicles used. He turned south and made his way closer to the dirt path. Dead leaves and twigs crackled under their feet. He stopped. "We're making too much noise," he whispered in her ear. "Let's stay at the edge of this road." They slipped through the trees and brush and started down the wide trail. After about a half mile, the trees ended. He reached an opening and stopped, pulling her back into the brush.

Beyond sat a smattering of ramshackle structures that appeared to serve as buildings, configured in a semblance of a semi-circle. Tempest tapped him on the arm and pointed. At their right, a small building sat near the entrance of the camp, and beyond it, in front of a longer structure, a man sat against a door with a rifle laying across his legs. Probably the artillery shed. The guard seemed to be asleep, but Chance couldn't risk the possibility of the guy simply resting. He held up his hand to tell Tempest to stay put, then silently slipped behind the two buildings. Moving quickly, he crept along the length of the back side, then slipped around the end, up to the door, and pounced on the man. Chance had his hands around the guard's neck before the man could budge. He fell to the side in a heap. Chance grabbed the guard's rifle and turned around to find Tempest, but she had disappeared. Hand shielding his mouth, he whispered to Leon. "Where the hell is she?"

"Across the grounds. Behind the smaller building."

His stomach tightened as he scanned the grounds until he saw her emerge, gun drawn, into a narrow space between the two structures across the way. He made a slicing motion across his throat. Damn the woman. Having her run through this place on her own was not part of the plan.

Using hand signals, he kept Tempest's attention and pointed at the long building situated about twenty yards away at the back of the camp. "*Stay put*," he gestured, his motions emphatic. He skirted to the side of the artillery unit and began to ease toward the front of the cell block, nerves prickling. This building was too exposed, the camp too quiet. In his experience, that usually meant bad news.

"Is that you headed to that back building?" Leon's voice came through the earphones.

"Yeah."

"Shit. Trouble. I see some movement in the big building across from you. I think there's some people in the barracks. They must have come in after we brought the baby home."

"How many?"

"Three or four. Camera's acting up. I'm taking her lower."

Damn it. No rescue is ever easy. And Tempest is

right between the barracks and the house. He slid along the front of the cell block to the first barred door.

"Movement in that building, too. Just one."

Chance started to lift on the rod. The heavy iron dragged against the metal braces at each end. The scraping clang echoed through the air, amplified by the silence of the night.

Shit.

Chapter Twenty-Eight

A small compound in South Ossetia
Thursday, March 30—1:00 a.m.

Tempest scoped the layout of the compound and took off down the opposite side from Chance. She crouched behind the first building, heart pounding, and pulled the 9mm from inside her suit. When she slipped the magazine into the weapon, the click seemed magnified in the silence of the compound. She cringed and held her breath. No lights filtered through the three windows in the long structure...if the barracks held anyone, they were asleep. She made her way along the back and stopped between it and the small house. Chance saw her and poked at the air, telling her to stay there, then he took off toward the long building they presumed was the cell.

She scooted behind the house next to the barracks. Again, nothing but darkness came from the windows.

A loud scraping sound assaulted her ears.

A shout echoed, and she dashed back to the front of the buildings and stopped in the shadows. A man headed across the grounds in the direction of the fallen guard and fired at Chance. The bullet hit the doorframe, sending splinters of wood flying. Chance shot off a round and disappeared inside the structure. As Tempest aimed, she caught sight of another man running along the open space toward her.

"Останови ть! Ostanovit'!—*Stop*!"

Russian. They spoke Russian. So her suspicions had been correct. Did that mean Alexei was here? The man she glimpsed drew closer, and Tempest fired. He dropped to the ground. Then she pointed her weapon at another man across the way and pulled the trigger again. The bullet hit a metal barrel with a ping, but she shot once more, and he screamed and fell, clutching his leg. She slipped back between the two buildings.

Cold steel pressed against the back of her head.

****

Chance slipped into the cell and let his gaze sweep across the small space. A man huddled in the corner, crouching. "Sloan?" He removed his NVGs and with caution, moved toward the figure. "Sloan? Can you walk?"

The young man straightened, back still against the wall. "Yeah, but—"

Chance's earphones crackled to life. He held up his hand.

"Three down outside, fourth just came from the barracks, headed your way. Two close together between the buildings. I think one of them is Tempest, but I don't know if she's the one in front or behind."

"Shit." He motioned to Sloan. "Here." The young man moved forward, and Chance handed him the rifle. "Get against th—"

A man burst through the entrance and fired. The bullet hit the wall.

"Get down!" he yelled at Sloan, but the kid had already cocked the rifle and fired.

The shot threw the Russian against the wall, and he

crumpled to the ground.

Jesus. Ballsy kid. Tempest didn't raise a wimp. "Come on. Let's get out of here."

"Я так не считаю." Two figures blocked the doorway. A man stood behind Tempest, his gun pointed at her head.

Chance switched his brain to Russian. *I do not think so.* The guy wore a military uniform—this was not Alexei. With a quick glance at Sloan, he halted and lowered his weapon.

Sloan hesitated, then did the same.

In stilted English, the man said, "Gun on ground." He pointed with his free hand. "Hands behind head."

Chance needed to buy some time. He threw a glance toward Sloan, but the young man weaved and staggered, clutching at his gut.

"You! Stop!" The Russian's voice filled the quiet cell.

Sloan crumpled, and Tempest cried out.

The man loosened his grip on her to aim at the young man, then started to pull the trigger.

She thrust her elbow into his ribs. "No!"

The yell and movement made the Russian jolt as he fired. His bullet ricocheted off the wall. Chance yanked up his gun and fired, his shot nearly simultaneous with the man's. Blood spewed over Tempest, and she fell.

Chance's heart stopped. He bolted toward her at the same time Sloan sprang up and reached her.

"Mom."

Blood cascading down her neck, she pushed herself upright, gaze on her son. An unspoken communication passed between them.

"Tempest—"

"I'm fine." She swiped her hand across her face then tipped her head and pressed against her neck. Blood oozed between her fingers.

Shit. Chance gently pulled her hand away. The Russian's bullet had grazed her neck. Blood spilled from the wound. "She's hit."

Sloan started to yank off his shirt. "Do you have a knife?" His muffled voice came through the thin fabric.

Chance dug inside his jumpsuit and handed him his Navy-issue MK3.

The young man sliced the shirt and ripped off the front. He tossed it to Chance and started to rip another piece into a strip.

Chance folded the dirty piece of fabric and pressed it against her neck. When Sloan handed him the strip, they gently wrapped it around her neck to secure the square, and Chance tucked in a corner of the strip to hold it in place.

"How bad is it?" Sloan knelt next to her.

He glanced at the kid. "We need to get out of here."

"Stop talking about me like I can't hear you." She pressed her hand against the wound. "I'm fine." She stood, wobbled, and planted her hand on the wall to get her balance.

Sloan slipped his arm behind his mother. "That shirt is filthy."

Chance scanned the two dead men. "It'll have to do for now." He pressed a button on his mic. "Leon. What've we got?"

"Quiet. I don't see any movement, but I'm still having trouble with the camera."

"Tempest got hit. Get Pavel in the air. We're

heading out." He reached over and snatched the dead man's gun from the ground then dug in the man's pockets until he found Tempest's 9mm. He shoved it into her hand, surveying her face. "Do you feel weak?"

"I'm fine. Let's go."

Chance tightened his mouth. She wasn't fine—she looked pale. But they couldn't hang around here. Sloan had moved away, so he slipped his arm around her. "Try to keep pressing on the cloth. The 'copter's on the way—we need to find that clearing." His grip strong on Tempest, he moved toward the door. "Sloan, let's go."

The young man hovered over the first guard then started to pull off the man's shoes and socks. He put them on and laced them up, speaking over his shoulder. "Go on. I'll catch up." He jumped up, then moved toward the other dead Russian, rolling the body over and tugging off the man's jacket.

As Chance crossed the cell, Tempest squiggled from his grasp. "Let me go. You're slowing us down. I'm okay."

God, the woman aggravated him. "Yeah. Until your adrenaline rush fades." He dropped his arm but took her hand. "Come on." His mic came to life.

"Something's coming down the road. Not a truck—smaller. Jeep maybe."

"How far out?"

"Two, three minutes."

"Fuck." He pulled on Tempest.

"What's wrong?"

"Nothing. Come on. We need to hurry." He angled his voice back toward the cell. "Sloan!"

The young man dashed out the door, shifting two weapons from one hand to another as he shrugged on the stolen jacket. They took off across the grounds toward the road.

A blast of gunfire roared through the air behind them, splintering the dirt and gravel. Chance pulled on Tempest and dropped face-down. The crunch of light shoes came across the compound yard. The footsteps stopped, and Chance rolled slowly onto his side to look up.

"Commander Adams, I assume?" The heavily accented English clipped the quiet. "You have come to rescue Sloan after all."

Chapter Twenty-Nine

A small compound in South Ossetia
Thursday, March 30—0130 hours

Chance rose to a sitting position. "Baranov."

"Ah. My Storm has told you of me. How kind of her." He inched forward. "Did she also tell you we are lovers?"

Fury launched through Chance. The son of a bitch. He snaked his hand across the dirt toward his gun.

Baranov cocked his weapon. "That would not be wise, Commander. Please remove your hand from your gun. I do not wish to kill my Storm, or you, just yet."

The muscles in his neck tightened, his body tensing as he drew back.

Alexei ambled toward them as if he had all the time in the world. He reached for Tempest, still face-down, and pulled her up to stand next to him. She staggered.

"She's hurt, Baranov. Let her sit."

The Russian shot a cursory glance at the cloth around her neck. "She will survive. Until we make love and I am ready to dispose of you all."

The anger building in Chance grew into a burning rage. If it ended up being his last living act, he would not let this maniac touch Tempest.

"You're full of shit, Alexei." Sloan twisted and

266

eased up on an elbow. He grasped the rifle and pointed it at him. "Is that what this is all about? Because you want her in bed? I don't think so. You might kill one of us, but you'll die before you get us all."

The man laughed. "Ah, Sloan. You have become so crass. You would sacrifice your mother? I do not believe this to be true. Set down the rifle."

"Do it, Sloan." Chance cut him a look. They needed time. Was the kid sharp enough to understand?

With slow, measured movements, Sloan eased away from the rifle. Under his breath, he muttered, "He's not going to survive this. No way in fucking hell."

What had Leon said? You have to believe it'll work, or it won't. As long as they didn't give up, they still had a chance to escape. Tempest's son had good instincts. He refocused, and in his ear, Leon's muffled voice filtered through. "Stall. Bird's on the way."

His grip on Tempest tight, Alexei motioned with his gun. "You two. Up. You can wait in the cell until I am done with her." Before he finished speaking, an aging, rusted Jeep careened into the open yard. A man hurtled from the vehicle, rifle in hand.

The slightest change in Baranov's expression didn't escape Chance.

"Yakov. You are here. Take these two to the cell and watch them. I will be there shortly." He yanked on Tempest, and she wrenched back. "Do not fight me, my Storm. We can make this pleasant or painful for you." He turned back to Yakov. "Remove that device from the commander's face. He is talking to someone."

Shit. Their lifeline. With a fading hope they could still flee, he slid the headset down to rest around his neck. Leon would still hear him. But the man came over and snatched it away, threw it on the ground, and crushed it beneath his heavy boot.

Their options diminished by the second.

****

Tempest pulled against Alexei as he propelled her toward the house. A wave of dizziness swelled through her, and she stumbled. He jerked her upright. "Do not play these games with me, my Storm."

Then Chance's voice filtered across the road. "You won't even let us watch, Baranov? I haven't had her. Let me have a shot when you're done. Consider it a dying man's request."

A jolt darted through her. She halted and turned to stare at him.

Sloan's hands drew into fists, and he glared at the SEAL. "You sick bastard."

Eyes narrowed, Chance peered at the young man, giving his head a subtle twist. "Sure. Why not?" Then he switched his gaze to Tempest.

For a fleeting second, his expression softened, and she understood. If they stayed nearby, maybe he could stop this madness. She struggled against Alexei's grip. "I'd sooner die than let either of you touch me." She started to move but pressed her hand against her neck. Blood spilled through her fingers. Light-headed, nausea swept through her. She faltered and sank to the ground.

Sloan lurched forward.

A shot rang through the air. Yakov pointed his rifle at them. "Enough. Stop." Using his weapon to point, he motioned to Chance and Sloan. "You two. The cell. Now. Baranov, do what you will with the woman, but do it quickly."

Alexei's lips pressed into a thin line.

Chance watched the two men. Whoever this Yakov was, he held some power or status over the Russian. KGB?

Yakov spoke. "Do you have the film?"

Baranov jerked and hesitated.

Chance nearly laughed. In Alexei's obsession with Tempest, he'd forgotten his own mission.

He tugged Tempest to her feet. "The film is in her pocket. I will retrieve it after I am done." He started toward the house, yanking her behind him.

Chance cocked his head. The faintest sound of rotors reached his ears. Had Leon directed the pilot to come straight to the camp? With Alexei's M16 and Yakov's high-powered rifle, the 'copter couldn't land—he'd be downed before he reached the open area. Had Leon lost his mind?

The rhythmic whump-whump grew stronger, and the helicopter circled the camp. Alexei started to run, dragging Tempest along. Yakov hesitated. If he shot at the 'copter, it would allow Chance and Sloan time to grab their guns from the ground. With only a glance in the air, the Russian kept his weapon on them. This man had some training.

But a rally of gunfire burst from the 'copter as it passed over, striking the ground just feet from them, leaving a trail across the hard-packed earth. The nearness of the blasts made Chance's skin crawl. Who the hell was up there, blasting at them that close? Not the pilot. Another scenario erupted in his mind. One of the Russians had hijacked the bird. They were fucked.

The shots made Yakov duck. If the Russians in the helicopter were going to kill them, Chance would make damn sure he took a few of their men out first. The diversion distracted Yakov, and Chance snagged his gun from the ground, aimed, and fired. Yakov's body jerked, and he dropped. So far no more shots had come from the 'copter. Maybe they were unprepared and had to reload. He could always hope.

With the lapse in gunfire, Chance targeted Alexei, but the Russian held Tempest too near, and Sloan had started to run toward them. He couldn't risk it, so he charged after them. Alexei pointed his gun over his shoulder and fired randomly as he headed for the house. A bullet whizzed past Chance's ear. *Crap!*

Then the 'copter circled back around, hovering, and a single shot rang through the air. Alexei lurched and blood spread across his back. He fell. Only one person Chance knew could shoot like that.

That was no Russian soldier. Leon was on that bird.

The 'copter lowered to the ground, and his friend's face appeared in the hatch. "Hoo-yah! Get yo' asses in here! Truck's comin'!"

Sloan grabbed his mother and forced her to the 'copter. Chance jumped on board and pulled them in. Before Sloan had cleared the opening, Pavel took off. Pings from the now too-close occupants of the truck resounded against the belly of the bird, but the pilot banked and headed away from the river, gaining altitude.

They had made it out.

Leon sat with Pavel, so Chance settled into one of the three seats behind them. With Tempest slumped in the middle and Sloan to her right, the young man began to unwrap the cloth from her neck.

"Is there a first aid kit?" He raised his voice to be heard over the spinning blades.

Leon translated to Pavel, and the man pointed to a metal box behind him. Chance dug through it and pulled out some packets of antiseptic wipes and gauze pads. He slid forward to watch while Sloan ripped open a pack and wiped his own hands. Using a fresh square, he cleaned his mother's wound, and then dug in the box until he found a couple of butterfly strips. He shoved them at Chance. "Open these."

In spite of his concern over Tempest, he raised an eyebrow at the kid's backbone. Outside of his men, the twenty-year-olds he'd seen rarely had this kind of level-headedness. Sloan gently pulled together the skin on her neck and stuck out his hand. Chance gave him the two strips, and he put them across the gash, closing the wound as much as possible with the bandages. Then he covered the wound with a gauze pad and secured the patch with some clean tape.

"Where'd you learn to do this stuff?"

Sloan cut a glance his way and shrugged. "Places we've been."

Vague answer, but the young man continued to impress him. Tempest shifted slightly and leaned toward her son, but after a few seconds she slipped her hand from her lap and brushed her fingers against Chance's thigh. He reached over to hold her hand. A perfect family picture.

Except they weren't.

With a deep sigh, a tightness gripped his chest as he closed his eyes. The bond between this mother and son needed no one else—no interloper to disrupt their lives. But Sloan would be leaving for college in the fall.

Maybe she'd be lonely. Would there be room for him then? He turned to look at her. A contentment colored her resting features, but then she grimaced and tipped her head. He squeezed her fingers. "Hang on. We'll be there soon."

She nodded and rested against him. Snatches of conversation peppered him. *Without pleasure there is no life. She cares for you. You are in love with her. Bring her back for a proper Greek wedding.* A soft chuckle formed in his throat. Would she like that?

But what if Dimitris was wrong? What if she turned him down? Maybe his brother's alternate scenario was true—she'd used him to rescue Sloan. He gazed at her delicate hand, snug in his. He couldn't—didn't want to—believe she didn't feel something more.

He sure as hell did.

The 'copter started to descend. Within minutes, it touched down and they climbed out and pulled all their gear from the aircraft. As soon as they'd cleared the rotors, Pavel gave them a salute, lifted off, and sped through the dark sky. Troy emerged from the shadows, spotted Tempest's makeshift bandage, and his lips pursed. He helped collect the equipment, and the five of them headed back toward the pier.

The need for expediency still urgent, Chance pressed them along. He wanted to return to Dimitris's island as soon as they reached the yacht. Remaining here presented too much risk. The truckload of men who barreled into the camp might have informants even in this area, ready to describe the late-arriving yacht with the strangers on board.

They made their way to *Elini's Promise* in silence, climbing on board. Dimitris popped from the bridge,

272

and Chance gave him a thumbs-up to pull out, then followed his team into the living area.

Because a team they had become. Each of them, even Tempest with her gunshot wound, had played an integral part in this rescue, which without, might have spelled disaster for them all. She stretched out on the sofa, weak and exhausted. Leon, discomfort flooding his features, sat upright, the driving force from his days on the teams still apparent, and Sloan, with his scraggly hair and beard, dropped on a seat and began to pull off the ill-fitting stolen boots.

In juxtaposition to Leon's posture, Chance slumped in the chair, studying Tempest and Sloan. He could see enough familial similarities to indicate they were related, but clearly, the boy must favor his father. And just as Tempest's eyes had rattled his brain, he had the same reaction to Sloan and searched for some lost memory. Something about the young man seemed familiar; yet, he couldn't cull it from his tangled thoughts. He brushed it aside as post-mission decompression and pushed from the seat to join Dimitris. As he passed Leon, he reached out and squeezed his friend's shoulder. Leon murmured a soft "hoo-yah" in response.

Troy followed him and grabbed his arm. "You made it out. What happened?"

They joined Dimitris at the controls, and Chance filled them in.

****

At the island villa, Elini directed them all to the sunroom. Bright sunshine flooded the view overlooking the sea, the azure sky reflecting off soft ripples in the water, hinting at a beautiful, warm day.

The scent of grilled meat drifted from a sidebar loaded with eggs plus sweet and savory pastries. Chance doubted if any of them felt like eating, but it would give them a little more time to unwind before they crashed. A doctor waited in the room and immediately took Tempest to a chair to examine her wound. Sloan followed.

The doctor began to peel off the tape. "Who cleaned this?" The man spoke in Turkish.

Chance started to respond, but Sloan said, "I did." *Geez. How many languages does the kid speak?* He moved a little closer to listen.

"Do you have medical training?" He studied the wound.

Sloan hesitated. "Informal. I guess you could say on the job."

The man nodded. "Where?"

"Israel."

The doctor glanced at him, brows raised. "Hmm. I see nothing more I can do here. This injury has been well-attended." He stood. "I am told you are leaving the area tomorrow. If the wound worsens or appears to be infected, call Mr. Thalassinos's physician in Athens. He may wish to prescribe some antibiotics." He opened his antique black leather medical bag and pulled out a small bottle, handing it to Sloan. A few pills rattled inside. "Pain medication. She will need them, but use them judiciously until you reach Athens and speak with the physician there."

Sloan thanked the man then focused on his mother. "Are you hurting?"

"I've felt better."

He opened the bottle and handed her a pill then

moved to the sideboard to pour a glass of water. After he handed it to her and watched her take the pill, he asked, "Do you want something to eat?"

"Not right now. You get something." She closed her eyes and leaned her head against the soft cushion.

After a pause, he turned and locked gazes with Chance for several seconds before moving toward the buffet.

Chance watched the young man load a plate with food—no doubt he was hungry. Alexei wouldn't have kept him well-fed. A fleeting recollection of another self-assured, cocky, twenty-year-old tugged at the recesses of his mind.

Yeah. And look where that cockiness landed you. He drew his lips in a line and sat next to Tempest. Desire rippled through him, but not of lust—a craving to hold, comfort, protect, and an unexpected need to believe she cared about him. "Tempest." He took her hand, and her eyes fluttered open, trying to focus. The pain killer from the doctor had already started its work. "Let me take you upstairs so you can lie down."

One side of her mouth curled up. "That sounds like fun." Her grip tightened on his hand, and she stood, bringing him up with her.

The expression on her face seeped through him. The meds had made her lose her filters, and he felt a twinge. But Sloan popped in front of him, plate laden with food, and Chance's growing desire deflated. Fast.

"Where are you taking her?"

Chance slipped his arm around Tempest and held her close. "To her room."

"I can do that."

"You need to eat and get cleaned up." He let his

gaze swipe over the young man. "You could use a shower."

"Who the hell—"

"Stop it, you two goons. You're acting like a couple of cavemen." Tempest slithered from Chance's grasp and marched off.

"Mom—"

"Tempest—"

Because Sloan had to set down his plate, Chance had the advantage and took off after her, but not before he caught Leon smirking at him.

Chapter Thirty

A small island off the coast of Turkey
Thursday, March 30—8:00 a.m.

Sloan cursed as his mother disappeared with the guy chasing after her. Debating his choices, he surrendered to his hunger and sat next to the black guy at a round table by a large window. The other two guys had stayed on the yacht, unloading a bunch of gear.

Focused on his food, he shoveled some eggs in his mouth. He was in pain, tired, hungry, more than a little weak, and kind of sick to his stomach. In the last ten days he'd been beaten, starved, and demoralized. But he'd survived, and now all he wanted was some order back in his life. After a few more bites of food, he put down his fork. Eating all this food too quickly would probably make him puke. "So who are you guys?"

The dude leaned back in the chair, stretching out his leg. His gaze skimmed over Sloan before he answered. "Friends."

He wiped his mouth and glanced at the streaks of dirt staining the napkin. For the first time, he looked down at himself. He was covered in filth. Shit. He did need a shower, but it could wait until he found out who all these people were. His patience thinned. "Your *friends* have names?"

The man looked amused. "Yep."

Asshole. He clenched his teeth. "Care to share?"

The guy studied him with piercing dark eyes until Sloan glowered at him and picked up his fork. "Sure. When you lose the attitude."

Anger crept through him, making his muscles tense. "Look, pal, I asked a simple question. I just spent ten days getting the crap beat out of me and thinking every day was gonna be my last. I don't need any lectures about attitude."

The guy shifted with a grunt, keeping his gaze steady. "I think maybe you do. Because if it weren't for these friends, today *would* have been your last day. Chew on that while you eat that sausage—*pal.*" He struggled up from the table.

Shit. What was wrong with him? He didn't usually act like this. "Hey, mister. I'm sorry. I appreciate it. I do."

With another long look, the man said, "I'm Leon. The guy with your mother is Chance, his brother Troy is still on the yacht, and the people who own this place are Dimitris and Elini."

Sloan digested the information. They couldn't be military. Captain Dickey wouldn't have approved an op like this. "You guys mercenaries? How did Mom find you?"

The amused look returned to Leon's face. "You'll have to ask Chance about that. I'm just the back-up guy." He started to limp off, but a quiet "Hoo-yah" slipped from him.

Sun blazed through the windows, and he squinted. The sudden quiet in the room closed in on him as Leon's words ate through him. Without these people, he *would* be dead. If not today, soon. His grandiose plans and efforts to stay in shape wouldn't have amounted to a molehill once Alexei decided he was done. The sudden, brutal awareness of his near-death roiled through his stomach. He bent over and vomited.

****

Chance knocked lightly on Tempest's door. "Tempest? Can I come in?"

A muffled response filtered through the wood, but he couldn't decipher the words. With a leap of faith, he opened the door. Tempest lay prone on the bed, so he moved over to her and sat on the edge. She didn't open her eyes. He combed back her hair with his fingers, stroking her cheek with his thumb. He started to unzip her jumpsuit. "Let me get you out of this thing."

"Okay."

He helped her into a sitting position, and she shrugged from the suit. He peeled it down, then she lifted her hips so he could pull it off. He tossed the heavy suit on the floor and sat down again, cradling her face with his palm.

She tilted her head against his hand, and he leaned over to kiss her on the forehead. A smile creased her lips.

He drew in a breath and bolstered himself. If not now, then never. "Tempest."

"Hmm?" Sleep was overtaking her.

"I love you."

Smile still in place, she nuzzled against his hand. "Lucky. I have two good men." Her muscles relaxed as she drifted off.

He watched her for a few minutes, tempted to curl up next to her in the oversized bed. But she needed rest, and he couldn't swear he would let her sleep. Instead of doing what he wanted, he stood and then left, closing the door behind him with a quiet click.

Chance went to his room, shedding his own jumpsuit and stripping down. Few things felt better after a mission than a hot shower. And sanctioned or not, this had been a mission.

One that they had remarkably all survived.

****

Sloan wiped his mouth and drank some water. He needed to lie down. But he grabbed some paper napkins from the sidebar and began to clean up his mess. He had almost finished when a woman's voice floated through the room.

"Sloan, what are you doing?"

"Cleaning up. I got sick."

The woman came over to him and pulled him up. "You do not need to do this. I have people who can clean it up. Come. I will show you to your room."

"Well, I—they shouldn't have to—"

"It is fine. They are well-paid." She led him upstairs to a bedroom with a private bathroom.

"Wow. This is great." Suddenly, nothing sounded better than a real toilet and hot shower. "Are you Elini?"

Her eyes sparkled. "Yes. My husband Dimitris and I own this villa. We have known Chance and Leon for many years." Her gaze coasted over his face. "They are good people, Sloan. You are very lucky to have such friends."

They studied each other in silence for several seconds until he nodded. "Thank you."

She smiled. "I believe everyone is resting. We can exchange stories at dinner tonight. My husband plans for us to return to Athens in the morning. Please make yourself at home. There are toiletries in the bathroom and some clothes in the closet that your mother brought for you."

Mom. Always the girl scout. Was she all right? He should go check on her. He stripped down and climbed in the shower, watching the rivulets of dirt and grime swirl down the drain as his mind recapped. The dude with the limp, Leon, really didn't give him any information beyond their names. But the other guy, the one with the weird name—Chance—something was going on there. He seemed a little too interested in his mother.

On the other hand, it wasn't fair of him to expect her to be alone forever. He was heading out this fall, and who knew where he'd end up? Didn't she deserve a life after she'd given him everything? He wasn't stupid or indifferent to the sacrifices she'd made to raise him. No. If this guy was interested in her and she liked him, Sloan wouldn't stand in the way.

After he vetted the dude. Thoroughly.

****

The setting sun cast a blaze of color across the sky. Shades of pink, purple, and orange reflected off puffy clouds in a glorious resplendence. Tempest sat with Elini and Dimitris on a patio nestled in the gardens, enjoying the warm afternoon. Now rested and feeling a bit more human, she let the colorful display soothe her scattered nerves.

If she allowed her thoughts to head in the direction of the past twenty-four hours, the events would choke her. She had killed a man—again. Would God forgive her? Were there divine, or even moral, rules regarding murder? Was it forgivable when committed in self-defense, or in defense of a loved one?

She couldn't answer that until her own personal judgment day came.

But God had given humans—even animals—the instinct for survival. Animals killed for food, for safety, and weren't human beings animals as well?

Elini asked her a question, and Tempest tore herself from her theological self-debate. "We would love to visit with you in Athens for a few days, Elini. I think Sloan could use some time to recuperate. That's kind of you to offer."

Some movement from the house caught her attention, and Chance, Troy, and Leon emerged and started across the lawn. The three men presented a potent bearing—even Leon, with his limp, still showed a stature that attested to his background. Neat, trim, strong—the training of SEALs. And Troy, although not a military man, favored his brother in build and had a self-assurance that spoke of success.

Her gaze settled on Chance, and her nerves tingled up her chest, through her neck. Her hand automatically pressed against the bandage. Chance had said *I love you* right before she fell asleep. It hadn't been a dream. Had it? Then fear sprinted through her. Her confession still had to be told. Dread draped over her like a shroud from the Grim Reaper. How could she possibly explain everything?

"Tempest? You look pale. Do you wish for me to have your medication brought to you?"

She jerked from her thoughts and faced Elini. "I'm fine. I was thinking."

Dimitris, with his usual optimism, said, "Ah! This

is in the past. All is well. We must focus on the present!"

She smiled, but it wasn't the present she was concerned about—just the future.

The men reached them, and Chance sat next to her while Troy and Leon moved to chairs by the Greek couple.

Elini addressed them. "I have invited Tempest and Sloan to extend their visit in Athens. Would the rest of you join us as well?"

Chance shook his head. "I can't, Elini. My week of leave ends Sunday. I have to fly home Saturday."

Leon also begged off. "I have a project with a deadline I put on hold to come out here. But I'd like to bring Hattie out here—sooner than fifteen years from now."

Troy shrugged. "I can stay for a couple of days." He smirked at Chance. "Might as well get my money's worth out of these plane tickets."

Chance rolled his eyes and shot him a dirty look.

"That would be wonderful!" Dimitris lifted his glass.

They toasted and sipped, and as conversation resumed, Chance grasped Tempest's hand. "Are you feeling better?"

She nodded and turned toward him, studying his face, his blue eyes, committing them to memory. She held no hope—none—that he would not disappear from her life forever. She blinked several times.

He pulled his chair a little closer and toward her, taking both of her hands in his. "You don't feel well. Do you want to go lie down?"

She shook her head. "I'm fine. It's nothing...just

that fading adrenaline rush you warned me about." She mustered a weak smile.

His lips tightened, and he shifted in the chair as a look of skepticism colored his features. He obviously didn't buy into her excuse and continued to watch her. Some movement from the house caught her eye, and she looked across the lawn. Her—*their*—son headed toward them. She sucked in a breath. He had trimmed his hair and shaved the beard. He looked ten years younger. And exactly like—

A small chuckle emerged from Elini. "Chance, that young man looks like he could be your son."

Chapter Thirty-One

A small island off the coast of Turkey
Thursday, March 30—2:00 p.m.

Tempest yanked her hands away from Chance. The blood drained from her face, leaving her dizzy, and she tensed.

With a slight frown, Chance turned and looked behind him. He stared at Sloan, then switched to look at her. She held his gaze for a moment then focused on her lap. She knew this time would come. Sloan looked exactly like Chance had at twenty. Marc and Sarah saw the resemblance, even Elini saw similarities. There was no question, no maybe—it was there in living color.

Chance got to his feet and reached over to grab her arm. "Come with me."

Leon cleared his throat, and Troy's voice cut through the thick tension. "Bro."

"Not now, Troy." He scowled at his friend. "You, either, Leon." He pulled at Tempest.

She rose, extricating herself from his grasp, and trudged behind him. He led her to a quiet area of the patio, behind a gazebo, out of earshot. He planted himself in front of Tempest and glared at her.

Tempest said nothing. If he had any questions, he was going to have to ask them.

Seconds passed, but it could have been an hour.

Perspiration began to collect between her shoulder blades, running in a rivulet down her spine. She shuffled her feet and started to back away.

He took hold of her arm again. "Oh, no, honey. You're not going anywhere. What the hell is going on?"

She coughed. "What do you mean?"

"Don't play games with me, babe. Who is Sloan?"

She managed to give him a questioning look. "He's my son. You know that already."

"Yeah, so you said. Where's his father?"

That was the question. Where was his father? She could say he was overseas, working for the government. She could say he was dead, because in a sense he was. She could say she didn't know, but that, under the circumstances, probably wouldn't fly, either. Or she could just play dumb. Dumb sounded good. "I haven't seen him in years." There. Good. Not a lie.

"That boy looks exactly like me. Or just like I did when I was in college. Even Elini noticed it. What the hell is going on?"

"He does look like you, doesn't he? It's an odd coincidence."

"Skip the games, Tempest. Who. Is. Sloan's. Father?" His clipped tone cut the question into tiny pieces.

She tried to pull away, but his grip on her arm tightened. Busted. This was the final roll of the die. The last spin of the wheel. All of the cards were in the dealer's hand, and the dealer was going for broke. "Let me go. You're hurting me."

His grip slackened, but he kept his hand around her arm. She yanked away but didn't bolt. Her chest filled with air and expelled as a long sigh. "Can we sit down?" She started to move around to the gazebo opening, and he didn't stop her. She stepped up the stairs and sat on a bench. His gaze followed her actions, and after a moment, he walked into the center of the gazebo and sat across from her. Not too close. As far away as the structure would allow. Maybe that was good. If he decided to lunge for her, maybe she would have time to make a dash for freedom and escape.

She paused and took another deep breath. Chance was being quite patient, but his continued stare tore at her. "Sloan was born twenty years ago."

He said nothing but his expression asked for more.

"His birthday is February tenth."

Chance stared at the foliage outside the gazebo. She could see his mind running backward, trying to calculate dates and time frames.

He spoke deliberately, "That would make it May…" His gaze returned to meet hers. "Early in May…?"

She nodded.

"That graduation party. At UVA. For Ginny Randolph…"

Tempest couldn't swallow. She couldn't breathe.

"A skinny little blonde with freckles. She—I was…crazy…and she talked to me all night. Probably kept me from killing someone. Or drinking myself to death." He tilted his head, studying her. "Ginny's sister."

There. It was out. Ginny Randolph's sister. The frumpy little wallflower, just-about-to-graduate-from-high-school, whole-life-ahead-of-her, sister of the glamour queen. Everyone loved Ginny. Tempest spent her entire life in the shadow of her beautiful sister.

Until she got pregnant and disbarred from the family.

"That was *you*? And you and I…?"

Tempest couldn't speak. She could only nod.

"Holy shit."

She peered at him. That was it? No anger? No questions? No—

"Wait a minute. Her name wasn't Tempest. I wouldn't forget a name like that. What the hell was your name? Teresa…no, Tammy. You're Tammy Randolph?"

"Chance…"

"What happened? I don't remember. How did this happen?"

"I—I…" she sputtered. "Ginny announced her engagement at that party."

He shot from the seat and threw up his hands. "Oh, yeah. I sure as hell remember *that*. I had a fucking ring in my pocket. We'd been dating for almost four years. Then she pops up with this character with three first names and a third at the end of it. Billy Bobby Tommy the third—"

"Charles Ernest James III."

"—and tells everyone they're engaged. Just like that. No warning. No *sorry, Chance, honey. I've met someone else*. She couldn't bring herself to marry a Navy boy. Not Virginia Randolph. That was way below her pay grade. Way beneath her station in life."

"You were angry—"

"Damn right I was angry! I was devastated. She wrote to me the entire time I was in Coronado. Signed every damned letter *Love always*. Yeah. Always my ass. Until Billy Bobby showed up."

Tempest listened to Chance's barrage. She had

heard it all that night, when he'd had too much bourbon and cried on her shoulder. Well, not cried—ranted would be closer. She'd never seen anyone so upset.

Until now.

But she had a massive crush on him then, and when he turned to her for solace, she'd provided it. All the way into bed.

"Bitch," he muttered. "Couldn't even look me in the eye and tell me to fuck off." His gaze settled back on Tempest. "But *you*. You just decided to have my son and not *tell* me?"

"Chance, it wasn't that simple. After we—you—"

"Fucked. Don't even try to make this out as rape."

She planted her hands on her hips and bit on her bottom lip. Her voice was tight. "I have no intention of accusing you of rape." She glared at him. "None. And I never did."

His eyes narrowed.

"The next morning, you jumped on your motorcycle and left." She paused. "I never saw you again."

He pushed up and crossed the few steps to hover over her, his voice strained. "You could have found me."

Her own anger spilled forth. "I tried! Do you have any idea how difficult it is to find…people like you? When I met Marc and Sarah, I asked him about you, and even he wouldn't say anything. He barely— *barely*—admitted knowing you. And then he said he had no idea where you were."

He ran his hand over his mouth, his muffled voice filtering through his fingers. "Dear God." His eyes closed, and he huffed a breath. Without opening them, he asked, "Why did you change your name?"

"When my parents found out I was pregnant, they wanted me to get an abortion. They said having a baby was going to ruin my life. I refused, so they sent me to a home in South Carolina for unwed mothers. But when the bus stopped, I got off and ran away. My aunt took me in." She leaned back and pressed her hand against her neck. The wound had started to throb. "I was afraid they would come looking for me and take Sloan away, so I changed my name." She paused and squeezed her eyes shut. "I even—I even moved to Norfolk because of the SEAL headquarters there. I thought…maybe I could find you." Her chest tightened as she struggled to swallow.

He stood and paced in a circle inside the gazebo. He looked over at Sloan, chatting with his brother and friends. "That's my son."

"Yes. Sloan is your son." Her voice was barely audible.

He pivoted. His voice rose. "Why didn't you tell me?"

"I just told you why!"

He advanced on her until his legs touched her knees. "Last week. You could have told me when you were in Marc's office."

His anger infused into her own. She shifted, propping her hands on the bench. "Oh, like you would have believed me then. You didn't want to help me as it was. If I had told you the whole story, you'd have thought I was lying just to get your help."

He shook his head, whether from pain or denying her words, she couldn't guess. "Twenty years." He straightened and his fists clenched. A low growl came from his throat. Then his posture slackened, and he turned to look toward the pool. "My son. I have a son."

"Chance, I didn't think—"

He whipped back around, and his gaze burned a hole in her heart. "And that's the bottom line, isn't it? You didn't think. You didn't think about anyone but yourself. Not about Sloan's father, your family, not even Sloan. You stole his heritage from him. You're no better than your sister. In fact, you're *worse*."

Tears stung her eyes, and she hugged her arms across her chest. Waves of regret flowed over her. Even with Marc's warning, never in a lifetime would she have guessed Chance would feel so strongly about family. He was so detached, trained as a SEAL, analyzing every movement and decision. She swallowed and put her hand over her mouth. What had she done? "Chance, I'm so sorr—"

"Sorry! You're *sorry*? How many lives have you affected and all you can say is *you're sorry*?"

She shot a glance at the pool. Everyone stared at them. Of course they could hear them shouting.

He jerked her from the bench and pointed behind him toward Sloan. "He's my *son*!"

Chapter Thirty-Two

A small island off the coast of Turkey
Thursday, March 30—3:00 p.m.

Sloan approached them, hands in his pockets. He wouldn't have let Baranov hurt his mother, and this guy…forget it. "Mom?"

Tears streaming down her face, she only looked at him in silence.

"What's going on? Are you okay?" He tore his focus away from his mother and toward the man.

The guy stood at one side of the gazebo, staring at him.

Who the hell did he think he was? His mother was hurt, and he had made her cry? She never cried. His vetting of this character was not going in the guy's favor. He turned his attention back to her.

Her head dropped, her voice so faint he took a step closer to hear her. "Sloan, there's something I need to tell you." She drew in a breath. "This is—this is Chance Adams. He's—" She stopped, eyes closed, then drew in a deep breath. "Chance is your father, Sloan."

Muscles tense, he stared at her then turned his attention to the man across from him. Words escaped him. He could only peer at the guy. Twenty years of questions, anger, disappointment, and resentment flowed over him. All he could muster was, "Why?"

His mother jumped up and grasped his arm. "No, Sloan. Don't be angry with him. It wasn't his fault." She tilted her head and looked away. "It's all on me."

He shook his head. "No." His world began to crumble. She'd been his rock, his strength, his comprehension of right and wrong. She could not have faults…imperfections…failings. "No."

She wrapped her arms around him, but he couldn't respond. "I'm sorry." She released him and left the structure. Left him with this man.

His…*father*?

They locked gazes, neither wanting, nor able, to speak. Finally, Sloan broke the silence with one simple question. "Why?"

"Because I didn't know."

He sliced through the air with his arm. "Didn't know? How could you not know? You know, *fucking* someone isn't like you just have a conversation in the park."

Chance's eyes narrowed. "Watch your language, young man."

"Why? Why should I? Apparently, you didn't watch your—"

He grabbed his arm. "Don't go there."

Sloan jerked away.

The man's expression tightened. "Obviously you didn't know anything more than I did. If she didn't tell you, why do you think she would tell me?" He waited, but Sloan had nothing to say. "What story did she give you?"

His anger swelled. This guy had no right to condemn his mother. "She didn't give me a *story*. She didn't say anything at all. For twenty years. I finally stopped asking. I figured the guy was dead or something." He stared at Chance and tightened his fists. "Or maybe she got raped."

Fiery rage flared in the man's blue eyes. Eyes the same color as his own. "I did *not* rape your mother."

"No? Just a fuck and run then?"

The visible anger expanded, flooding his face, and a low growl came from his *father's* throat.

For a second, Sloan understood how dangerous this man could be. Maybe that's why his mom hadn't pursued a relationship. He narrowed his gaze then closed his eyes for a second. His tone a bit lower, he asked, "Did you used to be a SEAL or something? Do you know Marc Dickey?"

Chance drew a deep, hitched breath. "I'm active duty. Marc is my CO." He steadied his breathing and lowered his voice. "I know you're angry. I'm angry, too." He sat across from him, skipped a beat, then said, "You're too young to understand being drunk."

Sloan laughed. He fell onto the wood slats across from the man. "Believe me, I've been way beyond drunk." He turned his gaze toward the man and added with insolence, "*Dad*."

The SEAL examined him for a long moment. He didn't push the issue. "Then maybe you can appreciate not remembering shit."

They studied each other for an eternity. Not just the man's blue eyes, but the hair color, build, and yes, even his personality—the resemblances were almost uncanny. Sloan backed down first. "You really didn't know?"

"No. I really didn't know. Until today. Right now."

Sloan looked toward the pool. His mother, Leon,

and this guy's brother…his *uncle*…had wandered to the edge of the gardens, deep in conversation. Dimitris and Elini had disappeared. He turned his attention back to Chance Adams. The man studied him, as if trying to learn him, understand him…make up for twenty lost years. His chest tight from conflicting emotions, his anger began to retreat, replaced by a deep sadness—for all of them.

"Let's get out of here." Chance stood. "Come on. I'll buy you a beer." He paused and a small smile flitted across his face. "Since you're no stranger to drinking."

Sloan hesitated. Did he really want to know this man? A few hours ago, he intended to vet the guy. But now? "I'm underage, remember?"

"Not on this island."

Torn between his need to stay with his mother and his desire to understand, he relented. With one final glance toward the gardens, he left with the SEAL.

His *father*.

****

Tempest watched Chance whisk her son—*their* son—away. She drew a ragged breath.

Leon rested his hand on her arm but didn't speak.

"I—I—" She shook her head, sniffed, and blinked.

"I need to give my leg a rest." Leon led her to a bench near some rose bushes. "Tempest, you were young. Don't beat yourself up."

She glanced at Troy then sat next to Leon, hugging herself as if it would stem the nausea in her stomach. "I could've done more. Tried harder. It's just…after a while, it didn't seem like it mattered anymore. He was gone. I couldn't find him…" The words caught in her throat, choking her. She looked at Troy. "It was easier to forget it happened." She directed her gaze to the rose gardens and squeezed her eyes shut. "But I couldn't forget. I never forgot. I thought about him every day." Tears flooded her eyes. "*Every* day." She swiped across her cheek. "What have I done?"

Leon slipped his arm across her shoulders. "We all make mistakes."

"No." She shook her head. "Not like this." The tears spilled over and cascaded down her cheeks. She met Troy's steady gaze. "Please don't hate me."

He sat on a bench across from them. "I have no reason to hate you, Tempest."

Leon pulled her close, letting her expunge her grief—and guilt.

****

Well after midnight, Chance and Sloan returned to the villa. The conversation had been long and hard, replete with anger and blame on both sides. But by the time they left, they had at least come to a tentative truce. And Sloan agreed to see him once they all returned to Norfolk. He couldn't ask for much more at this point. At least the boy—*his son*—was willing to try.

His son. The words still felt foreign, surreal. He had to put aside his anger, the devastating feeling of loss, and focus on now. Whatever it took, he would make this up to him, somehow. A part of him didn't want to take the blame for this, but Tempest—*Tammy*—didn't get pregnant by herself. During the evening with Sloan, snatches of that night came back to him. He had paced through Ginny's apartment, weaving around the other guests, speaking to no one, topping off his glass of bourbon in an endless succession. Finally, he'd plopped onto a sofa, absently watching the partiers, until Ginny's sister sat next to him. She'd been kind and caring, letting him fume, pour his heart out, and then he kissed her.

Oddly, now, he recalled that kiss vividly. Her soft lips, smooth skin, and a hint of red roots in her blonde hair. He'd been drunk—drunk enough to push the episode from his mind—but evidently never really forgotten.

But with the wrenching pain in his heart, he wanted nothing to do with Ginny or anyone in her family. He'd buried the memories and moved on. And never let a woman get close again. If he hadn't been so stubborn, hadn't allowed his ego to control his actions and thoughts, he might have called her, and Sloan wouldn't be a stranger to him now.

What had he done?

He headed to his room, but before he opened his door, Leon stuck his head from the room across the hall. "Wanna talk, C'mander?"

"Not particularly. I've done enough talking for a lifetime." *The lifetime of my son.* The words made his chest tight.

Leon emerged from his room and came up to him, pushing on his door. "Tough shit." He walked inside and settled into a chair by the window.

Troy ambled in behind him, and Chance scowled then turned back to Leon. Letting his anger spill out was easier than dealing with this ache in his heart. "When the hell did you get so ornery?"

"It's in my blood. Have a seat."

Chance spurted a laugh. "Thanks for offering me a seat in my own room."

Leon wasted no time. "What happened with Sloan?"

"We talked. We drank. The kid can down some booze."

Troy spit out a laugh. "So can his father."

Chance cut him a glance and grimaced. "So can his uncle."

Arms crossed, his brother ignored the comment and fixed his gaze on him. "Make amends?"

"We're figuring things out."

Silent, Leon stared across the room. He had something more on his mind.

"Out with it. What've you got to say?"

Leon's gaze returned to his old friend. He shook his head. "And Tempest?"

Chance tensed. He wasn't ready for ultimatums, advice, or insights from friends or relatives. He shrugged.

Leon's tone became terse. "It takes two to tango, they say."

Finally. Something he could respond to. "Yeah? Well, *they* can go to hell."

He stood. "Yep. They can. And when you meet up with 'em, y'all can dance together."

"Jesus. You've turned into a real pain in the ass, you know that?

"I've been told. Picked it up from my wife. You should try listening to someone else once in a while. You can learn a lot from someone you care about." He left the room.

Chance watched him leave then turned to his brother. "I suppose you have something to add."

Troy studied him for several seconds. "I lost two

years with my boys, Chance." He scratched at his neck. "So I get what you're feeling. But your situation is different from mine." He moved toward the door. "Don't throw something good away because of your ego."

He watched his brother leave and refrained from hitting the wall with his fist. Easy for them to say. They weren't the ones who lost twenty years.

The hell with all of them.

****

Tension permeated the plane ride to Athens the next morning. Tempest sat tucked in a corner seat, and Elini stayed with her for the entire flight, while Dimitris sat with his pilot in the cockpit. Sloan huddled in another corner, deep in conversation with his new family and Leon, occasionally laughing.

Bonding.

Another piercing pain shot through Tempest's chest. After twenty years of raising him, having her whole world revolve around him and his welfare, seeing him work to create that same connection with someone else sent a slow ache through her heart. As much as she wanted him to have a relationship with his father, it still hurt.

Maybe because she couldn't share in the new connections.

From the first day she'd laid eyes on Chance— briefly, during one visit before that fateful party—she'd fantasized about him. When she'd listened to her sister make teasing comments about him, her skin had crawled. He seemed like a good person, and Ginny had batted him around like a birdie in a badminton set.

Even at her young age, she saw the hypocrisy and

duplicity of her sister, and even that of her parents, and she wanted nothing to do with their insincerity and speciousness. Realizing the wrongness of their self-serving attitudes had been the catalyst that began to separate her from her family. At the same time, she'd learned that photography could cut through those falsehoods with brutal honesty, and she'd begun her mission to expose the deceit she witnessed, not only in them, but in the world around her.

The Randolphs were upper crust, upper class, a fixture of high society in the inner circles of Washington, and they and her sister hated the candid photos she snapped off, showing them with their guard down, their faults, their weaknesses. They'd belittled her passion and pushed her toward a more *respectable* profession in business, or at least *fine art*. Photography was a baser form of the craft that interested only the uneducated, the *lowbrow* of society. Their attitude only served to make her more dogged in her pursuit. But in the end, for all of her good intentions, she'd succumbed to their teachings and committed the ultimate act of selfishness.

If God didn't punish her for killing two men, he would certainly send her to hell for tearing her family apart.

Chapter Thirty-Three

The Thalassinos estate on the Aegean Sea—Athens, Greece
One week later

Tempest spent another minute putting on her makeup, and then took one final look around the opulent room, making a last check for any stray belongings. With a deep sigh, she picked up her bag and trudged down the hall to the house's elevator. The Thalassinoses's hospitality had given her and Sloan the chance to heal and get their strength back. Their conversations over the past few days had been civil, sometimes tempered with humor and reminiscences, but pointedly avoided the albatross that hovered over them.

Troy had stayed for a couple of days, giving Tempest and Sloan the opportunity to get to know him. After her initial discomfort over his probing stares when they first met, she'd found Chance's brother to be warm and easy to talk to, with a dry sense of humor that kept her laughing. It gave her a small sense of gratification to develop that friendship.

In the foyer, Dimitris and Elini were talking with Sloan. A tote sat at his feet, holding some personal items and clothing that they had graciously provided. With the grace of a model, Elini seemed to float up to

Tempest and gave her a hug. "It will be all right," she whispered. "Time changes things."

Tempest didn't argue but doubted there was enough time left in this millennium to fix her disaster.

"Tempest," Dimitris said, "You are welcome to visit us anytime. You and Sloan both."

"Hopefully soon," Elini added.

She forced a smile and thanked them both. They went outside where a limousine waited in the drive. She and Sloan climbed into the back and were whisked off to the airport.

The ride was quiet. Too quiet. Sloan barely spoke to her. She wanted to hold him in her arms like a little boy. She wasn't a bad person—just human like everyone else. She had done the best she could. She only did what had seemed right at the time. Every cliché and stereotyped phrase in the English language went through her mind—all the words she once thought were nothing more than lame excuses for poor parenting.

They were settled into the seats on the plane for New York before Sloan said in a soft voice, "You know, Mom, we didn't talk about it, but I'm not mad at you."

Tempest turned to look at him. "You have every right to be."

He shrugged. "I'm going to see him when we get home."

Tempest nodded. It was only right. For both of them. "Okay," she croaked.

He shifted slightly in his seat. "I'm not trying to hurt you." He hesitated. "I think there's been enough of that for all of us. But I'd kind of…like to get to know him." Then he plugged in some earbuds from an iPod Elini had given him and turned away from her. But she heard him say, "I love you" before he closed his eyes.

The simple words, spoken with sincerity and a bond between mother and son, sliced through her. In her thoughtlessness, her immaturity, her selfishness, she had hurt everyone in her life who meant anything to her. Chance was gone. She no longer held any illusions that they might have a life together. Not now. But her son still loved her.

And her parents and sister were still out there. She could at least find them and try to make amends. It was never too late, right? That was what the television psychologists preached. She looked over at Sloan. He would have the opportunity to get to know his father, and with luck, the rest of the family.

She, on the other hand, had been plunged into her own personal hell. And well-deserved at that. She inhaled a ragged breath and closed her eyes.

****

Sandbridge, Virginia Beach, Virginia
Tuesday, the Fourth of July

Tempest sat on her balcony, considering the events of the last few months. Her photos and Sloan's stories had run in *Newsweek* and the *New York Times*, and they had even been interviewed on the *NBC Nightly News*, something that went completely against her reclusive personality. The entire story of Sloan's abduction, Alexei Baranov and his connections to the KGB…all of it had become public knowledge. The countries of the free world were now in an uproar over the Georgians' plight. But the satisfaction it gave her dulled with the tightness in her chest when images of Chance crossed her mind.

The patio door slid across its track. Sloan stood at the threshold with his girlfriend behind him. "Mom, Becky and I are heading out. Are you sure you don't want to come watch the fireworks with us?"

Depends on what kind of fireworks you have in mind. Probably not. She smiled and stood. "No. You two go on. I can see them from the balcony if I want to."

His brow creased, but he gave her a quick hug and then Becky did the same. "I'll call you tomorrow." He hesitated. "Dad's going to show us around the base a little bit. As much as he can."

His declaration made her jolt. Sloan had been cautious talking to her about Chance, partially because he feared hurting her, but he did admit to calling him *Dad* soon after they returned from Athens. The word still sounded odd, foreign, to her. But at the same time right. "I'll take you two out to dinner one night this week. Okay?"

Becky beamed. "That'd be fun."

"Come on. I'll walk you to the front door." She and Becky had hit it off from their first meeting. Sloan had met her through a friend of Chance's, so her son had kept the young woman under wraps for a few weeks, fearing his mother might not like her. But with Becky's upbeat attitude, she was good for him. An image of Leon and Hattie struck her. "I know what would be fun. Maybe we could go to Washington and see Leon." She glanced at Sloan. "You haven't met Hattie—and his UAVs are pretty cool."

His face lit up. "Yeah. Leon told me about his stuff before he left Athens."

She shooed them off. "Go on. It's going to be hard to find a parking place." They both gave her another hug and scooted out the door. With a tiny spurt of melancholy, she wandered back through her apartment to the balcony. The heat of the July day still lingered in the night air. A waxing moon rose over the ocean, casting glittering sparkles of light over the cresting white caps of the gentle waves. The soft cascading splashes of the water on the sand drifted toward her. The picture, the sounds, never failed to soothe her.

It would be nice to have someone to share it with. But she didn't want *someone*. She wanted Chance.

An immense amount of soul-searching had enveloped her in the three months. Looking back at the things she had accomplished no longer seemed worth the path she had taken. She was renowned as a feature news photographer, sought after by magazines and television stations. But all of the accolades, all of the awards, no longer meant anything.

She'd decided to retire. At the ripe old age of thirty-nine.

One afternoon, bolstering her courage on a shot of vodka, she'd contacted her family. Her mother answered the phone, and when Tempest said, "Umm, hi, Mom. It's...Tammy," the woman had burst into tears. *Tears*. Her *mother*. That, in turn, had made her cry also, and the next day she drove to Washington, with Sloan tagging along, to reunite with her parents— Sloan's grandparents. Some days later Ginny came to Virginia Beach to visit with her, bringing her husband... Tempest couldn't help but smile—Charles Ernest James III—to reconnect.

The depth of regret she felt threatened to swallow

her. The idea that Sloan didn't hold any of this against her was a testament to his kind heart. In her mind, however, she refused to take any credit for that trait in him. Instead, she attributed it to the genes of his father.

Chance.

How she longed to see him again. Even if they couldn't have a loving relationship, she'd hoped they could be civil and do some things together, with their son. But it seemed that was not to be. She might see Chance when Sloan graduated, or if he married Becky or someone else.

Or it might be one of those events that Sloan had to choose whom to invite. She hoped to God they could get past their...*past*, without putting their son through that angst.

In the distance, she heard the pop of fireworks, and she gazed northward at the shoreline and the bright, colorful lights streaking through the sky.

Wishing she had someone to share the beauty with.

With a sigh as deep as the ocean, she sat and let her thoughts drift along with the waves.

****

The scantily-clad dancer hugged the pole and threw back her head to smile and wink at Chance. He picked up his beer and drained it, then set the glass down with a decided clunk. Riding out to Newport News to watch some twenty-year-old, not even naked, try to make a few bucks for her college education didn't hold much enjoyment for him anymore. But then, since his return from Greece, boredom seemed to be the mode of the day. His life was running on cruise control. He paid his bill and wandered out of the bar to his bike.

A sliver of moon lit up the sky, just like the night

on Dimitris's yacht. A warm breeze, the smell of the sea, his arms wrapped around Temp—

He cursed and stopped the thought. Leon didn't lie—he may have pushed Ginny to a deep recess of his mind and all but forgotten her, but that relationship wove through every action he did and every quirk of personality that tempered those actions. Because of Ginny, he'd never allowed another woman to get close, focused only on his job, set aside any feelings or emotions he might otherwise have had.

What his friend didn't know was the accident that took Leon's leg affected Chance as much as the debacle with Ginny had. The fact the ex-SEAL's life outside the Navy probably did Leon and the world far more good than whatever he could have accomplished as a SEAL did nothing to assuage Chance's own feelings of guilt. Had he not convinced Leon to try for the SEALs, his friend would still have two legs, not be in pain, and odds were, he'd have gone on and accomplished what he did outside the Navy regardless.

He may not have ruined the man's life, but he sure as hell didn't do him any good. During some brutal days of honesty, he questioned how Leon could continue to befriend him at all.

And now, again because of past mistakes, he prepared to throw away something that might be his own ticket to happiness.

With a sigh, he shook off his thoughts and feelings of discontent, replacing them with an image of Sloan. The vague tugging he had always ignored about having a family had come to fruition. He had a son. His chest swelled with an unfamiliar pride. Not only was Sloan leaving for college this fall, he had talked about trying out for the SEALs. If he did, Chance was certain the young man would make it through the training. After listening to Sloan described the conditions of his capture, Chance could see that drive in...*his son*...the drive that sifted the weak from the strong. But he remained silent. He would not, could not, ever again encourage anyone, especially his son, to go down that road. He would never be able to make up for the twenty years he lost, but he refused to lose even more. They made plans to spend as much time together as possible. Sloan seemed to recognize, accept, and appreciate that.

Tempest. That was his problem. She crept into his head throughout his long days and even longer nights. His anger had waned, replaced by a dull ache. He stared across the parking lot at a couple engaged in some heavy kissing. Those times he and Tempest spent together surfaced—*again*—the softness of her skin against his while she dragged her nails lightly across his chest. The scent, the taste of her, filling his senses.

With a frown, he grabbed his helmet and threw a leg over the bike, straddling the thick padded seat. The question now was, did he want to see her again? His retirement started in two weeks. He could easily take his bike onto the highway, head west, and never come back to Norfolk. But would he be any happier?

Cursing, he strapped on his helmet and cranked up the bike. The deep rumble of the engine always calmed his nerves. He revved it up and skidded out of the lot, kicking up bits of gravel as he pulled onto the asphalt highway.

Sloan wasn't just his son. He was Tempest's. When he pushed aside his hurt and anger, he admitted she had raised the boy. Alone. She'd done a good job with him. He could not and would not ever argue that point. If anything, he was lucky Sloan wanted to spend time with him. Not that it was his fault he never got a chance to be a father to him, but Sloan seemed to understand that. If he held any anger toward his mother, it didn't show. The little boy in the photo in Tempest's car had grown into an exceptional young man. That was the bottom line.

He accelerated on the east-bound ramp of the interstate, merging into the left lane. At some point in his life, mostly when he'd been in his thirties, he considered what it would be like to be *normal*. Eight-to-five job, little wife at home fixing dinner, kids playing on the swing set. But that was a throwback to the 1960s. Hell, he didn't know anyone who had a life like that. Yet, it would have been nice to give it a shot.

You still could, Chance. You're retiring in two weeks. You could ride right up to that fancy condo of hers and whisk her away like—

Like what? A knight on horseback? An officer and a gentleman? That was fiction crap. And the girl in the movie hadn't hidden Richard Gere's kid from him for twenty years.

You need to get over this, pal. You're forty-two. Are you going to spend the rest of your life riding around on this damned bike, with a long gray ponytail flapping in the breeze? Hell, why don't you just go ahead and have Hell's Angels tattooed all over your back now?

He gunned his bike and sped around the traffic. Let the cops give him a ticket, if they could catch him. He hit the entrance of the tunnel to the Southside and flew through the structure. This had to end. Now.

****

With a glance at the clock, Tempest snatched up the ringing phone. Eleven o'clock. Who would be calling her at this hour? Dread coated her as the thought of Sloan and Becky in an accident bombarded her thoughts.

"Ms. Raines, I'm sorry. There's a"—the voice hesitated—"person down here who insists on seeing a Tammy Randolph. I've tried to explain there's no one in the building by that name, but he says she's in your apartment. Should I contact the police?"

A chill slaked through her body. "No, Miguel. Keep him there. I'll be right down."

Tempest closed her condo door with a quiet click, trying not to disturb her neighbors. She boarded the elevator and pushed the lobby button. When the doors opened, she heard a commotion near the security desk. A biker argued with the guard. He wore jeans and a T-shirt with a black leather vest. A bandana circled his head. As she approached, the voice seemed all too familiar, and she stopped short. The biker turned and flashed her a grin. "Seems the security guard here won't let me up to your apartment, Ms…Randolph."

"Ms. Raines, I'm so sorry to bother you. This"—he shot a glance at the biker—"man refuses to leave."

Tempest ignored the guard. "What are you doing here?"

Chance shrugged. "Thought you might like to go for a ride."

"Now? At this hour? On your bike? Without a helmet?" Her heart pounded.

"Yes, yes, yes, and no. I happen to have a spare with me. Helmet, that is."

She stared at him for several seconds. What was he doing? Did he want to take her to the Dismal Swamp and leave her for dead? "Why?"

"Because I never know when I might want to give someone a ride."

She frowned. A flicker of longing surged through her. She tamped it down. "No. Why do you think I might like to go for a ride?"

"Well, because I'm a dashing knight on a fine specimen of a horse, and I've come to rescue you from certain perils." He gave her another grin.

Who was this person? Not the Chance she knew. He hated her. With good reason. Still, she could play along with his game until she figured out what he was up to. She crossed her arms and took a few steps closer to him. "Certain perils. I see. And what's the name of this fine horse you have?"

"Harley."

Tempest laughed. She couldn't help it. "Harley the horse."

"He's a fine specimen."

Her hand over her mouth to cover her smile, she spoke through her fingers. "I'm sure he is." She shook her head. The last time she had seen him, his anger at her was palpable. "Chance, what are you doing? Are you drunk?"

"No." His playful expression disappeared, and he stepped closer to her. "Tammy—"

"Don't call me that."

He slipped his arms around her. "Tammy, will you go for a ride with me?"

She relaxed against his body. She couldn't help that, either. "Chance, I—" She reached up to run her fingers over his lips. Longing, desire, hope, all flowed through her. "Are you giving me another chance?"

He caught her hand and kissed her fingers. "I'm giving you the only chance I have to give." Chance placed a finger across her lips to silence her. "Let's go for a ride."

She searched his face and saw no tricks, no deception. She stroked the stubble on his chin. He leaned down, slipped his hand through her hair, and pulled her closer. His lips met hers in a gentle kiss, just a few seconds, just enough to reawaken buried dreams.

"Will you go with me?" His deep blue eyes burrowed into her.

His expression, the tone in his voice—he wasn't asking about the ride. Tempest couldn't say how she knew, but the essence of the question held far more than a joyride down the beachfront. Hope swelled through her mind and heart.

He ran his fingers down her cheek. "Tempest?" His gaze swept over her face, then he slipped his hands over her shoulders and leaned down to kiss her again.

A whispered *I love you* came from his lips just as they touched hers.

She slipped her hand into his and smiled, feeling the guard's gaze on them. They walked across the lobby and outside.

Together.

All of her mistakes, her decisions, her sins, flashed through her mind in a blaze of light. Then they vanished.

He pulled a helmet from a saddlebag and helped her strap it on before they climbed onto the bike. Just before he started it up, he spoke to her over his shoulder. "By the way, have you ever been to a wedding in Greece?"

The engine roared to life, and they skidded from the lot into the night.

A word about the author...

Talia Logan is the pen name for an award-winning author of thrillers. She does her writing from the porch of a Chesapeake Bay-front home, where the seagulls caw by day, the waves crash by night, and the moon casts a sultry glow over the dark waters. Okay, that's fiction, but it's her goal.

www.talialogan.com